DESCENT INTO HELLIOS

A COLONIAL FLEET NOVEL

NEXUS HOUSE BOOK 2

RICK CAMPBELL

Severn River Publishing
www.SevernRiverBooks.com

ISBN: 978-1-64875-642-9 (Paperback)

ALSO BY RICK CAMPBELL

<u>The Nexus House Series</u>

The Final Stand: A Colonial Fleet Novel

Descent into Hellios: A Colonial Fleet Novel

The End of Time: A Colonial Fleet Novel

The Synthec War: A Colonial Fleet Novel

Annihilation: A Colonial Fleet Novel

The Seed of Destruction: A Colonial Fleet Novel

To find out more about Rick Campbell and his books, visit
severnriverbooks.com

MAIN CHARACTERS

A complete cast of characters is provided in the addendum

<u>NEXUS HOUSE</u>
Rhea Sidener Ten (Placidia) / Nexus One (The One)
Jon McCarthy Ten / Colonial Navy guide
Elena Kapadia Ten / Colonial Army guide
Noah Ronan Nine (Primus) / Legion Commander / Department Head - Defense
Lara Anderson Eight / Nine trainee
Carson Lieu Eight / 2nd Fleet guide
Angeline Del Rio Eight / 3rd Fleet guide

<u>CORVAD HOUSE</u>
Lijuan Xiang Ten (Placidia) / Princeps

<u>COLONIAL COUNCIL</u>
David Portner Regent - Inner Realm / Council president
Morel Alperi Regent - Inner Realm / Director of Personnel
Lijuan Xiang Regent - Terran (Earth) / Director of Material

COLONIAL FLEET
Nanci Fitzgerald Fleet Admiral / Colonial Fleet Commander
Jon McCarthy Admiral / Colonial Fleet staff
Khalil Amani Admiral / 2nd Fleet Commander
Natalia Goergen Admiral / 3rd Fleet Commander
Nesrine Rajhi Rear Admiral / Hellios cruiser task force commander

COLONIAL ARMY
Deshi Zhang Captain / Nexus escort platoon leader (Darian 3)
Trevor Romano Sergeant / Communications Specialist (Darian 3)

COLONIAL MARINE CORPS
Drew Harkins Major / Nexus Escort Platoon Leader (Hellios 4)
Ed Jankowski Sergeant Major / Nexus escort platoon (Hellios 4)
Narra Geisinger Sergeant Major / Nexus escort platoon (Hellios 4)
Liza Kalinin Sergeant / Nexus escort platoon (Hellios 4)
Chris Travis Sergeant / Nexus escort platoon (Hellios 4)
Deanna Riley Corporal / Nexus escort platoon (Hellios 4)
Tony Rodriguez Corporal / Nexus escort platoon (Hellios 4)

KORILIANS
Mrayev Pracep (war campaign commander)
Krajik Pracep Mrayev's executive assistant

OTHER CHARACTERS
Winston Albright Special Intelligence Division (SID) agent

PROLOGUE

It thinks the humans are preparing to strike deep into our territory.

Where and when?

It won't tell us. It's planning a trap, and is concerned our reaction will alert them.

It is being truthful?

I think so. But I fear it has ulterior motives.

It hates the humans as much as we do. Maybe more. Our common emotion binds us.

Should I try to make it tell us what we want to know?

No. It has become too dangerous to confront.

I can send in a slayer.

Slayers are too valuable in combat against the humans. We cannot risk losing one.

Then what do we do?

We wait. When it is ready, it will tell us where and how to trap the humans. And then we will annihilate them.

1

Rear Admiral Nesrine Rajhi, wearing the burgundy-and-crimson uniform of the Colonial Navy, stood on the bridge of her Resolute-class battleship. In command of the Excalibur battle group's one hundred starships, Rajhi assessed the status of her attack in the Antares planetary system. Thus far, the battle had progressed as planned. The Korilian Fleet was offering token resistance, much like they had done during the last three years. Elsewhere throughout the galaxy, the Colonial Fleet was pressing forward in a ten-pronged assault, each effort led by a Colonial battle group, with two additional battle groups in reserve.

Two jumps away in the Excelsior planetary system, 12th Army's ten million troops awaited the order to commence their assault on the fourth planet in the Antares system, eliminating the Korilian combat troops left behind. Thankfully, instead of engaging in close combat, Rajhi battled the Korilians from a distance. Through her starship's bridge windows, she watched the battle unfold as blue and red pulses impacted starship energy shields.

A burst of yellow light lit up the bridge, announcing the collapse of a nearby shield. Rajhi's eyes were drawn to the Korilian dreadnought. As its shield disintegrated, the pulse carved into the starship, its compartments brightening as explosions cascaded inside the crippled vessel. A moment later, several viper squadrons sped toward the damaged dreadnought. Although the immense starships were normally impervious to the small single-pilot vipers, once a shield went down and the warship's armor was penetrated, the vipers could tear a starship apart.

"Admiral," the communications supervisor called out, "the Korilians are targeting our communication pods."

Rajhi acknowledged the report, turning to one of the displays mounted along the front of the starship bridge. Korilian losses had been heavy, and Rajhi was convinced they were on the brink of defeat, with the remaining warships about to jump away. However, a Korilian cruiser on the flank had begun targeting the battle group's communication pods. Radio signals took millions of years to travel the vast distances between solar systems, so the Fleet used a series of communication pods, which jumped between systems to relay messages to and from the battle group.

Something was amiss. Why would the Korilians try to sever communications between her battle group and Fleet Command, unless...

White flashes illuminated the darkness through the bridge windows.

"Korilian warships!" the sensor supervisor announced. "Sector twelve-six!"

Six squadrons of Korilian dreadnoughts had joined the battle. It took Rajhi only a few seconds to assess the situation. Combined with the remaining Korilian starships, the enemy now outnumbered what was left of Rajhi's battle group. Additionally, the Korilian dreadnoughts—comparable to Colonial battleships—now had a two-to-one advantage over their Colonial counterparts. Reinforcements were required.

Although Rajhi could replace the communication pods and make the request, the nearest Colonial force, one of two battle groups in reserve, was three jumps away, normally a twenty-four-hour journey due to a twelve-hour hold between each jump to let the physiological effects of the jump dissipate before proceeding. A triple jump without recovery time between jumps would render each crew member nauseated, with many of them vomiting. Only in dire circumstances would Colonial starships enter battle with such compromised crews.

Fortunately, the situation wasn't dire. Rajhi's battle group could withdraw, delaying the assault on Antares 4, then return when additional forces were available.

Rajhi ordered her sensor supervisor, "Calculate optimal time for departure jump."

The sensor supervisor entered the commands, and the battleship's computer assessed the status of every Korilian warship, determining when the fewest pulse generators would be charged during the fifty-seven-second interval between firings. Shields would have to be dropped to engage the jump drive, and the starships would be vulnerable during those few seconds if enough Korilian warships with charged pulse generators had a clear shot.

The supervisor made his report, then Rajhi announced, "Operations officer, order all ships to jump at the mark."

The operations officer acknowledged, then relayed the command to the battle group. Yellow symbols appeared on his display, their color shifting to red or green, indicating the status of each ship's jump drive.

The operations officer reported, "All ships report ready to jump."

As Rajhi awaited the designated jump time, she reflected on the unfortunate situation. This was the first battle in three years that the Colonial Fleet had lost, and she would wear that dishonor. However, she had distinguished herself in battle and had destroyed more Korilian warships than any other starship captain. She was tempted to continue the battle in the faint hope she could emerge victorious and keep her reputation unmarred. But an entire battle group was at risk, not a single battleship like in the past, when she had beaten the odds. She reluctantly concluded that retreat was the prudent decision. Her battle group would fight another day.

When the clock reached the designated time, Rajhi gave the order. "Jump!"

2

When Admiral Jon McCarthy entered the conference room in the Fleet command center, buried a half mile beneath Earth's surface, he immediately registered the tension in the room. He joined the other dozen admirals around the table, surveying their concerned faces as they waited for Fleet Admiral Fitzgerald. The intelligence pre-brief had painted a grim picture. The advantage might shift to the Korilians again, and this time, they might not be able to stop them.

The Korilian War was nearing the end of its thirty-third year. For the first three decades, the Colonial Defense Force had been steadily pushed back, losing star systems and their colonized planets. As the Korilians pressed forward, they took no prisoners, left no one alive. After thirty years of conflict, humanity had been on the brink of extinction; the Korilians had destroyed every human star base and colony.

Three years ago, with only Earth remaining to conquer, the Korilian armada had jumped into Earth's solar system, where the Colonial Fleet had made its Final Stand. Led by Admiral McCarthy, the Fleet had defeated the Korilians, destroying every enemy warship in the process. Even though it had suffered severe losses, the Colonial Navy pressed forward immediately, initiating the Liberation Campaign, wresting control of the former human colonies back from the Korilians.

During the Liberation Campaign, the respective roles had reversed. Like humans during the first thirty years of the war, the Korilians saturated each planet with millions of ground troops. As the Colonial Defense Force —the Navy, Army, and Marines—regained lost territory, the advance was slowed by the need to painstakingly eliminate all Korilians who remained.

For the first three years of the Liberation Campaign, Korilian fleet resistance had been light. Over the last few weeks, however, opposition had unexpectedly stiffened.

Fleet Admiral Nanci Fitzgerald entered the conference room, her arrival announced by one of the Intelligence staffers. "Attention on deck!"

"Be seated," Fitzgerald said as she took her seat at the head of the table, then addressed the officer at the front of the room. "You may proceed."

Captain Tom Wears stood beside a large hologram displaying the relevant section of the galaxy. Earth-controlled planetary systems were colored green, and Korilian-controlled systems, red.

A thin vertical scar ran the length of Wears's face, passing through the center of his left eyelid. He'd been commanding officer of a battleship defending the Piunia planetary system a few years ago. A Korilian pulse had collapsed his ship's bow shield with enough energy bleeding through to demolish the battleship's bridge, injuring Wears in the process. His eye had been replaced, and he now served as Fleet Admiral Fitzgerald's liaison with Fleet Intelligence.

Wears began with a status of the Colonial Navy. Since the Final Stand, the Fleet had been rebuilt from the remaining ten battle groups to twenty-four, divided into six fleets. Four fleets were committed to the Liberation Campaign, with three fleets in action at all times, while a fourth fleet refitted, receiving replacement starships and supplies. The final two fleets were retained in Earth's orbit to defend Earth from a Korilian attack.

After briefing each assault in process, Wears addressed the overall status of the Liberation Campaign. "We've enjoyed tremendous success over the last three years, regaining over half of the territory we lost in the preceding thirty years. After our Final Stand, we thought we had destroyed the entire Korilian fleet, and that supposition seemed true as we encountered no Korilian warships during the first six months of the Liberation Campaign. Resistance gradually stiffened as replacement Korilian warships arrived. The increased opposition we're seeing is not unexpected, however. The Korilians have traded solar systems for time, rebuilding their fleet much like we did during the last five years of the Retreat."

Captain Wears had used the term the Colonial Defense Force had coined for the first thirty years of the Korilian War, when they had been steadily driven back, their star bases and colonies on distant solar systems overwhelmed by the Korilian assault. The thirty-three-year war had been neatly divided into three phases: the Retreat, the Final Stand, and the Liberation Campaign, with the Final Stand serving as the fulcrum upon which the war's tide had turned.

Wears continued, "Following the Final Stand, the Korilians were able to increase their warship construction rate, which we estimate is now fifty percent greater than ours. While we still hold a significant numerical advantage, they've rebuilt their fleet enough to amass local superiority. Yesterday, the Korilians forced a full battle group to withdraw, our first defeat in three years.

"However, what happened yesterday goes beyond sheer numbers. We think there's something else going on. The Korilians were able to predict our most vulnerable point of attack—the sector farthest from reinforcements—and begin routing sufficient forces toward Antares *before* we began the attack. While this might seem like an isolated incident, this isn't the first time it's occurred; it's just the first time they've been successful. We think the Korilians have developed a sophisticated intelligence model that can predict our assaults, or at least narrow the possibilities so they can concentrate their forces at the likely engagement points.

"We're still assessing the situation," Wears added, "attempting to determine to what extent they may be able to predict our campaign strategy, and are evaluating our options to counter. Subject to your questions, this concludes my brief."

There was a short silence while McCarthy and the other admirals assessed the information. Fleet Admiral Fitzgerald spoke first.

"If the Korilians have truly developed the ability to predict our assaults, it will become difficult, if not impossible, to defeat them, even with Admiral McCarthy's assistance."

Fitzgerald and the other admirals turned to McCarthy, who had led the combined Fleet to victory during humanity's darkest hour. During the Fleet's Final Stand against the Korilian armada, McCarthy had been given command of twelve battle groups. Never before in the history of the war had an admiral been given direct control of so many warships, because experience had shown that satisfactory command of more than four battle groups could not be achieved. McCarthy, however, was no ordinary admiral.

McCarthy was a Nexus, a member of a group of prescients that had guided humanity for thousands of years. After the Korilian War began, Rhea Sidener, the ruler of the Nexus House, had pledged her support, assigning a prescient guide to each of the six fleets. In addition, she had assigned the House's most precious assets, level-ten prescients, to the war effort. One of them, and the last remaining Ten alive aside from Rhea herself, was McCarthy.

He had been assigned to the Fleet at the age of sixteen, gaining experience in battle for another sixteen years, eventually ascending to command of 1st Fleet. As humanity prepared for its Final Stand against the Korilian Empire, Fleet Admiral Fitzgerald had devised a plan that relied on McCarthy's prescient ability, and he had led the combined six fleets to victory.

Although McCarthy had been dubbed by the public as the Hero of the Korilian War, he paid no attention to the accolades. He remained focused on achieving complete victory, defeating the Korilian Empire. In that endeavor, Fleet Admiral Fitzgerald had reassigned McCarthy to a staff position where he could provide guidance to all six fleets. Thus far, his strategic direction during the Liberation Campaign had been flawless. However, McCarthy had not foreseen the concentration of Korilian starships in the Antares system, which was cause for concern. Whatever the Korilians had developed was capable of countering the Fleet's most critical asset.

Fitzgerald asked Captain Wears, "Is it possible an artificial intelligence is providing guidance?"

She levied the question in light of the constraints on human artificial intelligence. Twice in Earth's history, artificial intelligence had attempted to eradicate humanity. After the 1st and 2nd Cyborg Wars, sentient machines and their cyborg variants—machines covered with human flesh or humans with brain implants—had been banned. There was no more sacred law.

"Yes," Wears replied. "We believe it is some form of artificial intelligence."

Silence enveloped the conference room. The Colonial Defense Force was prohibited from developing an artificial intelligence sophisticated enough to counter the Korilian version, if that was even possible. That left McCarthy, or perhaps another Ten trained by the Nexus House.

"Can Rhea assist in this matter," Fitzgerald asked McCarthy, "or are there others approaching level ten?"

McCarthy answered, "There are two others with potential to reach level ten, but both are having difficulty reaching the next level. For now, Rhea is the only other Ten I can confer with. With your permission, I'll meet with her this afternoon."

Fitzgerald nodded her concurrence.

3

Carved into the eastern side of the Ural Mountains lay Domus Praesidium, the three-millennia-old Nexus House stronghold. In the north wing, Lara Anderson and Siella Salvos sat in The One's office, facing her desk. Rhea Sidener, referred to within the Nexus House as The One, wore the shimmery blue Nexus jumpsuit with ten white stripes around each arm. Fastened around her waist was a white sash with gold embroidery, which signified her position—The One who ruled the House.

Siella and Lara were being trained primarily by Rhea, while other Nexus students were trained by instructors in groups according to level, which ranged from two to ten. Levels two through four focused on prescient capabilities in the present, levels five through seven exploited the past, while Nexi at levels eight through ten could view the future to varying degrees. Both Lara and Siella were students with significant potential, and Rhea had decided to conduct a portion of their training separately.

Lara was a level-eight Nexus, able to garner occasional glimpses of the future, akin to looking through a foggy window with small circles of clarity. Siella was a Nine, able to perceive the future clearly. Level ten, however, was a quantum leap above nine. A Ten could look into the future and postulate different actions, each one creating a timeline branching off from the Prime. Each timeline could be followed into the future, evaluating additional actions. A Ten's view of the future could be visualized as a tree, with the current future—the prime timeline—being the trunk of the tree, and the alternate futures being the numerous and ever-increasing branches. A level-ten Nexi could guide the future to the optimal leaf on the tree.

Few Nexi had the ability to become Eights, and even fewer became Nines. Those capable of becoming a Ten were extremely rare; about once a decade someone accomplished the feat. The Nexus House was now overdue for a new Ten. It had been twenty-one years since McCarthy passed the Test, and Rhea believed that either Siella or Lara would succeed. But time was running out, especially for Siella.

Siella had been recycled in her class twice, stuck at level nine. Under the edict from the Colonial Council, in its zeal to obtain level-ten prescients for the war effort, the Nexus House had been directed to push all Nines to the Test. If they passed, they were certified at level ten. If they failed, however, they became a Lost One, their mind trapped in an alternate reality, permanently insane.

Although Siella's potential was promising, Lara was even more special. She lacked a prime timeline, the artifact that Nexi and other house psychics followed into the future or past. Because Lara didn't have a line, her future or past could not be evaluated, which was both a source of consternation and hope. In addition to lacking a prime timeline, Lara, as well as Siella, was much older than any other Nexus at this stage of her training. Due to initially living on Outer Realm planets, both women hadn't undergone the standard testing, normally conducted at the age of five. It wasn't until both women were in their late teens, upon relocating to Inner Realm planets as the Korilians advanced, that they had been evaluated.

Lara's testing had revealed enormous latent talent, but she was initially passed over because she had the Touch—the ability to look into someone's mind by touching their skin—a talent banned within the Nexus House. However, ten years later, just before the Final Stand, the Nexus House had found itself in dire straits. The 1st Fleet guide had been killed, and a replacement was required. Unfortunately, the backup guide in training had been killed a few weeks earlier, and the next in line had failed her final evaluation. The Nexus House needed a replacement, and Lara had been identified from her initial screening—a rare full spectrum—prescient in all five senses.

Lara was inducted into the House, then rushed through an intense training regimen preparing her to be the 1st Fleet guide, assisting Admiral McCarthy. While McCarthy focused on specific sectors of the battle, evaluating the various futures, disaster could befall in an area he wasn't paying attention to. Nexus guides came in handy, able to focus the attention of each fleet admiral, including McCarthy.

Her contribution during humanity's Final Stand had been limited due to her incomplete training, but she had provided valuable insight during the crucial moments. Afterward, Lara had progressed quickly through the levels, a testament to her talent, becoming an Eight in only three years. However, she was currently stuck at level eight, unable to see clearly into the future. Lara's inability to achieve level nine was on The One's mind today.

Finally, Rhea spoke. "You *must* exclude emotion from your view."

Lara had heard it a thousand times; it was Nexus House mantra— *Emotion is the source of all evil.*

"It seems to help," Lara replied.

Rhea offered a disapproving frown. "The Corvads used emotion to propel their view."

Corvads were the Nexus House's arch nemeses. Three thousand years ago, there had been twelve major houses of psychics, with the Nexus House being one. For three millennia, they had waged war against each other, with the twelve houses split evenly between two factions: the Nexus House and their allies, and the Corvads and their ilk.

Thirty-three years ago, just before the outbreak of the Korilian War, there had been a final confrontation between the two remaining major houses—the Battle of Domus Valens. After three millennia of conflict, the Nexus House had finally prevailed, annihilating the Corvads.

The One continued her rebuke. "Emotion helps at first, but then you become enslaved to it. The Corvads fell into this trap and became addicted to emotion like a drug, requiring stronger and stronger doses. The strongest emotions are the negative ones—hatred, rage, and fear—and there is no emotion stronger than the terror created by the certainty of death. Corvad

Tens slaughtered innocent men and women, using the intense emotion to fuel their views. They were cruel and despicable.

"To avoid becoming addicted like the Corvads, emotion has been banned from Nexus views for three thousand years. That policy will not change. You *must* purge all emotion from your view. If you cannot, or choose to go down that path, the consequence is extreme."

The One didn't have to elaborate. After three millennia of warfare, enduring the slaughter of tens of thousands of their own, the Nexi were ruthless when it came to protecting their House and would exterminate anyone they considered a threat.

Lara took a deep breath and tried again, using a technique taught to her by Dewan Channing, the Deinde Eight. Within the House, there were nine primuses, each one in charge of all those in their level, plus nine deindes, second in command of their level. Channing, tasked with training fleet guides since they were normally Eights, had trained Lara before the Final Stand.

She imagined herself standing on a beach, the waves breaking onto the sand. In the distance, a thick white fog rolled quickly ashore, enveloping her. She concentrated, trying to force a tunnel through the mist, creating a portal into the future. A funnel began to form, the fog spiraling outward. But just before she was convinced she'd be able to see through the mist and into the future, the funnel collapsed.

Lara's frustration must have been evident on her face, because Rhea said, "Perhaps we need to try a different technique. What Channing taught you works well for level-eight premonitions and below, but there are other methods we can employ at level nine." She checked her wristlet. Their training session was almost over. "We'll try something new tomorrow."

Rhea's door tone beeped, and after she acknowledged, Noah Ronan, the Primus Nine and responsible for training the House praetorians, entered. Ronan was one of the few Nines who had survived the final battle thirty-three years ago at the Corvad stronghold of Domus Valens.

"What is it, Primus?" Rhea asked.

Ronan answered, "The communication center informed me you hadn't responded to their message. I assumed you were in training and put your wristlet on *Do not disturb*."

"You're correct," Rhea replied, then tapped her wristlet, returning it to normal operation. Messages began scrolling down her wristlet display. She looked up as Ronan informed her of the pertinent issue.

"McCarthy is on his way here. He offered few details, other than the Korilians forced a battle group to retreat at Antares, and wants to discuss the matter with you."

Rhea leaned back in her chair. "He didn't foresee it?"

"It seems so," Ronan replied. "I've already viewed a portion of our upcoming meeting with him; he saw a victory at Antares instead."

"This is troubling," Rhea replied. "The future was somehow guided down an alternate timeline."

"That's not all. His battle-related views are dissolving four weeks into the future."

Rhea's eyes widened. After a moment of reflection, she returned her attention to Lara and Siella. "We're done today. Continue with your other scheduled training, and we'll meet tomorrow morning, same time."

Both women excused themselves and soon parted ways, with Siella proceeding to praetorian combat training while Lara made a quick detour to her room. McCarthy always managed to spend time with her while visiting Domus Praesidium, and she wanted to ensure she was presentable. During their training together in preparation for the Fleet's Final Stand and during the intense battle itself, they had formed a strong bond. One that Lara hoped would develop further. She hurried down the marble-walled corridor, then slipped into her quarters.

Inside The One's office, Ronan brought up Siella's status again. "We're wasting our time training Siella as a praetorian. She doesn't have the build or aptitude."

Siella was an off-worlder, unusually slender and frail for a Persean. Due to the stronger gravity, Perseans were normally stocky and muscular, but Siella had inherited recessive Terran genes. Her progress as a praetorian had been less than stellar; Ronan's assessment was that she lacked the strength and natural talent required. There were other uses for Siella, but the options were dwindling, since she had also failed to become a fleet guide.

"I am aware of the issue," Rhea said. "Her future is difficult to predict for some reason; her line dissolves after only a few weeks. Perhaps that's why I hold hope for her. She's the only one, besides Lara, whose limitations are unclear."

When Rhea mentioned Lara, Ronan revisited an issue they disagreed on. "My recommendation against training Lara still stands. She has no line to follow, so you have no idea what her future is. She also has the Touch."

The reason the Touch was forbidden within the Nexus House was because those who had mastered the ability were predisposed to join the Corvad House. As a result, for three thousand years, the Nexi had terminated all who had the Touch. However, since the Corvads had been recently vanquished, Rhea had disregarded three millennia of House policy, letting Lara live.

"We've been through this before," Rhea replied. "The Corvads have been eliminated, and there is no house for her to join. If she adopts the Corvad view, it will be obvious, and we'll deal with it."

"She's an abomination. Without a prime timeline, she shouldn't even exist."

"The Sevens are working on the issue, rebuilding the pertinent section of the Codex."

The Codex, the repository of three millennia of Nexus wisdom, had been destroyed by a Corvad assault five centuries ago. However, the Codex had been partially rebuilt, revealing a reference to *the One with no line*. Unfortunately, the guidance was incomplete, and Rhea had directed her Sevens to focus on recovering additional references.

"We should save the trouble and kill her."

"That's enough, Ronan. Lara is a Nexus now, and you're obligated to defend her."

"Don't remind me," he said.

Changing topics, Rhea said, "When McCarthy arrives, bring him here."

4

After applying fresh makeup for McCarthy's visit, Lara stopped before the full-length mirror in her bedroom. As she examined herself, she caught movement in the mirror's reflection. Fog was seeping under her bedroom door, spreading across the floor toward her. Lara tensed, awaiting the pending premonition; fog was the one common element in her visions. The cold white mist swirled around her feet, then rose, completely filling her bedroom. Then it suddenly vanished, revealing a woman standing behind her by the door.

Lara turned quickly toward the apparition. She was a young blonde, perhaps twenty years old, with a dirt-smeared face and emerald-green eyes that complemented her tattered Colonial Army green-and-olive uniform. She appeared exhausted, staring into the distance. She paid no attention to Lara, which was unusual, since apparitions in her visions normally interacted with her.

The woman spoke without shifting her gaze, oblivious of Lara's presence.

"This is Major Elena Kapadia, attached to the last operational Third Army Group—"

The apparition froze and flickered with static, then resumed speaking, freezing momentarily every few seconds.

"...will be our last transmission. Whoever receives this message, pass to...of the utmost importance. Billions of lives are at stake. In eighteen years...but I have found a way to end the war. You must destroy the Korilian complex on the fourth planet in..."

The apparition froze and flickered with static again, then the woman repeated the message, which broke up at the same spots and ended at the same place. She began to repeat her message a third time as fog seeped beneath Lara's door again, filling her bedroom. Then the mist vanished, taking the apparition with it.

Lara took a deep breath and tried to process the vision. The woman's name and appearance seemed familiar. She searched her memory, recalling that the Army major was the woman in one of the videographs displayed above McCarthy's desk in his quarters aboard the 1st Fleet command ship. She was a few years younger in the videograph, standing by a troop transport as columns of soldiers boarded. Then the woman's name clicked—*Elena*. McCarthy had named his shuttle *Elena*, in memory of his close friend and fellow Nexus Ten who had been killed on Darian 3, the bloodiest campaign in the history of the Korilian War, consuming over one billion soldiers during the five-year conflict.

The vision had been a message from the past.

That Lara experienced this vision now meant Elena's message was important and somehow relevant to what was occurring today. She recalled Ronan's comments about the reason for McCarthy's visit. The Fleet had just lost its first battle since its Final Stand. The defeat at Antares and Elena's message were somehow related.

Lara hurried to The One's office, where she was meeting with McCarthy. The door clicked open after she requested to join them, and she entered to find McCarthy and Ronan seated before The One's desk.

"I apologize for interrupting," Lara said, "but I just had a vision about the war that might be important."

"Go ahead," Rhea directed.

"A message was sent from Darian 3 near the end of the battle. A message from Elena."

When she mentioned Elena's name, Lara felt a burst of emotion from McCarthy. One of Lara's talents that the Nexi seemed uninterested in developing further, in addition to her Touch, was that she was an empath. McCarthy hadn't revealed the extent of his relationship with Elena, but it was obvious they had been close.

"What did Elena say?" Rhea asked.

Lara relayed what Elena said in the vision, but then McCarthy said, "We never received a message from her, at least not that I'm aware of. But I wouldn't have been informed unless it rose high enough for Army Command to share the details with the Fleet. Or maybe the transmission didn't make it through. During the Korilians' final assault on Darian 3, they jammed all Third Army Group communications. Only sporadic transmissions were received near the end."

After a moment of contemplation, McCarthy said, "I'll have Army Command search their archives and see what they can find."

5

The following day at the Fleet command center in Brussels, McCarthy took his seat at the conference table, joining Fleet Admiral Nanci Fitzgerald and the fleet deputy commander, Admiral Liam Carroll. Also seated at the table was Captain Tom Wears, who relayed what had been discovered.

"Army Command located a message from Elena in their communication archives. It was the last message received from Third Army Group on Darian 3. The message was garbled and didn't contain any actionable information, so the communication center archived it."

Admiral Fitzgerald addressed McCarthy. "You have to understand that the Army kept Elena's talent a secret, just like we did yours, fearing the Korilians would focus their efforts on killing you and Elena if they discovered your abilities. The communication center personnel wouldn't have understood the significance of who sent this message."

McCarthy nodded, then Fitzgerald returned her attention to Wears.

"We have a copy of the message," he said.

He tapped his wristlet, and the lights dimmed as a grainy hologram of a female Army major appeared at the front of the conference room. There were dark circles under her eyes, and her face was smeared with red dirt. After three years on Darian 3, Elena would've been nineteen, and even through the grime and exhaustion, it was clear that she had developed into a beautiful young woman. Captain Wears tapped his wristlet again, and the message began playing.

The transmission was of poor quality, with occasional breaks in the message every few seconds. The hologram shook during each break, and once it resumed, dirt drifted down from above as a deep rumble echoed in the Army command bunker.

Elena spoke, and her voice was just as McCarthy remembered it.

"This is Major Elena Kapadia, attached to the last operational Third Army Group...will be our last transmission. Whoever receives this message, pass to...of the utmost importance. Billions of lives are at stake. In eighteen years...but I have found a way to end the war. You must destroy the Korilian complex on the fourth planet in..."

The apparition froze and flickered with static. Wears tapped his wristlet again, and the hologram disappeared as the conference room lights returned to their former illumination. It was quiet in the room until Wears spoke.

"As Fleet Admiral Fitzgerald mentioned, the Army communication center didn't know Elena was a Nexus Ten. They thought the transmission was the rambling of an overstressed officer as the Korilians closed in on her command bunker."

It was silent in the conference room for a moment, until McCarthy said, "In eighteen years..." to no one in particular. Then he looked at Wears. "When was this message transmitted?"

"Eighteen years ago."

"Elena viewed this future," McCarthy replied. "She was able to look beyond the Final Stand."

McCarthy locked eyes with Fleet Admiral Fitzgerald. He had never been able to see past the epic battle, his view dissolving only minutes after the Korilian assault began. Somehow, Elena had accomplished the feat.

"Elena's view penetrated the Final Stand, and she was able to follow the prime timeline eighteen years into the future. She saw what happened at Antares, and more. The tide is turning against us, and Elena learned how to stop it."

Fitzgerald continued McCarthy's line of reasoning. "A Korilian complex we must destroy. Perhaps one that contains the artificial intelligence the

Korilians have developed. But where is it? The location of the facility in her message is garbled."

McCarthy turned to Captain Wears. "What is the status of Darian 3?"

"It is now under Colonial control. The planet was declared Korilian-free by the Army less than a week ago. Why do you ask?"

"If Army communication gear is like the Fleet's, then the command center where Elena transmitted her message would have a recording. The transmission was garbled, but the recording would be complete. If Elena's command post wasn't destroyed and we can locate it, we'll learn where the Korilian facility is."

"Good idea," Admiral Carroll said. "I'll have the Army search for the command post."

McCarthy shook his head. "That will be like looking for a needle in a haystack. It could take months or even years to find it."

"What do you recommend?" Fitzgerald asked.

"I'll find Elena's command center," McCarthy replied. "Send me to Darian 3."

"That's out of the question," Admiral Carroll replied. "The Army has certified the planet Korilian-free, but they've been wrong before. And there's no planet with more subterranean tunnels than Darian 3. We can't risk it."

"The situation is serious," McCarthy replied. "Since our defeat at Antares, my war-related views have been dissolving four weeks into the future. I believe the Korilians will mount a major counteroffensive, one that I cannot adequately predict. I think it has something to do with the facility Elena mentioned, and we have to find and destroy it within the next four weeks. We don't have time to let the Army search for Elena's command center."

There was no response from Carroll or Fitzgerald as they evaluated McCarthy's revelation about his view and request to visit the potentially dangerous planet. McCarthy added, "I'll be able to view my own timeline on Darian 3 and foresee any Korilian attack. I'll be safe."

Fleet Admiral Fitzgerald finally spoke. "I agree with your assessment. However, I'll have to get Council approval to send you to Darian 3. When it comes to your tasking, the Council keeps me on a short leash. They still consider you our most valuable asset."

"I understand," McCarthy replied. "How long will it take to get Council approval?"

"I can request an emergency meeting for this afternoon. I'll know by the end of the day."

6

Five minutes before the scheduled conference with the Council, Fleet Admiral Fitzgerald arrived at the communication center and entered a twenty-foot-diameter conference chamber. At the appointed time, twelve holograms appeared, equally spaced along the chamber circumference.

The white-robed Council members were evenly split between men and women, with the twelve regents representing various constituencies of the 110-planet human realm. Four regents represented the Inner Realm worlds closest to Earth, four more spoke for the Outer Realm, while two represented the Ore Belt planets, which lay between the Inner and Outer Realm. Rounding out the twelve-member Council was the Fringe Worlds regent, representing the planets beyond the Outer Realm, plus the Terran regent, representing the inhabitants of Earth.

Each of the three senior members held a staff in one hand: Regent David Portner wore a red stole around his neck, signifying his role as Council president, while the next two highest-ranking members—Inner Realm Regent Morel Alperi and Terran Regent Lijuan Xiang—the directors of Personnel and Material, respectively, wore orange stoles.

"Greetings, Council," Fitzgerald began. "Thank you for the opportunity to address you on short notice."

Portner replied, "I hope you bring good news; that you have devised a plan to avoid additional defeats after your failure at Antares."

Fitzgerald did her best to hide her disdain for the Council. The arrogant regents had no idea how difficult it had been to defeat the Korilian armada during humanity's Final Stand, and the Fleet had reeled off three straight years of victories, regaining over half of the territory they had lost in the first thirty years. After a single defeat, she had to endure a reprimand from a regent who'd be in over his head in a parking lot puddle. Fitzgerald pushed her resentment aside and answered.

"I bring promising news," Fitzgerald answered. "We discovered a message sent by Elena, just before she was killed on Darian 3. She foresaw our victory in the Final Stand and the stiffening Korilian resistance we are experiencing now. She also advised us to destroy a Korilian facility, which will supposedly help end the war."

"Is this the facility where the Korilian intelligence center is located?"

"We don't know, but we think it's likely."

"This *is* good news," Portner replied. "How soon will you be able to destroy it?"

"We don't know where it is yet."

Alperi interjected. "What good is Elena's message if she didn't know where the facility is?"

"We think she knew, but her message was garbled. If you concur, I'll play her message so you'll understand what we're dealing with."

"Go ahead," Portner said.

Fitzgerald tapped commands into her wristlet, and Elena's hologram appeared in the center of the chamber. After another tap, Elena delivered her message.

After Elena's image faded from the chamber, Alperi was the first to speak. "I don't understand why you've requested this meeting. Even if Elena knew, she's dead. So how does that help us?"

"We think we can recover her message. We now control Darian 3, and if we can find Elena's last command center, we may be able to obtain a complete copy of the message."

"That's it?" Alperi asked. "You requested an emergency Council meeting to inform us you found an eighteen-year-old corrupted message? One you *might* recover?" He leveled a stern gaze at Fitzgerald. "Council members are extremely busy, attending to critical issues. You should request our time more judiciously in the future."

Lijuan Xiang joined the discussion. "Don't be too hasty in your judgment, Morel. I believe Fleet Admiral Fitzgerald has a plan that requires our approval."

As usual, Lijuan was the most perceptive of the three senior members. She kept more of an open mind than Alperi, who was a pompous ass as far as Fitzgerald was concerned, impressed with his position and the power he wielded.

Fitzgerald took Lijuan's cue and explained. "Admiral McCarthy believes there will be a major Korilian assault in four weeks, but his view destabilizes before he can determine what the Korilians are planning. I believe it's imperative that we quickly locate and destroy the Korilian complex Elena mentioned in her message. To do that, we need to locate her final command center within the next few days." Fitzgerald hesitated a moment, preparing herself for the Council's reaction, then made her request.

"That means we send McCarthy to Darian 3 to find it."

The Council erupted in discord, with all twelve members speaking at once. Fitzgerald drew a deep breath and waited until Alperi pounded his staff on the floor.

"Absolutely not!"

The bickering between regents died down, and Alperi continued. "We cannot risk McCarthy. If the Korilians launch a counteroffensive, we'll need his guidance."

"I don't disagree," Fitzgerald replied. "But our best odds of defeating the Korilians starts with destroying the facility Elena mentioned. The fact that she saw it in her view eighteen years ago convinces me it's critical to the Korilians' recent success, and we must destroy it. But we have to locate it first, and fast. That means we need to send McCarthy to Darian 3."

Alperi started to respond, but Lijuan cut him off. "As usual, Morel, you fail to heed the recommendations of our senior military commanders. Three years ago, as we prepared for our Final Stand, you opposed Fitzgerald's plan to send McCarthy on a mission to capture a Korilian cruiser, which was critical to our success. The admiral's request today is no different. We must risk McCarthy on a small mission ahead of a larger conflict. As Korilian resistance stiffens and they potentially begin an offensive of their own, McCarthy's mission to Darian 3 may be the deciding factor, just as his cruiser mission was three years ago."

Alperi's jaw muscles tensed as he searched for words to counter Lijuan's rebuke. Before he could respond, Council President Portner spoke.

"The decision facing us is straightforward. Is McCarthy's mission to Darian 3 essential or not?" After a slight pause, he added, "Is further debate desired, or do I have a motion to put Fleet Admiral Fitzgerald's request to a vote?"

"I so motion," Lijuan replied.

Another regent seconded the motion.

"All in favor of ending discussion?" Portner asked.

All Council members except Alperi replied, "Aye."

"It is time to vote," Portner continued. "*Yes* to approve Fleet Admiral Fitzgerald's proposal. *No* to oppose." Portner turned to Alperi.

"No," he said.

The voting continued around the chamber, reaching Lijuan with the vote at six in favor and four against. The motion would pass if either Lijuan or Portner supported it.

"Yes," she said.

Portner announced, "The motion is approved." He then focused his attention on Fitzgerald again. "I trust that you know what you are doing."

7

Having just finished lunch, Lara was departing the crowded main dining room in Domus Praesidium, which could seat ten thousand, when her wristlet vibrated. She checked the display, surprised by The One's command to report to her office immediately. It took only a few minutes to ascend to the first level of the mountain complex, where she pressed the intercom button beside The One's door. After Lara announced her presence, the door unlocked, and The One beckoned her inside.

Rhea was seated at her desk, examining a holographic image of a solar system on her desktop: a bright red star with five planets. Rhea had expanded one of the planets, examining it closely. She gestured toward the three chairs in front of her desk, and Lara settled into one as the hologram disappeared.

"The Army found Elena's message," Rhea said. "But it was identical to your vision, and they weren't able to determine where the Korilian facility is."

Lara nodded her understanding, then replied, "I'll see what I can do about invoking a better vision. Maybe I can recover the key information."

Although she spoke with confidence, she harbored little hope of success. Her level-eight visions were still mostly random, and she had no idea what had caused Elena's message to appear the previous day.

"Do that," Rhea directed. "However, we can't wait for a vision that might never come. Something significant in this war is going to happen soon, and not even I can discern what that is. Not only does Jon's view dissolve four weeks into the future, but so does mine."

Lara saw the concern in Rhea's eyes, a departure from her normally confident air.

"Is there anything we can do?" Lara asked.

"It's possible that there's a complete copy of Elena's message in her command center on Darian 3. Jon is going to search for it. Hopefully, he'll find the message and it'll be intact. However, Jon is ill-equipped for the search."

"But Jon is a Ten," Lara replied. "How could he not find Elena's command center?"

The One smiled. "Tell someone that you can see the future and they think you know everything. That's far from the truth. We can follow specific timelines into the future or past. In this case, however, there is no timeline to latch onto. Every *living* thing has a line. Elena and anyone who might know where her command center was located have been dead for eighteen years. The only method Jon can employ in this situation is to view various searches that crisscross the region where Elena's command center was located. But if it's well hidden, he could walk right past it in his view without discovering it."

Rhea added, "There are other Nexi who are better suited for this type of search, but Jon insists that he be sent."

"Why does Jon want to go?"

"Because he wants to be there when they find the command center; when they find Elena's remains." She paused for a moment, then added, "What happed to Elena has been a source of friction between Jon and me for eighteen years. He holds me responsible—I sent Elena to Darian 3, sentencing her to almost certain death.

"It's important that this issue be resolved. I'm convinced that Jon will eventually become a Placidia Ten and will co-rule the Nexus House with me. By the time that occurs, the friction between us must be eliminated. I believe his trip to Darian 3—finding Elena—will bring closure to this contentious issue.

"He will need help," Rhea added, "which is why you're here. I'm sending you to Darian 3 with him."

"Me?" Lara asked. "Why me?"

"As I mentioned, Jon doesn't possess the optimal talent to search for Elena's command post. But you do. You're an empath, and there are a lot of residual emotions on Darian 3. When the Korilians located Elena's command center and slaughtered all within, you can imagine the horror experienced by those slain. You should be able to sense those emotions once you reach Darian 3."

"Are you sure I'll be able to find the command center?"

"If you can lock onto Elena's residual emotion, then yes. But I cannot foresee the outcome because you have no timeline to follow into the future. However, I do know that without you, we don't find Elena's command center in time."

"When do I leave?"

"Tonight. Jon will stop here on his way to a starship in orbit, which will take you to the Darian system."

8

Later that day, Lara sat at the back of a classroom with forty students honing their level-eight skills. In the various Nexus classrooms, Lara was a novelty. At thirty years old, she was twice the age of most students. She had to explain each time she joined a new class that she hadn't been inducted into the House until she was twenty-seven, instead of five as was standard. She omitted the reason why—her Touch—due to the sensitive nature of the issue.

Today's training session had just finished when her wristlet vibrated. She had been waiting for McCarthy's arrival, stopping by Domus Praesidium to pick her up for the journey to Darian 3. A message from him scrolled down the display.

Meet me in the atrium.

Lara headed toward her rendezvous with the Nexus Ten, wondering why he had asked her to meet in the garden atrium instead of the spaceport. She was convinced there was a connection between them that would eventually lead to a more intimate relationship, but had been unable to confirm her suspicion. Their interactions so far had been purely professional. She hadn't broached the topic with him, and her visions hadn't clarified the matter.

She entered the atrium, with tropical vegetation filling a chamber that rose over a thousand feet through the mountain rock to a glass-dome roof. She followed the winding path through the foliage until she made it to the center—a thirty-foot-wide circle with stone benches along the perimeter. McCarthy was sitting on one of the benches and stood when Lara arrived. He gestured toward the bench as he sat back down, and she joined him.

They sat in silence for a moment until McCarthy spoke. "This was Elena's favorite spot. When we were kids, we'd sometimes play hide-and-seek here during our time off from training. She was always good at hiding, and I'd often give up and sit on this bench and wait. She'd eventually emerge from wherever she was hiding and sit beside me. Sometimes we'd talk until it was time for our next training session. Other times we'd just sit in silence, enjoying each other's company.

"When we were older, we found more exciting places. Elena never liked being cooped up inside a mountain, and we'd often escape to one of the eastern balconies. We'd sit on the ledge, our feet dangling over a two-thousand-foot drop. But we were Nines by then, and we knew we were safe. We'd sometimes get up early, climbing onto the ledge in the darkness to watch the sunrise. Each new day brought a glimmer of hope. Something we sorely needed back then."

Lara knew little about Elena and why she meant so much to McCarthy, other than she had been another Nexus Ten.

"Were you and Elena in a relationship?"

McCarthy shook his head. "We were like brother and sister. I'd lost both parents to the war by the time I was seven, and Elena was already an orphan when she arrived here as a five-year-old. We grew close, becoming the family we'd both lost. We thought about including other kids, but we both had the feeling there would be no one else left at the end of our training. That the others would be held back or worse—be pushed to the Test and fail, becoming a Lost One. Losing each other would be hard enough, and we didn't want to endure more heartbreak."

As McCarthy spoke, Lara could tell from his voice and face that he was struggling to contain his feelings. She reached over and touched his hand to convey her support. She hadn't planned to use her Touch, but her vision clouded in a white mist as she looked into McCarthy's mind.

The fog cleared quickly, and it was as if she were in McCarthy's body, recalling one of his memories. He sat in a small, dimly lit classroom with no windows. There were twenty student desks, worn by years of use, with eighteen empty chairs while McCarthy and a teenage girl occupied two seats in the front row. An office desk sat at the front of the room, cluttered with papers, the stacks almost falling over. There was a video bulletin board on a side wall with pictures loaded onto it: eighteen photos, each of a different teenage boy or girl with their name on the bottom.

Two women stood at the front of the room. The nearest stood with her hands clasped behind her. She was Rhea—the Nexus One—except she looked twenty years younger. The other woman stood in a corner, her head tilted, looking down at the floor. The teenage girl beside McCarthy was Elena. The petite blonde seemed about sixteen years old, with her hair pulled back into a single ponytail.

Elena looked toward the front of the classroom, her eyes focused on The One as she held McCarthy's hand. Her grip was tight and her hand ice cold; her arm was trembling.

She was terrified.

The emotion was so palpable that Lara's pulse quickened. She reflexively withdrew her hand and the vision faded.

"It's been years since I thought about Elena like this," McCarthy said. "About the years we spent together. About how close we were."

Lara explained that she had accidentally looked into his mind using her Touch, then asked, "Why was Elena so afraid?"

McCarthy searched her eyes, appearing to choose his words carefully, then answered. "I need to tell you a few things that you're not supposed to know yet, so you'll understand." He paused for a moment, then began.

"Out of our class of one thousand children, twenty of us were evaluated as having the potential to reach level ten. We advanced steadily through level nine, but once we began level-ten training, progress became more difficult. Finally, one of us achieved the feat.

"Zaheer was the first to open an alternate timeline. We crowded around him afterward as he told us about his experience and how he did it. Amira was next, then me. In total, twelve of us accomplished the feat. We couldn't believe it—a dozen Nexus Tens! We were thrilled. We thought we were an unprecedented boon crop of level-ten Nexi.

"We continued our training and with each passing day were able to create more branches. Some alternate lines were easy to follow. Months, even years, into the future. Other lines were more difficult, overwhelming us with their unpredictability only minutes into the view. But we honed our skills, enabling us to follow the lines farther.

"However, our instructors stipulated that we were never to follow our own timeline or the timelines of other students more than a day ahead, and never more than ten years for others. Not until after the Test. They told us the mind would have difficulty finding its way back if we followed a line too far into the future and viewed events we weren't ready to handle.

"When we reached level ten, our instructors began to distance themselves from us. We had spent years training with them and we'd become close, but they pulled away. We should have realized something was about to happen. They were preparing themselves for the inevitable. They had watched it happen, year after year."

"Watch what happen?" Lara asked.

"We weren't a boon crop of Tens. Every year the Nexus House develops a dozen or so Tens. But our instructors didn't tell us that. They also didn't tell us that a few months later there were none."

"What happened to them?"

"What our instructors didn't tell us was that we weren't really Tens yet. A true Ten can open and process alternate timelines at will, shape those lines with hypothetical scenarios, and simultaneously open new lines and shut down others.

"When a Ten is done viewing, he must terminate each line until only the prime timeline remains. But it's sometimes difficult to distinguish between the Prime and the alternate timelines. Our instructors drilled into us the importance of shutting down the alternate timelines, leaving the Prime as the only one open at the end. *Never* terminate the Prime. They knew what happened if you terminated it, and they deliberately withheld that information from us. They kept us ignorant of the danger we faced until it was too late to turn back.

"It happened to Chenglei first. We were in training, taking turns opening alternate lines. Two Tens viewing at the same time creates turbulence when their lines intertwine, so we took turns. After each view, we discussed the experience and any lessons learned, how to force a line to branch at a specific time, and, always, any difficulty terminating a line.

"We were almost done for the day. Chenglei was the next to last. We waited quietly while he finished his view. We could sense he was terminating his lines. He had this habit of tapping his fingers on his desk. A steady rhythm that helped him concentrate. Then his fingers stopped moving. After a minute, Amira went over and spoke to him softly, then gently shook him. He didn't respond. He was still viewing. But something was wrong.

"One of our instructors walked over, examined him closely, then turned away. She brought her hands to her face and started crying. The other instructor told us our lessons were over for the day. Back to our rooms. We never saw Chenglei again.

"The next day, our instructors explained what happened. Chenglei had terminated the Prime. If you terminate the Prime, you're stuck forever in an alternate line and the mind can't find its way back to the present. You're stuck in a fantasyland, forever detached from reality. Permanently insane.

"When we realized what would happen if we terminated the Prime, we were terrified. Some of us refused to continue training. But our instructors explained that we had no choice. By learning how to open alternate lines, we had opened Pandora's box. There was no turning back. We would either learn to master the view and become Tens or eventually make the same mistake Chenglei made. We were trapped.

"Amira said she would simply stop viewing. Never again open an alternate line and risk becoming insane by terminating the Prime by accident. Then The One told us the Council had given the House a mandate. Anyone with the potential to become a Ten would not be released from the House until they either succeeded or failed. The need for Tens was so great that it justified the means. We would either succeed, go insane, or be confined for the rest of our lives.

"There were eleven of us left, and we debated the issue. We knew that if anyone succeeded in becoming a Ten, he or she would be able to save millions of lives in the war. Eleven lives, versus millions. In the end, we all decided to continue.

"Five of us made it to the *carcerem cellula*, typically referred to as the Test. A final exam of sorts for a Ten. No Nexus who passed the Test had ever shut down the Prime. Unfortunately, the first three failed, leaving only Elena and me. I passed the Test, and a few weeks later, it was Elena's turn.

"The Test is fairly straightforward. Select a Prime to follow. Then open ten alternate lines. Then for each alternate line, force it to branch into ten more. One hundred lines open simultaneously. Ten by ten. A fitting test for a level ten. By the time I took the test, I had already proved I could open and follow a hundred lines. But a Ten has to be able to act in the present as well. He has to be able to talk, respond to situations, and in an emergency, terminate all lines immediately. Terminate all lines but one in a split second. That is the Test.

"I passed, barely. Our instructors warned us repeatedly about keeping emotion from affecting our views. *Never let emotion affect the lines.* They drilled it into us, but I didn't really understand what it meant. But only a few seconds before the end of my Test, before I had to terminate the alternate lines, I finally understood the danger emotion poses to a Ten.

"Imagine an alternate future, a line where everything you've ever wanted comes true—love, wealth, fame—whatever is important to you. Then you have to terminate the lines, but events haven't yet occurred such that this line has become the Prime. You'll lose this alternate line, this future. The line is so compelling that the mind has difficulty letting go. When the decision is made to shut down all lines but one, the mind chooses to shut down the Prime and keep you living in the alternate line, forever. A choice between the Prime, a life filled with the carnage of war, the sorrow of death, the unending loss of everyone precious to you. The choice between reality and a life where everything you want comes true.

"That's the danger emotion poses to a Ten. It almost trapped me. If I had been given a different Test, one where I had to choose between a future where Elena lived and one where she died, I wonder if I would have passed."

Lara saw the pain in his eyes. "I'm so sorry about Elena, Jon." She reached toward him to offer comfort but then stopped, her hand hovering over his, knowing that she'd be able to look into his mind once she touched him. She didn't want to intrude again without asking, but she wondered what Elena was like.

"Jon..." Lara said. "Can I...can I see her?"

McCarthy nodded.

She touched his hand, and white mist obscured her vision. The fog began to clear, leaving her in McCarthy's body again, seeing and hearing everything he had. She knew from previous occasions that she'd also experience the emotions he felt at the time, and she appreciated the intimate nature of what he was sharing with her.

The mist dissipated, leaving McCarthy in the small, dimly lit classroom again. He was sitting beside Elena as she focused on The One. Lara felt Elena's cold, tight grip and her body trembling in fear.

Today she would undergo the *carcerem cellula*. McCarthy had passed the Test several weeks ago. Although Elena had been excited for him, it only helped seal her fate. A Ten came along once every decade on average. The odds that there were two Tens only weeks apart were infinitesimal. Today would be her last day of sanity.

An elderly man entered the classroom. Dmitri was his name, and he was a Metu Lectorum. His special talent let him look into someone's mind and discern what they feared or desired the most. After a nod from The One, he ambled toward Elena, stopping before her. He placed his hand on her forehead and closed his eyes. After a long moment, he withdrew and conferred with The One, whispering something McCarthy couldn't hear. McCarthy viewed the future, trying to discern the outcome of Elena's Test, but her line dissolved as soon as the Test began. In his view, however, he was able to glean an item of interest—Elena would be given the same Test he'd been given a few weeks earlier.

The One approached Elena and provided the initial instructions. "Before we begin, I want you to follow the Prime into the future, focused on me. Follow me until I'm beside my mother's deathbed, then tell me what you see."

Elena tilted her head back slightly and concentrated. After about thirty seconds, she spoke. "I'm there. I'm eight years into the future. You're standing beside your mother's bed. She just closed her eyes. She's dying."

"There's a clock on the wall above her head," Rhea said. "What time is it?"

"It's 8:23."

"Good," Rhea said. "Beside me is a young child, holding my hand. Do you see her?"

"Yes."

"Someone is going to speak her name. What is it?"

"Stephanie. Her name is Stephanie."

Rhea paused before continuing. "Now follow her as she grows up."

"But you said never—"

"Yes, I know. Never follow a line more than ten years into the future. But today you will. You'll be fine. Now follow Stephanie's line."

Elena concentrated again, a faint smile creasing the corners of her mouth as she watched Stephanie grow up. Then she squeezed McCarthy's hand sharply, and the smile disappeared from her face. Her eyes opened wide, her pupils vacillating. A word formed on her lips.

"*Noooo!*"

Tears streamed down her face as she shook her head from side to side.

McCarthy knew what she saw. He had watched Stephanie grow up during his Test. And he had watched as she was incinerated as the Korilians began their attack on Earth. The Colonial Fleet had been destroyed, and the Korilian warships in orbit bombarded Earth with pulse after pulse. And it wouldn't be long before assault ships landed millions of Korilian combat troops on Earth.

Elena looked up at The One. "Tell me this won't happen. That this isn't the future. Please!" Elena pleaded with The One as she started sobbing.

"I'm afraid that what you saw is the future. Now look at me, Elena. We must begin your Test."

Elena looked at McCarthy, then back at Rhea, and her sobs subsided. She sat up in her chair, wiping the tears from her eyes with one hand, the other still holding McCarthy's.

Rhea gave Elena her next set of instructions. "Follow the Prime from the time of my mother's death, focused on Stephanie. Open ten alternate lines from the Prime. Then force each of those to branch ten more times. One hundred lines, minimum. You must shape each line until you find one where the future you saw does not come to pass. A line where Stephanie survives. When you find that line, tell me."

Rhea paused, then asked, "Are you ready?"

Elena nodded.

"Begin."

Elena tilted her head back slightly as she began to open alternate time-lines, searching for one where Stephanie survived. A line where the Korilians were defeated. Several minutes passed quietly as McCarthy waited nervously for Elena to find the line. Elena sat there, immobile except for her steady breathing. Then a smile flashed across her face.

"I found one! I have it."

"Keep following it," Rhea said, walking slowly toward Elena. "Follow it until you're sure." Rhea stopped directly in front of her.

"Yes, this is it. It works. I see Stephanie, and her children."

Rhea slammed her hands on Elena's desk. "Terminate your view! Now!"

Elena squeezed McCarthy's hand tightly, squishing his bones together with enough force to send pain shooting up his arm. McCarthy turned toward Elena.

She sat there, frozen in place.

McCarthy looked at her eyes. They were fixed, staring straight ahead.

Please, no!

But then her eyes began moving, and she looked at Rhea, her face barely a foot away. Rhea took a step back, a relieved expression on her face. Elena turned toward McCarthy, then threw herself into his arms, her legs straddling his waist, her arms wrapped tightly around him, her cheek pressed against his. She was crying. Tears of joy. And tears of grief.

"Oh, Jon. It was horrible!"

"I know," McCarthy said as he caressed her back.

"We have to do something," Elena said. "We have to guide the Prime into the right line. Please tell me we can do that. Tell me we'll be able to change the future."

"We'll try, Elena. We'll try together."

McCarthy's hand twitched and the classroom began to waver and fade, like one video dissolving into another. The classroom disappeared, and Lara found herself in another room. She was still in McCarthy's body, experiencing the emotion he felt at the time. Lara was no stranger to anger, but the rage that consumed him was more intense than anything she had ever felt.

9

"You can't let them take her!"

McCarthy slammed his hands on The One's desk. They were in The One's office, three months after Elena's Test. Rhea sat behind her desk looking up at McCarthy.

"She's only sixteen!" he said. "She needs time to develop! She'll be able to accomplish so much more if she's allowed to continue her training here."

Rhea replied calmly, "The House is powerless in this matter. I voiced my objection, but the decision has been made. The Council informed me last night. Elena has been assigned to the Army and will assist on Darian 3."

"Darian 3! You can't be serious! That planet's a meat grinder!"

"The Council assured me we will be victorious. They've committed to fully replenishing Third Army Group losses each week. With Elena's help, we will hold Darian 3 and turn the tide against the Korilians."

McCarthy stood there fuming, slowly realizing there was nothing he could do. The House, as influential as it was, had to acquiesce to the Council's orders, however ill-advised they were.

"When does she leave? I want to say goodbye."

"I'm afraid it's too late. An Army colonel stopped by to pick her up earlier this morning."

"What!" McCarthy said. "She's already gone!"

"We had very little notice, Jon. We were informed late last night."

"How could you do this to us? You could have at least let us say goodbye!"

"It wasn't my decision. It was Elena's. She requested I not tell you until she was gone."

"I don't believe you! There's no way Elena would leave without saying goodbye. We've been like brother and sister since we got here. Why are you lying to me?"

"You don't understand, Jon."

"What don't I understand! That you and the House are cold and calculating—inhumane in everything you do! In everything you've done to us!" McCarthy's body shook with anger. "We're nothing but a commodity to you! Something you discard if we're defective or fill a delivery order if not!"

"Elena took your place!" Rhea shouted, looking up at McCarthy. "You were the one who was supposed to go to Darian 3. I told Elena last night so she could prepare herself to say goodbye. Instead, she begged me to let her take your place. She pleaded with me. And I agreed. The Council directed me to assign a Ten to the Army, and I complied. They didn't specify which one of you it had to be."

The room reeled as McCarthy grappled with what Elena had done. She had sacrificed herself for him. McCarthy lowered his head, his hands still planted on Rhea's desk as tears began to flow.

"Jon," Rhea said softly. "I know this is hard. But your time here has ended as well. You've been assigned to the Navy, and an officer is here to escort you to your duty station."

McCarthy looked up, then slowly stood erect. Rhea waited patiently as he dried the tears from his face. Then she pressed one of the buttons on the comm panel on her desk. The door to her office opened, revealing a Navy captain standing in the doorway. She was tall and fit, with dark blonde hair tucked neatly into her officer's cap. There was something reassuring about her, something about her steel-blue eyes that exuded both confidence and compassion.

"Hello, Jon," she said. "I'm Captain Nanci Fitzgerald, commanding officer of the battleship *Tulaga*. You've been assigned to my command."

"Are we headed on a suicide mission, like Elena?" McCarthy asked bitterly.

Fitzgerald glanced at Rhea before answering. "No. We're not headed to the Darian system like your friend. I assure you the Navy will not place your talent at risk until the appropriate time, when you are ready. You have much to learn. About the Navy, about commanding a warship, a battle group, and eventually a fleet. We will protect you to the best of our ability while you learn how to best use your talent."

McCarthy stood there, not sure what to say but somehow reassured by the Navy captain.

"Come," she said. "We've already packed what you need." She nodded toward a small duffel bag on the floor outside Rhea's office. "We have a long journey ahead of us."

McCarthy pulled his hand away, and the vision dissipated. Lara was moved by the memories he had shared with her.

"What happened to Elena?" Lara asked softly.

"The Darian campaign was supposed to bleed the Korilians dry, but the opposite occurred. We sent over a billion men and women to their deaths. The Korilian casualties were four times ours, but reinforcements just kept coming. Then the Korilians severed the Fleet's supply lines. Rather than lose more ships while attempting to reestablish a supply route, we abandoned Darian. We left everyone on the planet to die, including Elena. An incredible talent, wasted due to the Council's unwise decisions."

McCarthy paused for a moment, then continued. "After Elena's Test, I told her that together, we'd change the future and defeat the Korilians. Maybe the message she sent from Darian is her way of holding up her end of the bargain. If so, I will hold up mine."

He stood and extended his hand, helping Lara to her feet. "Thank you for joining me here. I wanted you to understand who Elena was and why she was important to me. Plus, I want you to be aware of things about the level-ten view that Rhea would have kept hidden."

"Thanks," Lara said. "I appreciate it."

McCarthy checked his wristlet. "We need to get going. Our ride to Darian will be departing soon."

As they left the atrium, leaving behind the stone bench that McCarthy and Elena had shared as kids, Lara sensed McCarthy's bitterness over Elena's death. She wondered if she would ever love him enough to make the kind of sacrifice Elena had.

10

Lara and McCarthy entered the Domus Praesidium spaceport and headed toward McCarthy's blue-and-white shuttle. She joined him inside the four-person transport, finding her duffel bag already loaded behind their seats, beside McCarthy's bag. The shuttle lifted off, passing slowly through the spaceport doors before increasing speed.

The shuttle shook as it streaked upward through the night sky. Several minutes later, the vibration eased and Lara sensed the spacecraft tilting forward, leveling off from its upward trajectory. Looking out the shuttle window, Lara spotted hundreds of gigantic white starships resting in space, with countless transports flying between them.

"Second Fleet," McCarthy commented, "refitting for battle."

Several of the warships were heavily damaged, with black trenches excoriated in their armor or gaping holes melted through the entire ship. A small gray ship approached a damaged battleship, then slowed and turned around. A sparkling green beam shot out from behind it, completely enveloping the battleship. The gray ship began accelerating toward a repair shipyard in the distance, with the damaged warship in tow.

As they threaded their way through 2nd Fleet, Lara's mind drifted to the pending journey, wondering which starship would take them to Darian 3. "Are we headed to the Second Fleet command ship?"

McCarthy shook his head. "Second Fleet returned from battle today, and it'll take a few weeks to replenish their supplies and receive replacement starships. We'll be joining Third Fleet, which just finished refit and is about to depart."

When McCarthy mentioned 3rd Fleet, Lara's mood brightened. Angeline Del Rio, who had mentored Lara during her hectic training before the Final Stand, was the 3rd Fleet guide.

They left 2nd Fleet behind, approaching another formation in the distance, and 3rd Fleet soon took shape. The 3rd Fleet command ship appeared in the distance, built like a battleship except it had a command bridge—an operations center for the fleet's admiral—above the starship bridge, and extra sensors and communication systems.

The shuttle angled toward the command ship's spaceport, a large opening in the ship's port side. Lara sank into her seat when they entered the spaceport, evidence they were under the influence of the starship's gravity generators. The shuttle slowed to a hover, then settled onto the deck.

The shuttle door opened, and she followed McCarthy down the steps, where they were greeted by Admiral Natalia Goergen and two of her aides wearing the crimson-and-burgundy uniform of the Colonial Fleet, plus the 3rd Fleet guide—Angeline Del Rio—wearing a blue Nexus jumpsuit with eight white bands around each arm.

"Welcome aboard, Jon," Admiral Goergen said as she shook McCarthy's hand.

It was obvious from her smile and demeanor that they were good friends.

Angeline approached Lara and hugged her tightly. "It's so good to see you," she said.

Lara returned the hug as Angeline's words brought tears to her eyes. Her preparation for the Final Stand had been stressful. She had been plucked from Ritalis and inducted into the Nexus House, then thrust into an almost impossible situation—learning enough to become McCarthy's guide for the most important battle in human history. She held onto Angeline for a few seconds, not wanting to let go, but then she heard the rumble of the spaceport doors behind her. They were sealing the command ship, preparing to jump.

Admiral Goergen led the way from the spaceport, with McCarthy walking beside her as they talked. They took an elevator to the command bridge, where fifty men and women manned five tiers of consoles descending to a curved row of display panels mounted below the bridge windows. Goergen took her seat in one of two consoles overlooking the command bridge, while McCarthy stood beside her. Angeline, who was accustomed to the physiological effects of the jump, offered Lara her seat beside Admiral Goergen, which she accepted.

The operations officer turned to Goergen. "All ships report ready for the jump."

Goergen ordered, "Jump at the mark."

The operations officer entered the command into his console, and a few seconds later, five deep tones reverberated throughout the command ship, followed by the computer's female voice over the ship's intercom.

"One minute to the jump."

Ten seconds before the jump, five deep tones reverberated throughout the ship again. When the time reached zero, Lara's vision went black, and she tumbled down a spiraling hole.

11

From her suite atop the 120-story-high Terran Council headquarters building in Beijing, Regent Lijuan Xiang watched 3rd Fleet depart Earth's orbit, then deenergized the display. She stared at the dark monitor, her thoughts drifting into the past. She lamented what had become of her powerful House, almost destroyed by the despicable Nexi thirty-three years ago. Only Lijuan and a few disciples had survived, rebuilding their House at Domus Salus, the last remaining Corvad compound.

After the Nexi prevailed at the main Corvad stronghold of Domus Valens, they had swept the other Corvad compounds, slaughtering all within. After searching Domus Valens, the Nexi had obtained the Corvad registry, identifying all Corvads embedded in public organizations, and had hunted them down. However, a few names and the existence of Domus Salus had been omitted from the registry as a safety measure.

Although the Corvads had been decimated, the Nexus House was also weak. The Nexus One, in her arrogance, had not reconstituted her praetorians, pushing most of her Nines to the Test, and had allowed her Tens to be siphoned off to support the war. She had only one Ten remaining and barely a hundred praetorians. The Nexus arrogance was infuriating but would be used against them. The Nexus One had stood before Lijuan many times and never suspected she was a Corvad Ten.

As McCarthy departed Earth's orbit with 3rd Fleet, Lijuan realized it offered an opportunity to strike a significant blow. The Nexus One was a fool, taking unwise risks in her belief that the Corvad House had been destroyed. Her only Ten was embarking on a mission without a contingent of praetorians to protect him.

Lijuan smiled.

For eighteen years, she had waited patiently for the opportunity to kill Jon McCarthy. Years earlier, with the Korilians advancing toward Earth, it had been too risky to assassinate McCarthy, who might have been humanity's only hope. Her assessment had proven correct, with McCarthy's skill making the difference in the Fleet's Final Stand against the Korilian armada.

But things were different now. Despite the recent defeat at Antares, the situation was still well in hand, with the Fleet outnumbering the Korilian armada two to one. Lijuan still hedged her bets, however. Until she knew more about what the Korilians were planning in four weeks, she could not significantly impair the Fleet. She would let McCarthy complete his mission, then strike. If he found Elena's command center and retrieved her message, it would be provided to Fleet command. If he failed, it would not matter.

Either way, McCarthy would not leave Darian 3 alive.

The Nexus Eight accompanying him was another matter. When Lijuan met Lara before the Final Stand, she had been both stunned and intrigued that Lara had no line to follow into the future or past. However, as their hands touched, she had looked into Lara's mind and discerned that her indoctrination into the Nexus House had been rushed. Her allegiance wasn't firm. Additionally, Lijuan had detected something more important— Lara had the Touch, which made her an excellent candidate for the Corvad House. Perhaps she could be turned.

Lijuan entered a code into her communication panel, establishing an encrypted link to Domus Salus. Her Primus Nine appeared on screen.

"Yes, Princeps."

"I have a mission for you. McCarthy is headed to Darian 3 to search for Elena's last command center. When his mission is complete, kill him and bring the Nexus Eight with him to Domus Salus."

12

Even though jumps took only a few seconds, it seemed much longer as Lara spiraled through the darkness, until she was suddenly on the brightly lit starship bridge again. Although they had completed the jump, the turbulent, swirling sensation didn't cease. The bridge kept spinning, and Lara tried to keep down the gurgling contents of her stomach. She stumbled toward the slot of jump bags, opening one just in time. She braced herself on a console, waiting for the deck to stop spinning as urgent reports echoed in her ears.

"Shields are up!"

Lara felt a tingle as the starship's shields formed, and a glance at the nearest control console showed the command ship in the center of a sphere of twelve battleships, their shields melded together to form a protective outer bubble, augmenting the command ship's own shields.

"No Korilian warships in this sector!"

As the bridge's spinning slowed, Lara looked around. The starship crew sat at their consoles, attending to their duties. Seated in her command chair, Admiral Goergen calmly examined the sensor displays, while Admiral McCarthy stood nearby with Angeline at his side. The Nexus Eight moved toward Lara.

"How do you feel?" she asked.

"Awful," Lara replied. "The same as the first jump I made on *Atlantis*. I haven't made any jumps since that mission."

"It takes about a dozen jumps to get your jump-legs, when the body is able to partially weather the effects of the jump. After three years without jumps, you're starting from scratch."

"How many more jumps do we have?"

"Another eleven to the Darian system, where we'll drop you and Admiral McCarthy off. Unfortunately, we won't be employing the normal twelve-hour jump holds along the way. Fleet command has directed we proceed with ten-hour holds until we reach Darian 3. Apparently, we need to get you two to the planet as soon as possible."

Lara nodded. "Admiral McCarthy's views dissolve in four weeks. He thinks the Korilians are planning a major counteroffensive and that Elena's message holds the key to defeating them. We need to find Elena's message quickly so we have as much time as possible to prepare."

The spinning deck slowly stabilized, but the nausea didn't subside. She sealed her jump bag and dropped it into a disposal slot, then looked out the bridge windows, spotting a barren planet framed by an orange star behind it.

The sensor supervisor announced, "No Korilian recon probes in this sector."

Normal conversations between watchstanders resumed on the starship bridge, and Admiral Goergen rose from her command chair.

McCarthy turned to Lara. "Admiral Goergen and I have a few things to discuss." His eyes shifted to Angeline, who responded to the cue.

"I'll get something to help settle Lara's stomach, then show her to her quarters."

As McCarthy left the command bridge with Admiral Goergen, Angeline turned to Lara.

"We have a lot to catch up on."

Sitting in the crew's lounge across from Angeline, Lara sipped a cup of hot chamomile tea to help ease the nausea.

"How have you been?" Lara asked.

"Things are easier now," Angeline replied, "with starship losses substantially less than during the Retreat. Since the Liberation Campaign began, we've lost only two guides, both assigned to Second Fleet."

Even with the light Korilian resistance, being a fleet guide was a dangerous assignment. Korilian warships targeted the fleet command ships during battle, and although they were heavily protected, the Korilians were occasionally successful. 2nd Fleet had been annihilated during the Final Stand and rebuilt from scratch. Although a few dozen veteran starships had been transferred from the remaining five fleets, it lacked the critical teamwork that developed over time. 2nd Fleet was already on its third admiral and guide since the Final Stand.

"But I've been busy," Angeline said. "Three years nonstop, the same routine: resupply, then battle. After clearing a planetary system of Korilian warships, we support the ground assault from orbit, with the Fleet pulverizing Korilian defensive positions on the planet."

Lara had never witnessed it firsthand but had seen the images—battleships and cruisers aiming their pulses down toward the planet. Although the pulses weren't as strong due to traveling through the planet's atmosphere, given enough time, a Fleet in orbit could reduce the landscape to a wasteland.

"Enough about me," Angeline said. "How are you doing?"

"I'm frustrated, stuck at level eight."

Lara immediately regretted her choice of words—Angeline was an Eight—and Lara didn't want to make it seem that being stuck at level eight was a disappointment. After all, the invaluable fleet guides were Eights. Tens were too rare to be fleet guides, with McCarthy and Rhea being the only Tens, and Nines had an Achilles' heel in complex scenarios. Lara recalled McCarthy's explanation:

Although Nines can view the future, in battle involving thousands of external decisions, a Nine's view is perilous. Think of the future as a maze, and what a Nine might choose as the optimal path at the first intersection might lead to a dead end and disaster. Nines cannot see farther down the line and evaluate all the paths like a Ten can.

With Tens too rare and Nines unsuitable as fleet guides, that left the Eights, whose glimpses of the future provided valuable information.

If Angeline was offended about Lara's comment about being stuck at level eight, it didn't show. "I wouldn't worry," she said. "It will come with time. You've achieved level eight faster than anyone in recent memory, and The One is confident in your ability."

Lara was surprised by Angeline's comment. Rhea rarely praised her, focusing instead on her failure to advance as quickly as hoped. "I didn't realize you've talked with The One."

"Oh, not me," Angeline said. "Channing is Deinde Eight and has special access to The One."

"The One's got me fooled," Lara said. "I don't think she's ever said anything positive."

"Don't take it personally. The One sees many things, and her methods do not always make sense to those who can't see the future as clearly as she does. But she expects great things from you. Channing has been itching to get his hands on you again and complete your fleet guide training, but The One refuses. She believes you'll achieve level ten, and may even become a Placidia Ten."

Lara recalled the conversations she had overheard at Domus Praesidium. Placidia Tens could view the future without creating turbulence, and two or more Placidia Tens could view the same timeline simultaneously, propelling their combined view farther. The exponential ability of multiple Placidia Tens, viewing the same line simultaneously, led to remarkable discoveries and revelations.

"A Placidia Ten? You're kidding. Not even Admiral McCarthy is one, and he's been a Ten for twenty years."

"McCarthy has been preoccupied," Angeline said. "He was a Ten for only a few months before being assigned to the Fleet, and he's been focused on honing his views for battle. Once this war is over, he'll return to the House for additional training, and he might become a Placidia Ten or develop additional talents like The One."

Lara had heard stories of The One's talent, like the time she had taught the arrogant praetorian, Brandon Dargel, an unforgettable lesson, immobilizing him with her mind and almost suffocating him to death. She had felt

The One's power herself, when Rhea had begun to strangle her aboard *Mercy*, the 1st Fleet hospital ship. Thankfully, Channing had intervened upon McCarthy's request, convincing Rhea to let her live.

"Don't be discouraged," Angeline said. "You're only an Eight, yet talents have emerged. Not only are you an empath, but you can discern the drivers behind each emotion, which is no small feat. Plus, you developed the Touch without training. I have no doubt that you have enormous talent, and your empathic and Touch abilities are trivial compared to what you might be capable of." Angeline leaned forward. "I'm with The One. I expect great things from you."

"I wish I shared your optimism," Lara replied, "but I can't even decipher most of my level-eight visions."

"Don't worry," Angeline said. "You'll get there. I trained for over a decade before I reached level eight, and you did it in only three years. Give it time."

Angeline's encouraging words helped, but Lara still wasn't convinced she'd succeed. As she sipped the last of her tea, she felt Angeline's eyes on her.

"So," Angeline said, "how are you and McCarthy getting along?" She added a smile.

"What do you mean?" Lara had an inkling of where Angeline was headed but feigned ignorance.

Angeline leaned forward again, lowering her voice as she spoke. "I don't have to be an empath to realize what's going on. You and McCarthy."

"Oh, that," Lara said. "Another failure."

Angeline stared at her quizzically, and she could tell the Nexus Eight was evaluating whether she was being honest. Lara explained. "I can't figure out where I stand with him. I get the feeling he's interested in me—he always makes it a point to see me whenever he stops by Domus Prae-sidium—but he's never moved forward in that area. And his emotions are so damn hard to detect. I can't get a bead on him from that aspect either."

"You're such a pessimist," Angeline said. "Just like achieving level ten, a relationship with McCarthy will take time. His lack of emotion and reluc-tance to enter into a relationship are perfectly understandable."

It was Lara's turn to offer a quizzical look.

Angeline smiled. "First, he's a Nexus Ten. What was the first House mantra you learned?"

"Emotion is the source of all evil."

"Correct. It's drilled into every Nexus from the day we're inducted into the House, and the issue is even more critical for Tens. Emotion propels the view farther, but it also clouds the view, leading to inaccurate interpretations as to which branch in the future is the prime timeline. McCarthy has been trained to restrain his emotion, and then there's what happened with Teresa."

Lara recalled the discussion she'd had with McCarthy just before the Final Stand. He explained that he had fallen in love and become engaged to Teresa, an officer on his staff when he was in command of the Normandy battle group. When her tour of duty ended, he arranged for her assignment as executive officer of one of the ships in his battle group so he could protect her.

A few months after she transferred, McCarthy's battle group was involved in a fierce engagement, and the situation deteriorated. The battle group needed to jump away, but Teresa's ship was damaged, its jump drive temporarily disabled. McCarthy had to choose between leaving her behind or sacrificing other ships to save her.

He couldn't leave her. He delayed the battle group's departure until her ship's jump drive was repaired, losing five battleships in the process. Thousands dead, sacrificed to save one woman. When he told Teresa what he'd done, she was horrified. She requested a transfer to another battle group to ensure he'd never be tempted to sacrifice anyone for her again. Her ship was destroyed three months later.

"Jon told me," Lara said.

Angeline expounded. "You can understand his reluctance to enter another relationship while the war continues, even if you're temporarily safe within the walls of Domus Praesidium. You're very talented, and I have no doubt that you'll be involved in the war effort again in some way. I'm sure McCarthy is weighing the potential consequences of a relationship with you, not wanting to have the blood of another Teresa on his hands."

Lara reflected on Angeline's words for a moment, then Angeline said, "You don't need to worry about Teresa, or Jon being an emotionless Ten.

He'll come around when he's ready. Trust me," she said, pointing to her head. "I see things." She added a smile.

Lara didn't know whether Angeline was telling the truth or just offering encouraging words, but she accepted the Eight's statement at face value.

Angeline checked her wristlet. "It's late, and I'm sure you're tired from the jump. I'll show you to your quarters. The next jump is scheduled for early morning, so I recommend you keep breakfast light."

"Good idea," Lara replied.

———————

Lara woke an hour before the jump and joined Angeline in the admiral's wardroom for breakfast. Unlike lunch and dinner, breakfast aboard the starship was an informal affair, with food cooked to order as officers—or Nexi in this case—straggled in. Lara ate lightly as advised, and the two Nexi were deep in conversation when they were interrupted by five deep tones reverberating throughout the ship, followed by the computer's voice over the intercom.

"One minute to the jump."

Fifty seconds later, the five deep tones sounded again as the ship's computer counted down the remaining ten seconds. When the time reached zero, Lara's vision went black.

13

Ten jumps later, Lara tumbled through the darkness again, emerging on the starship bridge beside Angeline, who sat in the fleet guide chair. This time, after the twelfth jump of the trip, the nausea was minor—nothing more than an upset stomach. However, her head throbbed and her body ached from the series of shortened jump holds during the four-and-a-half-day trip to Darian 3.

After dropping McCarthy and Lara off at Darian, 3rd Fleet would continue its transit using standard twelve-hour holds to let the physiological effects of the jump dissipate. With battle imminent upon reaching the front line of the Liberation Campaign, Admiral Goergen would arrive with fresh crews, unaffected by short-cycled jump holds.

The now-familiar standard reports were provided to Admiral Goergen, sitting in her command chair, with McCarthy standing beside her.

"Shields are up!"

"No Korilian warships in this sector."

"No recon probes in the area."

Lara's eyes moved to the bridge windows and examined Darian 3, a planet with white clouds partially obscuring orange continents and dark green oceans. But what caught her attention more were the hundreds of destroyed Colonial and Korilian warships strewn throughout the planet's orbit—darkened hulks, some shorn in half, spiraling slowly in space—a somber reminder of the carnage from five long years of combat in the Darian system.

Near the 3rd Fleet formation, a dozen troop transports orbited the planet, with occasional surface assault vehicles streaking up from the planet and entering the troop transport bays. In the distance, outside the orbiting debris of destroyed starships, was a flat gray complex with several dozen executive transports docked, each painted in the green-and-olive Army livery.

"The Eighth Army command center," Angeline said. "Time to say goodbye."

She rose from her chair and hugged Lara. During the long transit from Earth, Lara had gotten to know Angeline even better. Her affinity for the Nexus guide had solidified into a strong friendship, one she hoped to continue once the war was over.

McCarthy bid Goergen farewell, then headed to the spaceport with Lara, where they boarded McCarthy's shuttle. Seconds later, it lifted from the deck as the spaceport doors opened.

It was a short trip to the Army command complex, where they were greeted by an Army four-star general and several colonels.

"Welcome to Eighth Army Command," General Dutch Hostler said.

After a round of introductions, McCarthy and Lara were escorted to the operations center, where they joined Colonel Kurt Coleman around a circular data fusion table.

"Good morning, Admiral McCarthy, Miss Anderson," Coleman began. "We've been apprised of your mission and will provide a platoon that will accompany you down to the planet's surface. But first, I'll brief you on the status of Darian 3 so you'll know what to expect."

Coleman tapped a symbol on the fusion table, and a hologram of the orange planet appeared, rotating slowly just above the fusion table.

"Darian 3 was certified Korilian-free about two weeks ago, and we're in the last stages of retrieving Eighth Army troops and equipment from the planet's surface. However, it's possible a few solitary Korilians have escaped detection, hidden within the thousands of miles of subterranean tunnels. For your safety, you'll be escorted by a twenty-member platoon."

The colonel expanded the planet, showing one continent in more detail.

"Regarding Elena's last command center, we don't have an exact location. We know very little about the last two weeks of the battle before Third Army Group was eliminated, because the Korilians heavily jammed all communications during the final days. However, we know Elena was transferred from Third Army Group command before it was overrun, and reattached to Sixty-Fourth Corps, which was the last operational combat force. There were ten divisions in Sixty-Fourth Corps, which was assigned defense of this section of the final perimeter."

A blue outline of a defense perimeter appeared on the western edge of the continent.

"It's likely that after the Korilians penetrated the perimeter, Sixty-Fourth Corps pulled its flanks back, creating a circular defense, which means the ten divisions fought primarily in this area at the end." The perimeter morphed into a blue circle. "Elena's final command center is likely somewhere in there. That's the best estimate we have," the colonel said, his eyes shifting between the two Nexi. "You'll have to rely on your talents to find the command center."

"I understand," McCarthy replied.

"Once you reach the planet's surface," Coleman continued, "you'll be on foot. One of the weapons employed in ground warfare short-circuits all large electrical systems within range, and there are thousands of modules buried in the terrain. Body armor will still work, but anything requiring more power will shut down, so a hovercraft isn't an option. Your shuttle will land in an unaffected spot as close as possible to your desired location, but from there you'll be on foot. Do you have any questions before you head down to the planet?"

When neither McCarthy nor Lara replied, he added, "I'll escort you to your transport."

14

Seated beside Admiral McCarthy in the Army shuttle, Lara took an anti-nausea pill, then closed her eyes during the rough descent through the planet's atmosphere. Accompanying them in the transport was a twenty-member combat platoon wearing black armor, plus a communications specialist wearing the olive-green Army uniform.

The turbulence subsided, and Lara opened her eyes as the shuttle plunged through the clouds, emerging above one of Darian 3's continents. The planet had once been covered with lush vegetation, but after five years of war before it fell to the Korilians and another year of combat before it was retaken, the ground beneath Lara was barren, pulverized by years of ground combat and starship pulses. Deep trenches traversed the flat landscape, disappearing into the distance, and the ground was littered with damaged combat vehicles. The burnt hulks of Colonial and Korilian starships, which had crashed into the orange soil, dotted the wasteland.

Sitting beside McCarthy, Lara felt the chill from his view. After a moment, the sensation subsided, and McCarthy turned to her and shook his head. He had discerned nothing about the location of Elena's command center, which wasn't unexpected. Without being able to latch onto the time-line of someone in the command center, it was unlikely McCarthy would locate it. However, Lara's ability to detect emotions didn't rely on timelines. Hopefully, she'd be able to detect Elena's emotions and locate their source.

Although the land was barren, Lara sensed strong residual emotions. Over one billion men and women had died on Darian 3, along with an unknown number of Korilians. She could also sense the Korilian emotions —they felt similar to human emotions but were infused with complex elements she failed to grasp. It was as if emotions were a language for Korilians, much more than just feelings.

As Lara prepared to search for Elena's command center, she realized that McCarthy had planned ahead. It was one of the reasons he had invited her to the atrium, letting her use her Touch to look into his mind. During the vision, while McCarthy had held Elena's hand, Lara had felt Elena's emotion. She hoped that, like a fingerprint, she'd be able to discern Elena's residual emotion from the plethora of others who had died on Darian 3.

The shuttle stopped its descent one thousand feet above the surface and slowed, heading west toward the center of 64th Corps' last known position. McCarthy pulled up a display on his wristlet to monitor where they were during their search. As the shuttle crossed over the blue line representing 64th Corps' final perimeter, Lara followed the advice The One had provided prior to departing Domus Praesidium—she visualized Elena standing in the command center, imagining the final seconds of her life before she was slain.

Lara was overwhelmed by the number and intensity of the emotions emanating from the surface. There were *so* many—how would she find Elena in the sea of feelings beneath her? McCarthy must have sensed her apprehension because he gently squeezed her hand, offering encouragement.

As the shuttle passed slowly over 64th Corps' final combat territory, Lara searched for a trace of Elena's emotion. But although she could discriminate between the different emotions—with fear, despair, anger, and hatred being the most dominant—she couldn't differentiate between the sources. She closed her eyes and concentrated on one emotion, fear, trying to determine if there were subtle differences she could use to distinguish between them. Perspiration began to dot her face as she focused, trying to tune out everything except the fear emanating from below.

She had no idea how much time passed, but she eventually felt a nudge on her arm. After she opened her eyes, McCarthy said, "We've completed the transit across Sixty-Fourth Corps' assigned area. We're going to make another pass. Do you have any guidance?"

Lara shook her head, then McCarthy ordered the pilot to make the return pass farther south. After the shuttle reversed course, Lara closed her eyes again and concentrated, and not long thereafter felt McCarthy's nudge again; they had completed the second pass. The shuttle made a third pass, this time over the northern section. When Lara failed to discern anything useful, McCarthy directed the pilot to drop to five hundred feet above the surface and repeat the process.

Lara failed to detect Elena's emotion during the next pass over the center of 64th Corps' last known position, and panic began to set in. McCarthy must have sensed her despair, because he turned to her.

"Give me your hand and use your Touch."

Lara gripped his hand firmly, and she was suddenly back in the classroom where Elena had taken her Test. Lara was in McCarthy's body and Elena was sitting in his lap again, her legs straddling his waist and her arms clamped around him. Elena was sobbing, and Lara felt her tears on McCarthy's cheek. Elena spoke, repeating the same words she had uttered during the same vision a few days ago.

"It was horrible."

"I know," McCarthy said as he caressed her back.

"We have to do something," Elena said. "We have to guide the Prime into the right line. Please tell me we can do that. Tell me we'll be able to change the future."

"We'll try, Elena. We'll try together."

Elena's emotions swirled around her, the fear and despair from her Test almost suffocating Lara. As she wondered why McCarthy had shown her this scene again, Lara detected subtle emotions she had missed the first time she had looked into his mind. Beneath Elena's fear and despair were other emotions: a fierce determination to succeed, plus another emotion completely unexpected.

Hope!

Lara released McCarthy's hand, realizing her mistake. She had been searching for the wrong emotion. Despite the odds, Elena would never have given up hope—hope for humanity—even though her life would soon end.

She turned to McCarthy. "You knew I was searching for the wrong emotion? Why didn't you say something?"

McCarthy shook his head. "I cannot detect emotions. I don't know what Elena was feeling, but I wanted you to take another look."

This time, it was Lara who squeezed McCarthy's hand. "Thank you. I have what I need now."

McCarthy directed the pilot to reverse course and make another pass over the region. Lara concentrated again, and as the shuttle approached the area's center, she detected a faint trace of an unusual emotion considering the circumstances—hope. There was a familiarity to it, and she was certain it was Elena's. But where was the emotion coming from?

She looked out the shuttle window. The landscape rippled with deep ravines and ridges. Lara was certain Elena's command center was nearby, but there were miles of ravines crisscrossing below them, and it would take days or even weeks to search each one.

As she wondered how they could more easily find the command center, Lara's window fogged up. She pulled the sleeve of her Nexus jumpsuit over her hand and wiped the window, but the fog remained. Moisture must have condensed on the outside. But when she looked at the window in the row ahead of her and the one behind her, neither was clouded.

The window suddenly cleared as a cloud of fog leapt from the shuttle toward the planet, and Lara realized she was having a vision. As the fog descended toward the surface, it expanded and began rotating, creating a swirling, tornado-like cone. Lara followed the fog until it touched down on the planet's surface near a deep ravine.

"There," Lara said to McCarthy as she pointed out the window. McCarthy took a picture with his wristlet and Lara annotated the spot on the photo, then McCarthy forwarded it to the pilot along with instructions to land the shuttle nearby. The shuttle pitched downward and began its descent. A few minutes later, it landed gently on the orange soil.

Captain Deshi Zhang, in command of the Army platoon, approached Lara and McCarthy as his unit prepared to exit the shuttle, retrieving their assault carbines from stows near their seats. Information scrolled down the sides of Zhang's helmet facepiece as he spoke, his voice emanating from a speaker near his mouth.

"Admiral McCarthy, while on the surface, you and Miss Anderson will remain in the center of our formation. Let me know where you want to go and if you detect any Korilians in the area. We've scanned the region extensively and found no trace, but if your talents detect anything, let me know. Do you have any questions?"

"None at the moment, Captain."

"Wait inside the shuttle until we verify the surrounding area is clear."

Zhang informed the shuttle pilot that his platoon was ready to debark, and the shuttle ramp lowered onto the planet's surface. Zhang led the way from the shuttle, with his platoon forming a semicircle around the transport, assault carbines held ready. A moment later, he called to Admiral McCarthy. "All clear."

Lara and McCarthy, along with Communications Specialist Trevor Romano, headed down the ramp and joined the combat troops, whose armor had changed color to orange, matching the surrounding dry and dusty terrain. They moved toward the ravine, stopping at the edge. It was about a fifty-foot-wide chasm, dropping straight down over one hundred feet.

Zhang pulled up a satellite image of the area on his facepiece. He studied it for a moment, then said, "We can descend into the ravine a few hundred yards to the left."

He gave the order, and his platoon began moving again, forming a protective perimeter around Lara and McCarthy, as well as Romano. They followed the ravine's path until they found a section of the cliff wall that had given way, forming a steep path down.

After picking their way down the boulder-strewn incline, they reached the bottom of the ravine, then headed toward the spot Lara had identified.

They scanned the ravine walls as they traveled, looking for an indication of the command center entrance. But the walls were fairly smooth, with only sporadic shallow alcoves. Lara focused on Elena's emotion. It was more intense than it had been while flying overhead and was growing stronger.

They passed their starting point, with the shuttle on the plateau above them, and continued on without any sign of the command center. But Elena's emotion continued to strengthen. Then they reached a section of the ravine where the cliff walls had collapsed in several locations, crowding the path with rubble. As they traveled past the collapsed section, Elena's emotion began to fade.

"There," Lara called out, pointing to the landslide.

Captain Zhang gave an order, and two soldiers took station on either end of the ravine while the rest began clearing the rubble, moving the smaller rocks away and breaking the larger boulders into pieces with pulse blasts. After almost an hour, a small dark hole appeared.

They continued clearing the rocks away until the opening was large enough to walk through. Zhang led half of his platoon inside, leaving the other ten soldiers in the ravine protecting Lara and McCarthy.

It was quiet in the ravine while they waited, and the minutes passed slowly. Finally, Zhang and his soldiers emerged.

"All clear," Zhang reported. "There are no other entrances to the command center and no Korilians—alive—inside. Follow me."

He led the way, with McCarthy, Lara, and Romano trailing him into the dark opening. When they stepped into the darkness, Zhang activated a light in his helmet, illuminating a tunnel. It wasn't long until they reached thick metal doors that had been blown partially open, evidenced by black scorches and molten pulse marks. Beyond the door, the tunnel opened into a large cavern. As they entered the command center, they stepped on something crunchy for about twenty feet. Looking down, Lara spotted translucent exoskeletons—Korilian remains—piled knee-high, which crumbled as they waded through them.

Beneath the Korilian remains were dozens of human skeletons inside olive-green uniforms that had been slashed to shreds. The men and women serving in the 64th Corps headquarters had made a valiant stand as the Korilians forced their way inside. Lara focused on Elena's emotion again, wondering if any of the skeletons were Elena. But the emotion emanated from farther back in the cavern.

Romano pulled a lightstick from his backpack and activated it, illuminating several rows of dust-covered electronic consoles that stretched into the distance before fading into the darkness. Romano placed the lightstick on a nearby console and activated another lightstick, then Zhang led the way deeper into the cavern.

Elena's emotion grew as the darkness receded, and they soon reached the end of the command center—an alcove with consoles lining the wall and its floor littered with skeletons. Elena's emotion was strongest in the center of the alcove where a decapitated skeleton lay, its skull a few feet away.

When Lara focused on the headless skeleton, the emotions that flooded her body were so intense that she almost recoiled. She had been concentrating on the hope Elena had harbored until the very end, and hadn't prepared herself for the terror Elena had experienced as a razor-sharp Korilian limb sliced through her neck.

Romano surveyed the equipment consoles lining the alcove, then approached one, placing his lightstick on a nearby workstation. He examined the console, then removed and rummaged through his backpack, retrieving a fist-sized battery pack. He opened one of the console panels and swapped out the battery packs, then pressed the power button. The console energized, with messages scrolling down the display. He turned to McCarthy.

"This is the main communication console. Anything transmitted from this command center would have been routed through it. Give me a minute and I should be able to locate the transmission you're looking for."

Romano scrolled through the message directory, and a moment later, he called out, "I've got it. It's the last transmission sent. Do you want me to play it or just download it?"

"Play it," McCarthy said.

Romano entered a command, and a holographic image of Elena appeared in the center of the alcove, near where the skeleton lay. She was exhausted, with dark circles under her eyes—just as Lara remembered from her vision. Even though they were looking at a hologram, Lara sensed Elena's presence. She exuded a calm confidence that somehow put Lara at ease in this cavern filled with human and Korilian remains.

Romano tapped another command, and Elena's last transmission began playing. Her hologram shook every few seconds, accompanied by dirt drifting down from above, along with the deep rumble of nearby explosions.

"This is Major Elena Kapadia, attached to the last operational Third Army Group headquarters. This will be our last transmission. Whoever receives this message, forward it to the Colonial Council—they will understand. It is of the utmost importance. Billions of lives are at stake. In eighteen years, the war will turn against us again, but I have found a way to end the war. You must destroy the Korilian complex on the fourth planet in the Hellios system. Then you must send a strike force to the Korilian home world."

There was a loud rumble, and the hologram froze. McCarthy turned to Romano. "Is there anything else?"

Romano shook his head. "This is all there is."

McCarthy nodded his understanding, then Romano terminated the hologram and downloaded the transmission into his wristlet. Romano stood and donned his backpack. "I'm done here."

There was no response from McCarthy, then he knelt near Elena's skull. It was tilted slightly to the side, its vacant orbs staring at him. Slowly, he reached toward it.

It took a second for Lara to realize what he was doing—he was preparing to use a level-seven skill, the ability to follow timelines that had interacted with objects in the past. Although Elena's timeline no longer existed, anything she had interacted with would have a residue of her line, and nothing would have a stronger residue than her skull.

But to learn anything about Elena's last hours, McCarthy would have to relive the last seconds of her life—traumatic images that would be seared into his memory—the moment the Korilian severed her head and sent it rolling on the ground, her mind still conscious and gripped in unimaginable terror while the blood drained from her brain.

McCarthy paused with his fingers an inch from her skull. His hand hovered in the air for a few seconds, then he pulled it back and looked away.

Lara knelt down and wrapped an arm around him, pulling him close. Even though she couldn't see McCarthy's face and he was exceptional at controlling his emotions, she knew he was in pain. As a grief counselor on Ritalis, she had shared the emotional experience with the next of kin thousands of times. Kneeling beside McCarthy, however, an unusual emotion surfaced. She was jealous. She wanted McCarthy to care as much about her as he did Elena.

She pushed the selfish thought away as McCarthy stood. He asked Zhang, "Can you have Elena's remains transported to Earth?"

"Yes, Admiral," Zhang replied. "I'll arrange the transport, and you can provide routing instructions once her remains arrive in Earth's orbit."

McCarthy acknowledged, and Lara felt a chill as he began viewing the future again. His body stiffened.

To Zhang, he said, "We have company."

15

Captain Zhang spoke, but Lara didn't hear anything; he was attempting to communicate with his platoon outside via his armored suit comms. He spoke again, and this time his voice emanated from his helmet speaker.

"I've lost communication with my platoon. We're being jammed."

He moved quickly toward the command center entrance, with the others following, stopping beside the partially open door, assault carbine held ready. He tried to contact his platoon again.

"Still nothing. Stay here while I check things out."

Zhang slipped through the doorway and headed down the tunnel. To Lara's surprise, McCarthy followed.

"Captain Zhang said to stay here," Lara whispered.

"It's not going to matter," McCarthy replied.

Lara felt the cold sensation from McCarthy's view. If he said it wouldn't matter, that was good enough for her. She followed him, with Romano close behind.

They exited the tunnel to find Zhang's platoon lying on the ground. All were immobile and bleeding from their armored joints, and some had been dismembered. Standing among them were ten men and women, each wearing a shimmery gray jumpsuit. Each man carried two thin swords—katanas—strapped to his back, while each woman had two daggers sheathed in waist holsters. They wore no armor, although they had blue glowing pads wrapped around each forearm.

Zhang pointed his assault carbine at the nearest man. "All of you, step aside. Back against the ravine walls." He was clearing a route to the landslide they had descended from the plateau.

"I'm afraid we won't do that," one of the men in gray said. He appeared to be the oldest of the group, somewhere in his forties. Zhang swung his carbine toward him.

"Move aside," Zhang repeated. "I'm not going to ask again."

"Put down your weapon," the man said, "and your death will be relatively painless. If you do not..." He gestured toward the nearest dismembered soldier.

Zhang fired his pulse-rifle, but the man reacted even before he pulled the trigger, swinging his forearm in front of his body. Zhang's pulse reflected off the glittering blue arm pad, blasting a hole into the ravine wall behind the man. Zhang fired again, a three-pulse shot. This time, the man used the blue pads on both forearms, reflecting the pulses from one pad to the other, sending each pulse back toward Zhang. The pulses hit Zhang in his chest, blasting him onto his back. Wisps of smoke rose from his partially melted chest armor as Zhang pushed himself to his feet, leveling his assault carbine at the man again.

"You're a slow learner," the man said.

Before Zhang could respond, the man pulled a metal star the size of his palm from a thin pocket in his jumpsuit and flung it toward the Army captain. A few feet into its journey, the star separated into six pieces—five points and the center—each maneuvering independently toward Zhang.

Zhang got off three pulses, taking out the center and one point before the others reached him. The four remaining points sliced into Zhang's armor, penetrating the arm and leg joints, then detonated a second later, tearing Zhang's limbs from his body. His torso landed on the ground, blood pouring from the armored suit holes. Zhang groaned in pain for a few seconds before his face went slack.

Lara turned away as she splattered the ground with vomit, wiping her mouth with the back of her hand as she turned back toward the carnage.

Romano asked, "What do you want with us?"

He had barely finished speaking when a dagger went flying toward him. Lara turned in time to see the weapon impale Romano through his throat, its tip protruding from the back of his neck. He dropped to his knees and pulled the dagger out as blood gushed from the wounds. He clamped a hand over each opening, trying to stem the loss of blood as it also gurgled from his mouth. It wasn't long before he collapsed onto the ground.

Lara also wondered what the men and women wanted with them, but she wasn't about to ask now.

The man moved forward, stopping a few paces from McCarthy. The man grinned, then spoke again. "It's unbelievable how incompetent the Nexus One is, letting her only Ten travel outside the safety of a Colonial warship without a guard. She herself travels with only four praetorians instead of the standard ten."

McCarthy replied, "The One can take care of herself, and you will pay with your lives."

"I think not," the man said as he reached for a sword.

As the blade slid from its sheath, Lara felt a burst of heat inside her abdomen, like a furnace igniting. The warmth spread swiftly, radiating out to her limbs. Without thinking, she stepped in front of McCarthy with her hands up, her fingers curled into claws facing outward.

The man laughed. "What do you plan to do, Nexus wench? Scratch me to death? Gouge my eyes out?"

"You dare attack us, you witless fool?" The words tumbled from Lara's mouth involuntarily as the heat kept building. Her face felt flush, and her hands began tingling.

The man's eyes narrowed. "Step aside," he said, placing the point of his blade between Lara's breasts.

McCarthy grabbed Lara roughly by the shoulders and guided her behind him.

"You will deal with me," McCarthy said.

"My pleasure," the man replied.

Lara peered around McCarthy, wondering what his plan was. As far as she knew, he had no special talent and only basic praetorian training. As the heat kept building inside her body, Lara spotted movement. Ronan and nine other Nexi were rappelling down the ravine wall behind the men and women in gray. They were outfitted with the same type of weapons, wearing blue jumpsuits instead of gray.

The Nexi hit the ground simultaneously and withdrew their swords and daggers. The men and women in gray heard the Nexi land and spun toward them. McCarthy retreated toward the command center entrance, pulling Lara with him as they watched the fight unfold.

Several of the men and women in gray threw metallic stars at their opponents. The targeted Nexi raised their forearms perpendicular to their body, and Lara felt a pulse emanate from the glowing blue pads on their arms, detonating the stars midflight. At the same time, each Nexus raced toward a different opponent.

The women moved with blazing speed and catlike dexterity, evading sword swings and dagger thrusts as they attacked. The edges of their daggers glowed bright red, as did the men's swords. Likewise, the edges of the weapons used by the men and women in gray also glowed red once they were employed.

Ronan was the last to engage, attacking the man in charge of the gray-clad detachment. By then, one of the Nexi's opponents had already been felled while a Nexus lay sprawled on the ground. Ronan attacked with crisp, sharp movements, driving his opponent backward until he hit the ravine wall. The man's determination steeled, and he unleashed a furious assault, driving Ronan back a few paces. Behind them, two more men and women in gray went down, along with another Nexus.

Ronan halted the man's advance, then his tactics suddenly changed. His attack became more fluid, one move blending seamlessly into another as he drove his opponent back again. Lara sensed desperation from the retreating man as he warded off each of Ronan's blows a fraction of a second later than the previous one.

The man in gray was in pure defense mode now, hoping one of his comrades would come to his aid. But two more men and women in gray had fallen, along with another Nexus. The remaining four in gray were engaged by six Nexi, and another one fell. It was now six against three. There would be no aid.

Ronan's opponent had little time to contemplate his fate, because Ronan's sword finally pierced the man's defense, slicing deep into his left shoulder. His left arm drooped, but he continued fighting using the sword in his right hand, warding off Ronan's blows in increasing desperation, backing up more quickly. But then his back hit the ravine wall again, and after the next parry, one of Ronan's swords sliced through the man's right wrist, sending his hand and sword flying aside.

Lara figured the battle between Ronan and his opponent was over, but the man reached for one of the shuriken on his belt. A swift response from Ronan severed the man's other arm just below the elbow, with his sword slicing a third of the way into the man's waist. Ronan withdrew his blade as the man fell to his knees, blood gushing from two bloody stumps and the gash in his side.

Ronan turned to assess the status of the rest of the battle in time to spot the last man in gray fall to the ground, his head severed. Three Nexi were down and were quickly tended to by other Nexi while Ronan returned his attention to his opponent.

"What house are you from?"

The man glared up at him. Ronan placed the point of his blade on the base of the man's throat. "What house?"

The man remained defiant. "You will never find out."

"We'll see about that."

Ronan examined the other men and women in gray, identifying four who were still alive. But then all four began convulsing and foaming at the mouth. Ronan spun back toward his opponent, only to watch him begin trembling, then collapse onto the ground in convulsions. Foam oozed from his mouth into the parched ground, and not long thereafter, he lay still. After a quick survey, Ronan confirmed all of their adversaries were dead.

The heat inside Lara extinguished.

After a glance at McCarthy and Lara, verifying they were fine, Ronan stopped by each injured Nexus. As Ronan checked on his praetorians, McCarthy turned to Lara.

"What the hell were you thinking, stepping in front of me?"

"I don't know," Lara replied. "I felt this heat growing inside me, and I reacted instinctively, without thinking."

McCarthy gave her a curious look as Ronan approached.

"That's right," Ronan said. "You weren't thinking. Next time, leave the fighting to praetorians."

Lara didn't care for Ronan's rebuke. "At the time," she said dryly, "there weren't any praetorians in sight."

"That's because we weren't supposed to be seen. The One isn't as incompetent as our friend here believed. Once Rhea learned you were headed to the planet's surface, she assigned a standard guard detachment. I haven't been out in the field for a while, so I decided to lead. We were focused on protecting you from stray Korilians, however, not a house attack." He placed his hand on McCarthy's shoulder. "You did well with your continuous view, keeping theirs disrupted so they couldn't foresee our arrival."

Ronan's gaze swept over the ten dead men and women in gray. "Something is amiss. What would a minor house have to gain by killing you? Plus, they've hidden their affiliation, wearing gray instead of their house livery."

He turned to one of the Nexus praetorians. "Get retina scans and DNA samples, and run them through the databases. Find out who they are."

"Is it possible they're Corvads?" McCarthy asked. "That a cell survived?"

"It's possible. They fought like Corvads, although they weren't as good as they were thirty years ago. They could also be from one of the minor houses aligned with the Corvads during the House War. Their praetorians were trained by Corvads."

McCarthy knelt beside Romano, removing his bloodied wristlet, which had downloaded Elena's message. After rejoining Ronan, he said, "Elena's remains are in the middle of an alcove at the back of the command center." He gestured toward the dark opening. "Transport them to Domus Praesidium."

16

The injured Nexi were soon ambulatory, assisted by other Nexi, and the eight surviving praetorians escorted McCarthy and Lara to the Army shuttle, carrying the two dead Nexi and Elena's remains. Upon reaching the shuttle on the plateau, they found the pilot dead inside the cockpit, his throat slit. There was no sign of the ship the gray praetorians had arrived in, but Ronan spotted landing marks in the orange soil nearby. He examined the imprints.

"Class-two light shuttle with a jump drive. The pilot took off once he realized his detachment had been slain." He looked skyward. "He must have had proper authorization codes to make it planet-side with Eighth Army still controlling the Darian system." Ronan turned to a nearby praetorian. "Have House intel scan the Eighth Army transit database, identifying all shuttles departing Darian 3 in the last hour."

Three years ago, Ronan's order—revealing the Nexus House could infiltrate encrypted military networks—would have surprised Lara. But she had learned that the Nexus House held influential positions in every public, private, and military organization, providing access to critical information.

McCarthy and Lara were escorted to Ronan's shuttle, which was hidden in a trench not far away. It was similar to the Army shuttle except it was larger due to having a jump drive, and painted blue and white instead of Army green.

The shuttle lifted off from the planet's surface and soon docked at the 8th Army command ship in orbit. McCarthy and Lara, along with their Nexus guard, were escorted to the operations center, where they downloaded Elena's message from Romano's wristlet. The message was immediately transmitted to the Colonial Defense Force headquarters on Earth, as well as to the separate Fleet and Army command centers.

After learning Elena had directed them to destroy a Korilian facility in the Hellios system, Colonel Kurt Coleman manipulated the fusion table controls, and a three-dimensional hologram of the Hellios system appeared, floating above the fusion table. The system comprised seven planets orbiting a reddish-orange star.

Coleman scanned the data on the fusion table, displayed on the flat surface beneath the hologram. "We don't know much about the Hellios system," he said. "The fourth planet is marginally habitable from an atmosphere and temperature perspective, but we know nothing about its ecosystem. It could be a barren, rocky planet without life, or a lush world crawling with Korilians." He surveyed a screen across the operations center as several blinking new icons appeared on it. "Fleet Command just dispatched recon probes, so we'll learn more soon."

General Hostler examined another screen displaying a map of the galaxy, which was zoomed in on the area of interest. "This is not a good scenario," he said. "The Hellios system is deep in Korilian-controlled territory, within the original boundary of the Korilian Empire. Any force we send that deep into Korilian-controlled territory will be at significant risk.

"But it's not my call," Hostler added. "Once we know what we're dealing with on Hellios 4, the five-stars and Council can assess the risk and decide."

17

The Nexus shuttle materialized in Earth's orbit, completing the twelve-jump return trip from Darian 3. The shuttle was challenged by the nearest orbiting defense station, and the pilot transmitted the proper codes. A portal in the defense shield surrounding the planet opened, which the shuttle slipped through and began its descent through the atmosphere.

As Lara endured the bumpy ride, she looked forward to a long, hot shower in Domus Praesidium. The Nexus shuttle had no berthing or shower facilities, just standard shuttle seats and lavatories. While the Nexus Nines and McCarthy seemed capable of getting a good night's sleep in a reclining chair, Lara slept fitfully, awaking occasionally with her head on McCarthy's shoulder and his arm around her. Each time she woke in his arm, he simply released her as she sat up, making no comment, as if offering his shoulder was a service he'd provide to anyone.

The shuttle plunged through white cumulus clouds toward its destination—the snow-capped Ural Mountains. Turning eastward, it angled between two jagged mountain peaks, descending into a spaceport as its doors retracted open. A gentle bump announced the end of their transit.

The shuttle door slid open, and as they debarked, McCarthy told Lara to meet in the Nexus One's office in thirty minutes. Just enough time to clean up.

"They were clearly praetorians," Ronan said, "which is unacceptable."

He was seated between McCarthy and Lara in The One's office, facing Rhea at her desk. Ronan had forwarded a mission debrief to Rhea shortly after departing Darian 3, detailing the encounter with the detachment of gray-clad men and women outside Elena's command center.

Ronan asked, "Were you able to identify any of the attackers from the retina scans and DNA samples?"

"Nothing," Rhea replied. "Whoever launched this attack has the ability to alter the planet registries, deleting personnel records. Even a minor house would be capable, which doesn't clarify the matter."

She leaned back in her chair. "There are two main possibilities which must be dealt with. The first and most likely is that a minor house attacked us after learning of our current shortage of praetorians, going after our most vital asset." She glanced at McCarthy. "The second is that a Corvad cell survived and has gained enough strength to attack. As you stated, both are unacceptable and must be dealt with. How do you recommend we proceed?"

"You already know the answer," Ronan said sharply. "You must disregard the Council's edict and stop pushing all excess Nines to the Test. We have only one hundred praetorians, and there is no telling how many praetorians a minor house alliance or a Corvad cell might muster against us. We must reconstitute our strength as rapidly as possible."

Rhea nodded. "Done. How many Nines do we have in training that you expect to certify as praetorians?"

"About fifty in this year's cycle." Ronan paused before continuing, and Lara sensed the resentment in his words. "It will take almost two decades to rebuild the legion. For thirty *years* I've asked this of you, and now we are in crisis."

"We are not in crisis," Rhea replied. "But it is wise to rebuild our strength as quickly as possible. In the meantime, sweep all Corvad compounds again, looking for any sign that a Corvad cell survived. If so, find it and destroy it. I will deal with the minor houses."

Rhea turned to McCarthy. "Do you have anything to add before you depart for Colonial Defense Force headquarters?"

"Nothing."

Rhea examined Lara for a moment before speaking. "Do you have any insights on what you felt before you stepped in front of McCarthy on Darian 3?"

Lara shook her head. She was as perplexed as anyone regarding the heat she'd felt spreading through her body. The heat had dissipated even quicker than it had built and hadn't recurred.

"You're excused," Rhea said to McCarthy and Lara. "Ronan and I have a few other issues to discuss."

After leaving The One's office, McCarthy escorted Lara to her room before departing for the Colonial Defense Force headquarters. Lara walked slowly through the corridors, hoping to extend their time together.

"Why would another house try to kill us on Darian 3?" she asked.

"It's most likely residual animosity from the House War."

Lara recalled that Angeline, the 3rd Fleet guide, had mentioned the House War during Lara's initial training, informing her that she would learn more while studying with the Sevens, who were responsible for House lore. Due to Lara's accelerated training, progressing through eight levels in only three years, her history lessons with the Sevens had been truncated.

"Angeline mentioned something about the House War while I was training to be your fleet guide, but I don't recall the details."

"When the Corvads split from our House three millennia ago," McCarthy replied, "the other five major houses also split, and the six false houses attacked the six true, original ones. Over the last three thousand years, the Corvads destroyed the houses aligned with us, while we eliminated those allied with them. Many minor houses were also destroyed or devastated."

"Minor houses?"

"A minor house is one that doesn't have the ability to develop Tens.

That training is closely guarded by major houses for obvious reasons. Right now, the Nexus House is the only major house remaining, and there are about two dozen minor houses, most of which were aligned with us during the House War, but some were Corvad allies."

They reached Lara's quarters, and she lingered beside her door, continuing the conversation a few moments longer.

"What are you going to discuss at the Colonial Defense Force headquarters?" she asked.

"The Hellios operations brief. The reconnaissance is complete and we have a plan, but it requires approval by the Joint Chiefs and Council."

Lara was intrigued and wondered how difficult the mission might be, wanting to learn more. "Can I attend the briefing?"

McCarthy considered her request for a moment. "Yes. Since you were a former fleet guide and a potential future one, I can arrange your attendance. I'll have to ask The One for permission to take you, though." He paused, and a chill passed over Lara as she felt McCarthy's view. "But I already know her answer. We leave in ten minutes."

Still inside Rhea's office, Ronan asked, "What do you make of what Lara experienced on Darian 3?"

"I don't have an opinion yet," Rhea replied. "I've discussed the matter with the Primus Talentum, and he wasn't able to shed much light on what ability Lara might have. Internal heat is basic to many talents and is more an indication of her latent power than a specific ability. However, it's useful to note that her talent began to surface when she was in peril. Talents can sometimes be triggered if the wielder believes his or her life is in danger, and it appears that's the case with Lara.

"However, the Primus Talentum advised me to not attempt to trigger her talent until he's had a chance to work with her. If a talent is triggered too early, it can surface in unpredictable and unmanageable ways. That means we continue Lara's training as scheduled. Unless the situation becomes dire, we'll focus on her talent once she reaches level ten. Any questions?"

Ronan was uncharacteristically quiet.

"What concerns you?" Rhea asked.

"I felt it," he said. "I felt her power in the ravine. It was more intense than what I felt from The Three. A power stronger even than yours."

Rhea evaluated Ronan's words. Before she could respond, he added, "It's a mistake to train her. She's too old, and need I remind you—she has the Touch."

"That power you felt is exactly why I've decided to train her. I feel it as well, and I'm convinced she will be a tremendous asset once she develops her talent."

A scowl formed on Ronan's face. "I am responsible for defending this house, and you have disregarded my primary recommendations for thirty-three years. Only now do you acknowledge the need for more praetorians, and you continue to insist on training Lara. In addition to having the Touch, she has no line to follow and you cannot see her future. She could easily be used against us if she defects to another house."

"Then I suggest you be nicer to Lara," Rhea said sarcastically, "so she doesn't defect."

"I have a better suggestion. Kill her and eliminate the possibility she might be used against us."

"That's enough!" Rhea replied. "You are responsible for defending this house, which means protecting all Nexi, including Lara. Do not bring this recommendation up again unless you have new information to convince me my decision is unwise. Do you understand?"

Ronan hesitated for a moment, then replied, "Yes, One."

A vibration from Rhea's wristlet broke the tension between them. Chen Wei, the Primus Seven, appeared on the wristlet display.

"We have a new discovery concerning the Codex," Wei said. "We've recovered another portion of The Five's guidance concerning the One with no line."

"I'll be right there," Rhea replied.

She locked eyes with Ronan before leaving.

18

Rhea headed toward the south wing of the two-mile-long Nexus complex. As she traversed the passageways, her thoughts dwelled on Lara. She was an enigma, a person with no prime timeline to follow into the future or past. Until she met Lara, Rhea hadn't encountered the phenomenon before. Every living organism, even the tiniest microbe, had a line that could be followed.

After encountering Lara, Rhea had searched for guidance in the Codex, the repository of all crucial Nexus House wisdom. She had found a reference in the text of The Five, in the last segment of their wisdom, akin to the Bible's Book of Revelation:

Harken the arrival of the One with no line...

Unfortunately, the rest of the passage was missing. Five hundred years ago, the Codex had been destroyed during a Corvad attack that breached the Praesidium walls for the first and only time in three thousand years. It had taken over a century, but the Codex had been rebuilt, some of the knowledge pieced together from remnants of the original, other knowledge reconstituted from excerpts available elsewhere in the House, used for training the various levels. But the most crucial information was likely lost forever.

Only once in the history of the House had there been five Placidia Tens, whose ability to view the same timeline simultaneously led to remarkable discoveries and revelations, recorded in the Codex for following generations. Regrettably, The Five's wisdom and guidance had been destroyed and only partially reconstituted. The Sevens continued working with the remnants of the original Codex, hoping to recover the missing sections.

Rhea stopped outside a set of double doors in the Praesidium's south wing. After placing her palm on the identification screen, the doors whisked open, and she entered the laboratory where the Sevens worked on the remaining segments of the Codex. She found Chen Wei, the Primus Seven, waiting inside.

Rhea surveyed the busy laboratory, with twenty of the most capable Sevens interspersed between dozens of small robotic arms. Each arm was working with a section of the damaged Codex, organizing black flakes no bigger than the tip of a pen, attempting to reassemble the charred remains of burnt pages while the Sevens determined whether the hidden letters made sense grammatically in the order arranged and, more important, whether the letters and words they formed had previously existed beside each other before the pages had burned. Painstaking work, with success measured in a phrase a week.

Chen Wei approached. "We have finally made progress on the relevant text of The Five," he said.

"What have you found?"

"It is not much, but it confirms your assessment of Lara's importance. We have partially completed The Five's sentence. It now reads—*Harken the arrival of the One with no line, for she is the harbinger of...*"

Rhea mulled the new information, pondering its meaning.

The harbinger of what?

Death? Destruction? Salvation?

The phrase was too open-ended. Also unclear was whether Lara was a harbinger of events related to the House or something else, perhaps the Korilian War. And did Lara play a key role, or was she simply an indicator? If she played a key role, what guidance had The Five recorded in the Codex?

Help her, or kill her?

Rhea's frustration began to mount, building on her resentment of what the despicable Corvads had done, compounded by the slow progress of her Sevens.

"We must recover this entire section of the Codex," she said. "Focus all resources on this area."

"Yes, One," Chen replied.

Rhea's thoughts returned to Lara. It was clear that she would somehow play a critical role. But despite Rhea's strong words to Ronan, she wasn't yet convinced whether Lara was an ally or enemy. The guidance from The Five, once recovered, would hopefully answer that crucial question.

19

The Fleet transport pierced the thick gray clouds above Brussels, descending toward the Colonial Defense Force headquarters in the heart of the city. Peering out the shuttle window, Lara took in the ancient sites: the Grand Place medieval square, the Cathedral of St. Michael and St. Gudula, and the Parc du Cinquantenaire with its Triumphal Arch. McCarthy sat beside her, not interested in the landmarks, having visited Brussels countless times.

She felt the cold sensation from his view during the entire trip as he evaluated the assault on the fourth planet in the Hellios system, assessing various options and subsequent outcomes. In every view thus far, he could perceive the landings on the planet's surface, but no further.

As McCarthy had previously explained, in chaotic scenarios like battle, where thousands of decisions are made every minute, the prime timeline dissolved quickly. In some scenarios, a Ten could see only a few minutes into the future. It was clear that there would be heavy fighting on the planet's surface, but McCarthy seemed confident that during the engagement, he'd have a consistent five-to-ten-minute view ahead. Still, it would be better if the outcome could be predicted before the assault began.

As they prepared to land, Lara wondered if he had pierced the darkness during their trip.

"Any luck?" she asked.

McCarthy shook his head as the shuttle thrusters kicked in, slowing the transport's descent toward the two-hundred-story-high Colonial Defense Force headquarters.

The shuttle landed on a rooftop pad, and McCarthy and Lara were escorted by a Colonial Defense Force aide into an elevator, which descended to one of the secure levels several hundred feet below the surface. Fleet Admiral Fitzgerald had requested they talk before the meeting, and McCarthy and Lara entered a small conference room. Fitzgerald was waiting with her deputy fleet commander, Admiral Liam Carroll, and Captain Tom Wears, who was Fitzgerald's liaison with Fleet Intelligence.

After Lara and McCarthy joined the Fleet officers around a conference table, Fitzgerald opened the dialogue.

"You did well on Darian 3," she said, addressing both McCarthy and Lara. "We were able to fill in the missing information in Elena's message, and as you know, she was right. There's an important Korilian facility on Hellios 4." To McCarthy, she said, "You've reviewed the reconnaissance and proposed assault plan, but before we brief the rest of the Joint Chiefs and senior Council members, I need your assessment. Hellios is deep in Korilian territory. Will we succeed?"

"I cannot say with certainty," McCarthy answered. "Predicting the outcome of a battle so many jumps away is difficult, and my views terminate at the planet's surface. However, my assessment is—trust Elena's view. She was able to accomplish something neither I nor Rhea were able to do, foreseeing this critical junction eighteen years ago. If she believed the facility must be destroyed, then we do what it takes."

"Fair enough," Fitzgerald replied. "Do you have any recommended changes to the proposed plan?"

"I have one. Second Fleet has been assigned to the Hellios task force, but the Second Fleet guide is our newest. Third Fleet is being pulled back for resupply after their attack in the Pleiades cluster, which means the Third Fleet guide is available for this assault. Angeline is our most experienced guide, and I recommend she be assigned to this mission."

"Done," Fitzgerald replied. "I'll swap guides while Second Fleet is outbound. Finally," she added, "I take it that you and Rhea agree that you should accompany combat troops into the Korilian facility?"

"What?" Lara interjected. "You can't be serious. Admiral McCarthy's not trained for combat. Why would you risk your most valuable asset by sending him inside that facility?"

Before Fitzgerald or McCarthy could reply, the conference room door opened, and a Colonial Army aide entered. "The other Joint Chiefs and Council members are ready to begin," he said.

McCarthy turned to Lara. "It's the only way. We'll explain during the brief."

Fitzgerald led the way into the main conference room, taking her seat at the table between two five-star generals: Marine Corps Commandant Narendra Modi and Army Chief of Staff Sergei Lavrov. Beside them sat two civilians: Inner Realm Regent Morel Alperi and Terran Regent Lijuan Xiang, the directors of Personnel and Material, respectively. Lara and McCarthy took their seats opposite them with several other Fleet, Army, and Marine Corp admirals and generals.

Fleet Admiral Fitzgerald made a few introductory remarks, then handed the meeting over to Captain Wears, standing at the front of the conference room.

"As you're aware from the pre-brief," Wears began, "Korilian resistance is stiffening, and there are indications that they've developed a sophisticated artificial intelligence capable of predicting our assaults. Additionally, we recently discovered a message transmitted by Elena Kapadia, a Nexus Ten allocated to the Army at the same time Admiral McCarthy was assigned to the Fleet. The Army sent Elena to assist in the Darian 3 campaign, and she transmitted a message just before the last remnants of the Third Army Group were overrun.

"The transmission was garbled, but due to the efforts of Admiral McCarthy and Nexus Lara Anderson, we recovered Elena's message. She foresaw the increasing Korilian resistance we're encountering today and instructed us to destroy a Korilian facility in the Hellios system. We've sent reconnaissance probes to the system, and here's what we found."

Wears pressed a remote in his hand, and a hologram of the Hellios system appeared, hovering in the air above the conference room table. Wears zoomed in to the fourth planet.

"There is indeed something important to the Korilians on Hellios 4. To begin with, in orbit is a class-four Korilian star base—the largest one we've encountered thus far."

Wears zoomed in again, angling toward a flat gray object with five arms extending from a central hub, with Korilian warships docked along the star base arms.

"There are two hundred Korilian warships in this system. We estimate this represents about twenty percent of the Korilian fleet. At first, we thought Hellios was a staging ground for Korilian forces as they jumped to nearby systems. But reconnaissance has confirmed that the same contingent of starships is always there, with one hundred on alert on a rotating basis while the other hundred dock at the star base. We believe these ships are there to protect the planet from attack, which begs the question— what's so important on Hellios 4?"

Wears manipulated the remote in his hand again, and the hologram shifted to the planet, expanding to fill the center of the conference room. It slowly rotated as Wears continued.

"There are no Korilian cities, at least none above ground or close enough to the surface for us to detect. However, there are eighty identical facilities scattered across the planet." Wears zoomed in to the planet's surface, revealing an industrial complex emitting a hazy mist into the atmosphere. "We've analyzed these facilities and have determined the Korilians are terraforming the planet, increasing its temperature and modifying the atmosphere. But that still didn't explain the need for a two-hundred-warship defense force. Then we discovered this."

The image on the view screen shifted to a sprawling Korilian complex.

"This facility is structurally different from the others and also transmits thousands of messages each hour. We believe the intelligence center is located somewhere in this complex. Additionally, a few miles away are Korilian barracks that house over two million Korilians. How many of these are combat troops is unknown, but for now, we're assuming they all are. Also unknown is how many Korilians are in the facility, although we know the complex has one level above the planet's surface and nine more levels underground.

"Subject to your questions, this completes the reconnaissance phase of the brief."

"This paints a daunting scenario," Regent Alperi said. "What's the plan?"

Fitzgerald replied, "Before we discuss the proposed operation, we need to agree on the goal. There are two options. The first and most obvious is to destroy the facility and the artificial intelligence inside. However, if we simply destroy the intelligence center, the Korilians can build another one. Or perhaps they already have a backup and destroying the facility accomplishes nothing.

"The second alternative is to obtain the algorithms behind the Korilian artificial intelligence. We can then devise a method to counter what they've developed, no matter how many facilities they build. However, this option is more difficult, as we can't simply destroy the facility; we have to gain access and download the algorithms."

Fitzgerald continued, "I recommend the second option. If we're going to send a task force this deep into Korilian territory, let's take the extra step and obtain the algorithms. However, this option can't be accomplished by the Fleet alone. It requires significant ground forces, enough to hold off two million Korilians long enough to enter the facility, locate the intelligence center, download the algorithms, and extract all personnel."

Alperi asked, "Can we hack into the Korilian network from afar, instead of having to send troops into the intelligence center?"

"We've tried," Fitzgerald replied. "But we haven't been able to penetrate the Korilian network firewall."

Her response satisfied Alperi, so Fitzgerald remarked, "Unless someone objects, we'll proceed with the operational brief for option two." She surveyed the two generals and both Council members. After no one objected, she turned to Captain Wears. "Proceed."

"We'll start with the Fleet plan. There are two hundred Korilian warships in the Hellios system, so if our approach goes undetected, a single fleet of four hundred starships will be sufficient. Second Fleet has just completed refit and returned to full strength with replacement warships and has been assigned to this mission.

"However, time is the critical issue. The longer it takes to render the system safe for the troop transports, the longer the Korilians have to prepare for the surface assault and route additional starship reinforcements to the Hellios system. Reconnaissance of the surrounding systems shows no additional Korilian warships within four jumps, but we can't rule out subterranean starship bases on nearby moons.

"Speed is the critical element of the assault, so our plan optimizes how quickly the Korilian armada in the Hellios system is defeated. Second Fleet will be divided into two task groups: all cruisers in one group, with the battleships and carriers in the other, roughly two hundred starships each. The battleships will engage the Korilian ships on alert. We'll have a two-to-one advantage over the alert Korilian warships, but with all battleships against their mix of dreadnoughts and cruisers."

"What about the hundred ships docked at the star base?" Alperi asked.

"That's where the cruiser task group factors in. Thirty seconds before the battleships and carriers arrive, the cruisers will jump inside the Korilian alert perimeter and destroy or severely damage the starships docked at the star base."

Alperi interrupted. "I'm not following you. You said our cruisers are going to jump directly within weapon range of one hundred Korilian warships? It'll take a few seconds to generate shields, which means the Korilian warships will have a clean shot before shields are generated. The cruisers will be decimated."

"That's correct," Wears replied. "As I mentioned, we're trading losses for speed. Without shields, one fourth of our cruisers—those targeted by Korilian dreadnoughts on patrol—will be either destroyed or heavily damaged, and another one fourth will be targeted by the alert Korilian cruisers, and we expect to lose about half of those. However, we then get to return the favor. We'll have one hundred cruisers who weren't targeted, plus about two or three dozen more that survived the Korilian onslaught, who will target the Korilian warships docked at their star base. Those ships won't have shields up, and our counterattack will destroy or disable most of those warships.

"During the Korilian pulse-generator recharge, the battleship and carrier task group will jump into the Hellios system, joining the battle. We should then have over three hundred operational starships to their one hundred, and we hope to quickly destroy the remaining Korilian ships."

Alperi asked, "Should we consider sending two fleets to Hellios to ensure we have superior odds in case we've underestimated Korilian starship strength?"

Wears replied, "Unfortunately, we have only one fleet available at this time. Three fleets are tied down in other campaigns, leaving only Second Fleet and the two fleets assigned to Earth's defense. If we send two fleets to Hellios, it would leave us with only one in Earth's solar system, which we think is unwise."

Alperi nodded his agreement, so Wears continued. "Once we have control of the Hellios system and it's safe for troop transports to make the jump, we'll commence the surface assault, which is the riskiest phase of the plan. The problem is that we have only one Marine Expeditionary Force available right now, and it's only at eighty percent strength. All other Army and Marine Corps units are engaged or en route to other campaigns."

Army Chief of Staff General Sergei Lavrov interrupted. "A partial MEF against two million Korilians on the surface, plus an unknown number inside the facility? Are you serious?"

Marine Corps Commandant Narendra Modi replied, "In a prolonged campaign, you'd be correct. But we're talking about a few hours. We need to establish and hold the perimeter long enough for our forces to reach the intelligence center inside the facility. We intend to assign nine divisions to the perimeter and one to the facility insertion. With the element of surprise, plus a fleet in orbit providing ground support, we believe we can accomplish the task."

"I don't like it," Alperi said. "We have no additional troops?"

General Lavrov replied, "I'll have a new Army corps available in four weeks, which is the equivalent of a full-strength MEF, but they'll be mostly green recruits."

"With all due respect," General Modi said, "even at fifty percent strength, an MEF would be superior to an inexperienced Army corps."

"Oh, come on, Narendra. How can you say that? There's no way even a full-strength MEF can stand up to an Army corps."

"Let's not get into that debate again, gentleman," Fitzgerald said. "Besides, this isn't just any MEF. The Third MEF has just been extracted from the Pleaides campaign, and General Modi has allocated it to this important mission."

"The Third MEF?" Lavrov asked.

As Lara listened to the debate, she recalled the exploits of the Marine Corps' 3rd Marine Expeditionary Force. It had performed well during the first year of the Liberation Campaign, and since then, it had been the lead element of every major planetary assault over the last two years. *First unit down* had become their motto.

"There's no need to continue this debate," Fitzgerald said. "We're going with the Third MEF. I'm not going to put McCarthy's life in the hands of green troops. Besides, we can't wait another month for the Army corps. Admiral McCarthy believes the Korilians will commence a major assault in two weeks. We need to destroy the Korilian intelligence center and obtain its algorithms before then."

Regent Lijuan Xiang interrupted Fitzgerald. "Excuse me, Fleet Admiral Fitzgerald, but something you said just caught my attention. That you weren't going to put Admiral McCarthy's life in the hands of green troops. Please explain."

Fitzgerald and Wears exchanged glances. "I'll take it from here," Fitzgerald said, then answered Lijuan's question. "We were about to discuss that, Regent. As Captain Wears mentioned earlier, time is the most critical element, and locating the Korilian intelligence center could take an extended period of time. Time we might not have.

"The complex is over a mile in diameter with ten levels. We need to find the intelligence center quickly and won't have time to scour the entire complex. Admiral McCarthy will accompany a Marine contingent into the Korilian facility, guiding them to the intelligence center."

Alperi asked, "You're going to land our only Nexus Ten on the surface of a planet with two million Korilians nearby, then send him into a facility with hundreds, if not thousands of Korilians inside? Am I missing something?"

Lijuan responded instead of Fitzgerald. "You question the advice of our military leaders at every turn, Morel. Before the Final Stand, you objected to McCarthy's mission to capture a Korilian cruiser, which was both successful and crucial to our victory, and you also objected to sending McCarthy to Darian 3 to retrieve Elena's message, which was also successful. Fleet Admiral Fitzgerald is again recommending we harness Admiral McCarthy's unique talents to achieve success. When are you going to learn to heed her advice?"

"When she starts making sense," Alperi snapped.

"As the Personnel Director, maybe you should focus on providing the forces required to *fight* the war and let the generals and admirals *win* the war," Lijuan offered.

Alperi countered, "As the Material Director, if you had built starships faster, we would have already defeated the Korilians."

"I do the best I can with the limited personnel allocated by your committee. Perhaps you should reevaluate your priorities."

Lara listened to the terse exchange between the two Council regents, who outranked all others except the Council president. When President Portner retired, Alperi and Lijuan would be the leading contenders to assume leadership of the most powerful organization in the Colonies, and it was obvious they were already jockeying for advantage.

Fitzgerald broke into the Council member exchange. "The platoon McCarthy will accompany will be handpicked—the best in the Third MEF—and they won't enter the Korilian complex until the situation is well in hand. Yes, there's risk. But I believe the risk is worth the potential gain. If we don't figure out what technology the Korilians are using against us and how to counter it, we're going to lose our advantage, and the tide may turn against us again.

"Unless anyone has additional questions," Fitzgerald added, "it's time for a vote."

There were no additional questions, so Fitzgerald announced, "The Fleet votes yes."

"The Corps votes yes."

"The Army votes yes."

"Regent Alperi, Regent Xiang," Fitzgerald said. "The Joint Chiefs' opinion is unanimous. We request your support at the Council."

"Thank you, Admiral," Lijuan said. "Your proposed operation is not without risk, but your plan is sound. I will recommend Council approval." Lijuan turned to Alperi.

"As the director of Personnel, my opinion carries significant weight during Council deliberations. I take my responsibility seriously and will not recommend a mission that puts our resources at undue risk." Alperi studied Fleet Admiral Fitzgerald for a moment. "I approve of your plan and will recommend Council approval."

20

Seated at her desk in Domus Praesidium, Rhea terminated her videocon with the Council aide. This aide happened to be the executive assistant to Senior Member David Portner, head of Colonial Council, but more important—and unknown to the Council—the aide was a Nexus Four.

The Hellios decision had been made quickly. The full Council had been briefed and the mission to destroy the Korilian complex on Hellios 4 approved. Orders had been sent to Fleet and Marine Corps Commands to prepare the required forces, and the Council had also approved Admiral McCarthy's participation in the ground assault so he could help locate the intelligence center. Assuming, of course, McCarthy's view advanced into the future once he reached Hellios 4. That critical issue was what concerned Rhea this morning, as even her view became disrupted once McCarthy landed on the planet's surface.

She tapped her wristlet, and a few seconds later, a supervisor in the Nexus intelligence center appeared on the wristlet display.

"Any breakthrough in naviganti views?" Rhea asked.

Like most organizations within Domus Praesidium, the Intelligence Department employed Nexi from levels two through nine, tapping into their unique talents. Of interest to Rhea tonight were the navigantis—level-

nine Nexi who stood six-hour watches, viewing timelines as directed by
supervisors who identified critical gaps in their intelligence collection.

"No change, One. All naviganti views dissolve at the same point—when
Admiral McCarthy's assault vehicle lands on Hellios 4. It doesn't matter
which timeline we follow."

"I understand," Rhea said. "Inform me immediately if there is a breakthrough."

"Yes, One."

Rhea terminated the connection with the intelligence center, pondering
their inability to see the future more clearly. McCarthy suspected the issue
was battle related, with the prime timeline dissolving due to the uncertainty in outcome resulting from so many critical decisions in a short time.
But Rhea wasn't sure. In her thirty-three years of views during the Korilian
War, she had encountered similar situations where the timeline rapidly
dissolved and the outcome could not be discerned. But this felt different. It
felt more like her view was being—blocked.

Only twice in the history of the House had a Nexus Ten's view been
blocked, both times by a Corvad Ten who had developed the unique
talent. The first time was five centuries ago, when the Nexus Placidia Tens
had been blocked from predicting the Corvad assault that penetrated
Domus Praesidium for the first, and only, time in three millennia. Thirty-
three years ago, the views of the Nexus Three had also been blocked, but
in a more sophisticated way—their views had been altered. This time, the
Nexus House had struck first with their praetorian legion, annihilating
the Corvads at the Battle of Domus Valens. After the battle, Ronan and
the remaining praetorians had swept the other Corvad compounds and
eliminated all within, then hunted down all Corvads in the public
domain.

The specter that a Corvad cell had survived the Battle of Domus Valens
and subsequent purge had transformed from a suspicion hovering in the
periphery of Rhea's mind into an alarming possibility. McCarthy and Lara
had been attacked on Darian 3 by house praetorians, and now, her view
had the distinct feeling it was being blocked. But even if a Corvad Ten had
survived or been developed, why would the Corvads block views of the
Hellios mission?

At this point, she had more questions than answers. After assessing her options, she decided to visit Sanctuary.

———

At the outer reaches of Domus Praesidium's west wing, The One's footsteps echoed off granite walls as she wound her way through the passageways, eventually treading down a desolate, dusty hallway. At the end of the passageway, Rhea stopped before a rough-hewn granite wall where construction on this passageway had supposedly halted three millennia ago. Then she took a step forward, passing through the mirage.

Before her was another wall—this one real—with a three-foot-diameter bronze House seal. She touched the eye in the center of the Nexus House symbol, and the seal began rotating. After turning ninety degrees, a vertical seam appeared through the middle of the wall and seal. The two halves of the wall and seal split and pulled slowly apart, creating an opening into a twenty-by-thirty-foot chamber.

At the front of the room stood a podium made of quartz, and at the other end of the chamber were five circular daises. Rhea approached the podium, which contained the crystal memories of every Nexus Placidia Ten since the reign of The Five. She selected three crystals, placing each into a slot.

Holograms of two elderly men and one woman wearing blue robes—the three Placidia Tens who had ruled the Nexus House prior to Rhea—appeared atop the daises.

Rhea bowed her head slightly in respect. "Masters Tanner, Sokolov, and Klein. I seek your guidance."

Elias Tanner, who had been Rhea's mentor, replied, "What troubles you, Rhea?"

There were many things that troubled her, but she would keep the conversation focused on the reason she had entered Sanctuary. "I suspect my view is being blocked."

An anxious expression formed on Tanner's face, accompanied by worried looks from the other two Placidia Tens. "What is the status of our conflict with the Corvads," Tanner asked quickly, his calm tone replaced with urgency. "That you speak to us here tells me that we did not return. Were we successful in eradicating the Corvads?"

Rhea prepared to explain the outcome of the Battle of Domus Valens, as she had done during every previous visit to Sanctuary. Although the crystal memories could recall events and information from their past, they could not remember new discussions.

"You were successful. Every Corvad compound was seized and the Corvads killed. We obtained their master registry of Corvads hidden within the civilian population, and our praetorians hunted them down. The Corvads are no more, or so we thought for the last thirty-three years.

"Last week, a Nexus Ten was attacked by a contingent of praetorians from an undeclared house—they wore gray instead of their house livery. Additionally, all Nexus views appear to be blocked at the same point in time, when our Nexus Ten reaches the surface of Hellios 4, where we suspect the Korilian intelligence facility is located."

"Korilian?" Tanner asked.

Before departing for the final battle with the Corvads at Domus Valens, The Three had never mentioned the Korilian War. During Rhea's last visit to Sanctuary, it had finally dawned on her—The Three had never seen the war. Their views had been altered by a Corvad Ten, which had been the catalyst for the Nexus assault on Domus Valens.

Rhea went on to explain what had occurred over the last thirty-three years, including McCarthy's role in humankind's Final Stand against the Korilian Empire. They had won the battle, but the war was far from over, and it seemed the tide was turning against them again.

Tanner replied, "Before we begin with the premise that your view is being blocked by Corvads, tell us more about these Korilians. Do they have the same capabilities as humans? Are there some that can follow the prime timeline and evaluate alternate futures like our Tens?"

"We don't know," Rhea replied. "They're a telepathic species, which makes communication difficult. We cannot detect and translate their thoughts, and we can communicate with them only if they resort to speaking. Their verbal language is crude, conveying basic concepts only, which makes it difficult to have complex discussions with them."

"Without detailed knowledge," Tanner replied, "I think it's prudent to assume that Korilians may have similar abilities to ours. There could also be species on Korilian worlds with this ability, or even abilities that surpass ours." He turned to the other Placidia Tens. "What say you?"

"I agree," Valeriya Sokolov replied, and Klein added, "I don't think that prescient abilities are a human-only capability."

"So, let's set aside the source of the block," Tanner said, "and focus on how to extend your view past the block."

"That is why I'm here," Rhea replied. "Before the Battle of Domus Valens, you were able to partially pierce the Corvad block. How did you do it?"

"We used a combined Placidia Ten view. How many other Placidia Tens do we have now?"

"I am the only one," Rhea replied.

Tanner frowned. "Then you cannot pierce the block."

Rhea's chest tightened at the news. "There must be a way."

Valeriya joined the discussion. "Let's not be too hasty with the verdict. It's not impossible to break through a block with only a single Placidia Ten —it's just never been tried."

Tanner replied, "You need at least two Placidia Tens. You have to be able to combine views without creating turbulence. If Rhea combines her view with another Nine or Ten, her view will dissolve seconds later."

"You're correct," Valeriya said. "But it's the few seconds we must focus on. I do not know the solution, but we have a window in time to work with." She turned to Angus Klein. "What do you think?"

"The issue is view stability. A block isn't instantaneous. The view dissolves quickly, giving the impression the view is blocked. View speed and timeline stability are the critical elements. You want to select a timeline that is stable and can be viewed quickly, increasing the amount of the future that can be analyzed before the view dissolves."

Rhea focused on the last part of Klein's comment. Views of the future weren't real-time. In a few seconds, a Nine or Ten could view several minutes or even hours into the future, depending on the stability of the timeline and the ability of the Nine or Ten.

"I see," Valeriya said. "Rhea should combine her view with someone whose view of the future is strong and fast. In this case, I think a Nine's view would be optimal, as the view wouldn't be distracted by alternate timelines. What do you think?"

"I agree," Klein replied.

Tanner added, "It looks like you'll need to combine your view with that of a capable Nine. Do you have someone in mind?"

Rhea reflected on the options, her first thought going to Ronan. His view of the future was very stable, but not very fast. As a praetorian, his view was used primarily to disrupt his opponent's view, eliminating the ability that either combatant could predict their opponent's moves, reducing the outcome to whoever was more skilled. The speed of his view wasn't critical. There were several navigantis to choose from, but the speed of their views wasn't something they focused on. Then the obvious answer dawned on her.

Siella.

There was no doubt that Siella had enormous potential. In fact, the primary reason she was having difficulty making the transition from Nine to Ten was because her view was so strong, and in particular, very fast. If one were to consider the prime timeline a highway and the alternate futures the exits, Siella's problem was that she traveled down the highway so fast that she was unable to take an exit once it became apparent to her. This weakness—the tendency to follow the prime timeline too quickly— had suddenly become a strength.

"I have a good candidate," Rhea replied. "But I've never combined my view with another's. How is this done?"

Tanner went on to explain, with Valeriya and Klein also providing guidance. When they finished, Rhea thanked The Three, then removed their crystals from the podium slots, returning them to their storage locations. After the three holograms disappeared, she entered a command into her wristlet, and Ronan appeared on the display.

"Locate Siella and have her meet me in the intelligence center, immediately."

"Yes, One," he replied. "May I inquire why?"

"I intend to employ Siella as a naviganti."

"A naviganti? Are you terminating her level-ten training?"

Assignment as a praetorian, naviganti, disruptor, or combat pilot—all level-nine responsibilities—was normally done only after The One had decided the Nexus was incapable of achieving level ten.

"Her naviganti assignment is temporary," Rhea replied. "Only a single session."

"I recommend you inform Siella up front. Her confidence is as frail as her body."

"I'm aware of that. I'll explain when she arrives in the intelligence center."

Rhea reached the north wing of the Praesidium and entered the Nexus intelligence center, a sprawling complex with video displays lining the walls and hundreds of Nexi seated at control consoles reviewing the data gathered by the thousands of Nexi embedded in every important organization on Earth: the military, government, financial, and other entities whose decisions shaped humanity's future.

She entered the intelligence center's command cell, a suite one level above and overlooking the complex, and stopped beside the supervisors monitoring the navigantis. Ten Nexi were seated at a long console, each monitoring a video of the future. The videos were generated by the ten navigantis, each in an isolation chamber so their views wouldn't disrupt each another. Connected to each naviganti were electrodes that captured and translated the naviganti's brain activity into a visual display of what each Nine was viewing.

The views were monitored by the ten supervisors, who reviewed the data as it was sent into the repository database where analysts attempted to identify the critical events that guided the future down its current path. Sometimes the events were obvious, such as the outcome of a major battle. But sometimes the future was shaped by a single individual or a solitary act —the movement of a single pebble on a mountain slope that starts a landslide.

At the moment, all ten navigantis were analyzing prime timelines related to the assault on Hellios 4: one was following McCarthy as he descended to the planet aboard a surface assault vehicle, several followed the timelines of the accompanying Marines, while others focused on various 2nd Fleet personnel as they engaged the Korilian warships in orbit.

Rhea stopped by the naviganti director, overseeing all ten navigantis and their supervisors. "Any change in naviganti views?"

The director shook his head. "All timelines dissolve at the same moment—when McCarthy lands on Hellios 4." Rhea saw the concern in his eyes as he added, "We could be dealing with a cataclysmic event that annihilates Second Fleet and the MEF, or..." he hesitated for a moment, "... our views could be blocked. Do you have any guidance?"

"It feels more like a block," Rhea replied. "We're going to try to push through it."

"How do we do that?"

Siella entered the command cell, and Rhea waited for her to approach before answering.

"I'm going to replace a naviganti with Siella and guide her through the process."

Siella's eyes widened as the director's gaze shifted toward her. "It's only a temporary assignment," Rhea added for Siella's benefit, letting her know her level-ten training wasn't being terminated. "Hopefully for only a single session."

"Yes, One," the director replied. "Naviganti number seven is almost at the end of his shift. You can proceed to Isolation Chamber Seven."

An assistant guided Rhea and Siella to the isolation chamber, arriving just as the off-going naviganti exited. As he passed by, he bowed his head slightly in respect for The One.

They entered the chamber and Siella slid into the reclined naviganti chair, then the assistant attached two dozen electrodes to Siella's head. After confirming the equipment was operating properly by viewing images of Siella's thoughts on a display monitor, the assistant exited the chamber, the door closing silently behind him.

Siella looked up at The One, who sensed the Nine's tension and anxiety. Rhea placed her hand on her shoulder. "I have great confidence in you. I've selected you because, together, we have the best probability of piercing the disruption that is terminating our views on Hellios."

"Together?" Siella asked.

Rhea explained the plan, exuding confidence rather than revealing her doubts, uncertain as to how successful their effort would be.

"Ready?" Rhea asked. After Siella nodded, Rhea said, "I want you to select McCarthy's timeline as he boards the surface assault vehicle on the troop transport. When his SAV lands on Hellios 4, I want you to accelerate your view to the maximum speed possible. Once I combine my view with yours, we'll have only a few seconds before it dissolves, and we need to see as far into the future as possible before it does. Understand?"

Another nod.

"Begin."

Siella closed her eyes, and an image formed on the display—Jon McCarthy heading toward an SAV with a platoon of Marines. The speed of Siella's view was impressive, covering an hour as they waited in the SAV in only a few seconds.

When the SAV was launched from the troop transport, Rhea reached over and deenergized the monitoring equipment relaying Siella's view to the naviganti supervisor cell. There was no telling what they might discover if they pierced the block, and Rhea's intuition told her something significant was occurring farther down the timeline—something she might not want to share with others at the moment.

In Siella's view, the SAV descended quickly toward the planet. When it landed, Rhea reached out with her mind and latched onto the prime timeline, adding her impetus to the view.

McCarthy exited the SAV, and instead of the sudden termination Rhea and the navigantis had experienced countless times, the view continued. But it was quickly destabilizing, the view shuddering as hazy gray scenes sped by. But the combined view was exceptionally fast, traveling hours into the assault in only a few seconds.

They followed McCarthy as he accompanied the Marine platoon into the Korilian facility, trying to make sense of the images flashing by as the future dissolved: Korilians, Marines, close combat, blood. As darkness encroached from the periphery of their combined view, a hazy image sped by before the future faded into oblivion.

Rhea sucked in a sharp breath.

Her gaze shifted to Siella, who was attempting to contain her emotion as tears formed. Siella's lips trembled and her voice quavered as she said, "This can't possibly be the future."

Rhea evaluated how best to proceed. After a long moment, she placed a firm grip on Siella's shoulder and leaned toward her, stopping a few inches from her face.

"You will tell no one what you have seen tonight, not even Ronan. Do you understand?"

Siella nodded. "Yes, One."

In a darkened alcove adjacent to her office in Domus Praesidium, Rhea paced slowly around an empty pedestal. For the first twenty-five centuries after Domus Praesidium was built, the Codex had been maintained atop the pedestal in this small room. After it was destroyed five centuries ago and partially reconstituted by the Sevens, the new Codex now resided deep within the Praesidium, protected by measures not even she could overcome.

Rhea had already resolved the primary issue created by her combined view with Siella—whether to allow McCarthy to accompany the Marines into the complex on Hellios 4, or even to request the mission be cancelled entirely. After analyzing each alternative, the path forward had become clear: success on Hellios 4 was paramount, regardless of the cost. The question now was how to ensure a favorable outcome, and her thoughts shifted to the Codex and the frustratingly vague guidance from The Five concerning Lara Anderson.

Harken the arrival of the One with no line, for she is the harbinger of...

After postulating numerous scenarios and assessing their outcomes to the best of her ability, one alternate future stood out from the rest: send Lara to Hellios 4 with McCarthy. The inability to follow Lara's timeline meant she was a true wild card, the influence of her interactions on the future impossible to predict. It was risky—the outcome uncertain—but an alternate future with Lara involved offered the best potential for a favorable outcome.

Rhea considered how to broach the subject with McCarthy without revealing what she had gleaned during her view with Siella, then tapped her wristlet, requesting a communication link. A moment later, McCarthy appeared on her wristlet display.

"Jon, I'm concerned about the Hellios mission. The prime timeline dissolves quickly once you reach the planet's surface."

"I'm concerned as well," McCarthy replied. "Do you have any guidance?"

Rhea nodded. "Take Lara with you."

"Lara? She provides little value while risking her life. She's only an Eight."

"That's why I'm sending her with you. Your view dissolves once you reach the planet's surface, and there's no guarantee your view will be restored once you pass this point in the prime timeline. Lara proved her worth as your guide during the Final Stand, experiencing important premonitions at critical moments. She might prove useful again on Hellios 4."

"I don't think it's prudent," McCarthy said. "Lara's premonitions are still random and difficult to interpret. I think it's best if she were left behind."

Rhea replied sharply, "I don't need to explain myself further. Just do as you're told."

She tapped her wristlet, terminating the communication. She couldn't risk continuing the conversation. If what she and Siella viewed really was the prime timeline, it was best that McCarthy not know what awaited him.

21

Lara stood in the busy Domus Praesidium spaceport, waiting for McCarthy to pick her up for the journey to Hellios 4. Beside her stood Ronan, supervising the preparations for his journey to Domus Valens. He was taking ample precautions: ten blue-and-white Nexus cobras—the Nexus equivalent of Fleet vipers, but designed for atmospheric versus space combat—rose on elevators from the hangar deck, while forty praetorians were arranged into two contubernia of twenty praetorians each, standing beside two transports.

The praetorians were outfitted similarly to the detachment on Darian 3: each wore a utility belt containing several shuriken—metal throwing stars —and a holstered pulse-pistol. The men carried two swords strapped to their backs, while most of the women had a pair of daggers sheathed on their hips. There were several taller and more muscular women, however, who were outfitted like the men. Each praetorian had electronic pads strapped to their forearms, although the devices were deenergized—a dull gray color instead of glowing blue like on Darian 3.

Ronan was similarly equipped, his attention focused on schematics being projected from his left arm pad, appearing head-high about a foot from his face. Lara watched while he reviewed a facility's schematics, examining each level by manipulating the image with his right hand. Ronan had explained they were going to scour the Corvad compounds again, starting with Domus Valens, the historical stronghold of the Corvad House, from where their Placidia Tens had ruled. Lara had sensed Ronan wasn't in a good mood and decided not to inquire further, focusing instead on her upcoming journey with McCarthy.

An hour earlier, she had been summoned to The One's office, where Rhea had explained her assignment. She would assist Admiral McCarthy again, but not as a fleet guide. She'd accompany him to Hellios 4, where she would help guide the Marines to the Korilian intelligence center as quickly as possible. When she learned that she'd be heading into the facility with the Marines, she had a brief vision: of her standing before a Korilian—its limbs swinging toward her, about to slice through her body—and had to quell a panic attack.

That vision was again in her mind as the heavy overhead doors pulled slowly apart, revealing the dark sky. Pushing the thought aside, she soon spotted a descending vehicle faintly illuminated by a full moon. A Nexus blue-and-white shuttle entered the spaceport and landed nearby. McCarthy emerged and scanned the spaceport.

He stopped before Lara and Ronan, querying the Primus Nine. "Where is The One?"

"She directed me to tell you that she is not available tonight. I think that means she doesn't want to talk."

"I've deduced that," McCarthy replied, frustration evident in his tone.

Lara offered what little she knew. "The One told me that my task is to help you find the Korilian intelligence center. She's concerned that your view might not extend into the future once you land on Hellios 4 and believes my premonitions will be helpful, like they were during the Final Stand."

"That's what she told me as well," McCarthy replied. "At least that's what she wants us to believe. But there's an ulterior motive behind you accompanying me. I think Rhea has seen more than she's letting on. Something she doesn't want me to know."

"Why would she withhold information from you?"

"That's what I'm trying to figure out. As a Placidia Ten, her view of the future is more nuanced than others', plus you don't rule the House for thirty years without developing a keen intuition. I hope her decision to send you is based on a gut feeling and not her view of the future."

"What do you think she's seen?" Lara asked.

"There are several scenarios I can think of, most with unpleasant outcomes."

At the mention of *unpleasant outcomes*, several images flashed through Lara's mind, all containing Korilians and blood. On Hellios 4, they wouldn't be engaging in combat from the relative safety of a fleet command ship, protected by four hundred warships. They'd be heading into a Korilian facility with their lives in the hands of a few Marines.

"Won't the Marines clear a path before we enter the facility and protect us from the Korilians?"

"Of course. If everything goes as planned, we'll be safe, providing guidance to the lead Marines from a safe distance behind. But this Korilian complex is very large, filled with hundreds of passageways the Korilians can travel along. The Marines will try to seal them off, but we could easily end up in close combat."

"The One wouldn't send you to Hellios 4 if she knew you were going to be killed, would she?"

"As master of the Nexus House, Rhea has a responsibility to do what's best for the House and for humanity. Nexus Tens have sacrificed our own many times in the past and will no doubt do so in the future. At this point, however, I'm optimistic. I can't envision a scenario where my death is in the best interest of the House or humanity. My best guess is that she's viewed farther down the prime timeline than I have and doesn't like what she's seen, and is attempting to guide the Prime into an acceptable alternate future. That, it seems, is where you come in."

McCarthy turned to Ronan. "Can you provide any insight?"

"Unfortunately, no," Ronan replied. "The One has refused to discuss the matter."

McCarthy shifted his gaze back to Lara, his voice softening. "Perhaps we should accept Rhea's reasoning at face value. If my view doesn't extend into the future once I land on Hellios 4, I'm definitely going to need your help. In essence, you'll be the viewer and I'll be your guide, interpreting your visions."

Lara tensed at the prospect of the mission's success being placed in her hands. She forced a smile and tried to stay positive. "I'll do my best."

Ronan extended his hand to McCarthy. The two Nexi gripped each other's forearm as Ronan said, "Remember, Jon. The future is not set."

McCarthy led the way into his four-seat shuttle, and Lara sat beside him in the front row. As the door slid shut, McCarthy said, "*Elena*, proceed to the Second Fleet command ship."

The shuttle lifted off and passed through the spaceport doors, then accelerated quickly, pressing Lara into her seat as the shuttle increased speed. The shuttle shook for several minutes as it streaked through the atmosphere, then the vibration eased and the spacecraft tilted forward, leveling off from its upward trajectory. Lara looked out the window, spotting hundreds of white starships resting in space.

"Second Fleet," McCarthy commented. "It just finished refit and is ready to depart."

The 2nd Fleet starships were too numerous to count, but during her experience as the 1st Fleet guide, Lara had learned that a fleet at full strength contained four battle groups, each with one hundred ships: forty-eight battleships, the same number of cruisers, and four carriers. She spotted a squadron of battleships; each starship had a pulse-generator portal in the bow and hundreds of weapon batteries rippling down the sides. Cruisers were similar in design except smaller and faster but packing only half the punch. In the distance was 2nd Fleet's allotment of sixteen carriers, each capable of launching its complement of five hundred vipers in four minutes.

They approached the 2nd Fleet command ship, heading toward its spaceport, a large opening in the starship's port side. Lara's skin tingled as they passed through the spaceport's life-support shield, then she sank into her seat, evidence they were under the influence of the starship's gravity generators. The shuttle slowed to a hover, then settled onto the deck.

The shuttle door opened, and she followed McCarthy down the steps, where they were greeted by Admiral Khalil Amani and two aides, plus a Nexus Eight named Carson Lieu. Lara had met the fleet guide while he was training in Domus Praesidium. Both Lieu and Admiral Amani were relative newcomers to their positions, having replaced the previous pair after they

were killed when the 2nd Fleet command ship was destroyed six months
ago in the Excelsior planetary system. Lieu was still a teenager, only seventeen, the youngest fleet guide at the moment.

Admiral Amani spoke first, addressing McCarthy. "Welcome aboard
Controlador. Second Fleet is ready to depart for Hellios. Would you like to
join me on the command bridge?"

Lara sensed the deference in Amani's voice. Even though he was the
same rank as McCarthy, a four-star admiral and in command of one of the
six fleets, McCarthy's role in the Final Stand had earned him a debt of gratitude not only from the general population, but among those who served in
the Colonial Defense Force.

McCarthy accepted the invitation, and Amani extended the offer to
Lara as well, who also accepted. As they headed to the command bridge,
McCarthy talked with Amani while Lara conversed with Lieu, catching up
on events since she had last seen him in Domus Praesidium.

The elevator doors opened, and they emerged onto the command
bridge, with its familiar arrangement: fifty men and women manning five
tiers of control panels descending to a curved row of monitors below the
bridge windows. Amani took his seat in one of the two chair consoles overlooking the command center, while Lieu offered his seat to McCarthy.
McCarthy declined, and Lieu settled into his chair.

With McCarthy standing beside Amani and Lara next to Lieu, Admiral
Amani ordered his operations officer, "To all ships in Second Fleet, jump at
the mark."

The operations officer entered the command into his console, and a few
seconds later, five deep tones reverberated throughout the command ship,
followed by the computer's voice over the ship's intercom system.

"One minute to the jump."

Ten seconds before the jump, five deep tones reverberated throughout
the ship again. When the time reached zero, the starship bridge dissolved
into darkness as they began their journey to Hellios 4.

22

Two Nexus assault vehicles, accompanied by ten cobras above providing cover, sped along a deep ravine in the Carpathian Mountains, weaving through the narrow approach to Domus Valens, where Corvad principes had ruled for three thousand years. Along the sheer mountain walls on both sides of the ravine, the burnt-out hulks of defense batteries, destroyed during the Nexus assault three decades ago, littered the landscape. As the assault vehicles approached the Corvad enclave carved deep into the mountain, Ronan, who was seated at the head of the lead assault vehicle, let his thoughts drift into the past.

The Battle of Domus Valens had raged for five days. The defense batteries lining the approach to the Corvad stronghold had been formidable, and Domus Valens had been protected by an encapsulating energy shield. It had taken four days to destroy the defense batteries and obliterate the shield. Once the shield went down, several dozen Corvad cobras made it aloft before the remaining single-pilot fighters in the space-port were destroyed, but the Nexi had air superiority and quickly shot down the sallying aircraft. Only then, with the approach cleared and the shield disabled, had the legion of Nexus praetorians breached the moun-tain fortification.

The thousand-strong Nexus Legion had been divided into ten cohorts, each led by a centurion. In the center of the assault and protected by the 1st Cohort and their praetorian guards, the three Nexus Placidia Tens provided guidance to their advancing forces. Likewise, the three Corvad Placidia Tens, protected by their praetorians, directed the efforts of their legion.

Ronan was only eighteen during the Battle of Domus Valens but already a centurion and head of the Nexus Legion's 2nd Cohort. He was also one of only four Nexus praetorians who had mastered the highest level of Letalis-Tutela, the deadly House martial arts, which technically put him fourth in charge of the Nexus Legion, after the Primus and Deinde Nines and the 1st Cohort commander.

With both sides focused on killing the opposing Placidia Tens, the battles swirling around them were furious and bloody. The Corvad Tens had the upper hand, guiding the battle from the fortified Domus Valens command center. In a bold move, they left themselves defenseless, sending their praetorians into the fray, spearheading a Corvad surge that decimated the Nexus 1st Cohort. Ronan had received an urgent order directing 2nd Cohort to assist. But they had arrived too late. Although only a dozen Corvad praetorians had survived the assault, they had accomplished their goal, slaying the three Nexus Tens.

The remaining Corvad praetorians were quickly dispatched by Ronan's 2nd Cohort, and as he stood over the bodies of The Three and the Primus Nine, and after verifying the Deinde Nine and the 1st Cohort commander had also been slain, he realized he was the senior Nexus centurion alive— and therefore in command of the Nexus Legion. He also realized he had a decision to make. Retreat—pulling what remained of the Nexus Legion from Domus Valens—or forge ahead, attempting to reach and breach the Corvad command center.

After downloading an update from surveillance aircraft scanning Domus Valens, Ronan realized that the Corvad offensive that had slain the Nexus Placidia Tens had been successful but costly. There were more Nexus than Corvad praetorians remaining, and Ronan made a critical decision. He gathered the remnants of the other cohorts, then led them as they fought their way to the sealed Corvad command center. They reached the entrance, but before Ronan tried to breach the command center, he decided to ensure that any emergency escape route was cut off.

Surveillance craft above scanned the Corvad stronghold and identified an escape tunnel, and Ronan ordered it sealed with a bombardment of the mountainside exit.

With the Nexus praetorians fending off lower-level Corvads surging to the aid of their princeps, Ronan had the command center doors blasted open. Without praetorians to defend them, the Corvad Tens were easily killed. Although each had a specific talent and all three were capable of telekinesis, none were very dangerous and were easily overwhelmed. When the Battle of Domus Valens ended, only Ronan and thirty-nine other Nexus praetorians—from the original complement of one thousand—had survived.

The Nexus assault vehicles banked to the left and lined up on the final approach to Domus Valens, then slowed as they passed between the remnants of the two-hundred-foot-tall spaceport doors. They proceeded slowly as the vehicles' searchlight beams cut through the darkness in the rubble-strewn facility. After identifying a clear spot among the destroyed Corvad air and space transports, the two vehicles landed, and forty Nexus praetorians surged forth. Ronan surveyed the two contubernia and found it fitting that forty Nexus praetorians—the same number that had survived the Battle of Domus Valens—had returned.

Ronan broke the contubernia into ten squads of four praetorians each, then sent nine squads on predetermined routes through the Corvad stronghold. He remained in the spaceport with the remaining squad, surveying the cameras mounted to the walls. Three decades ago, after clearing the Corvad compounds, surveillance cameras had been installed throughout each facility to monitor for Corvad activity. A praetorian in each Nexus squad would examine the cameras as they passed by, verifying none had been tampered with and that all were relaying accurate video back to Domus Praesidium.

After the Corvads were vanquished three decades ago, Nexi had rummaged through the facilities collecting everything of value—primarily information—such as the Corvad version of the Nexus Codex, the registry of all Corvads, and all information stored in their computer networks. However, the three-millennium-old Domus Valens was an extremely large compound, with five levels above the spaceport entrance and another five below, covering an expanse of over fifteen square miles. Much material had been left behind.

Through the spaceport door opening, another vehicle arrived. A bulk container ship, contracted for this endeavor, hovered nearby as Ronan's squad cleared a landing spot. After the ship touched down, its rear ramp lowered, and several dozen hover-containers were off-loaded, along with a contingent of Nexus Fours with scanners capable of seeing through walls, aiding their search for hidden compartments or rooms. After the Nexus praetorians had verified Domus Valens was indeed abandoned, the Fours would forage through the facility again, collecting additional items of interest.

23

On the top floor of the Terran Council building, Regent Lijuan Xiang stood before the display console, almost shaking in anger. She'd been watching the video feeds of the Nexus intruders as they pillaged Domus Valens. As the despicable Nexi rummaged through the compound, the agony she had felt over three decades ago resurfaced.

Thirty-three years ago, as the Nexi launched their attack from Domus Praesidium, she had been sent from Domus Valens with a core of select Corvads, hidden away in Domus Salus as an insurance policy against the possibility the Nexi might prevail. That decision by the Corvad princeps—the most powerful of the three Placidia Tens and the ruler of her House—had proven wise. The Nexi had triumphed, slaughtering all within Domus Valens. The only consolation was that the Nexi had also lost their three Placidia Tens and their praetorian legion had been decimated. Additionally, the existence of Lijuan and her fellow Corvads, along with the existence of Domus Salus, had been erased from Corvad records before the battle began.

Lijuan was only sixteen when she became the de facto princeps of the Corvad House. Although not a Placidia Ten at the time, she was the only Ten remaining. Thirty-three years later, she had attained Placidia Ten status and other important talents had emerged.

She was a charmer, able to manipulate people's emotions. Additionally, she had the power of suggestion. Her most powerful talent, however, was one that had been mastered only once before in the history of the Corvad House. She could block timelines from being viewed, and she could also alter the views of Nines and Tens, fabricating fake timelines into the future.

She had put those talents to good use, hiding her identity as a Corvad while attaining a seat on the Colonial Council, manipulating its decisions for the last decade. However, her primary desire had been thwarted by the war. Although she yearned to orchestrate the destruction of the Nexus House, defeating the Korilians had been the higher priority. Unfortunately, the Nexus House—with its supply of fleet guides and, of course, Admiral McCarthy—played a crucial role.

With the war well in hand and the Korilian Empire in retreat, she had finally struck, sending a detachment of Corvad Nines to slay McCarthy on Darian 3. But something had gone wrong. Predicting the future when an opposing Nine or Ten was involved was problematic, but McCarthy and the Nexus One should have been caught unaware, their attention focused on other timelines. Lijuan had overestimated the Nexus One's complacency, not expecting her to send a full Nexus guard to Darian 3. That lack of insight had proved fatal to her plan.

Fortunately, Lijuan had blocked the timelines of the praetorians she had sent on the mission, preventing the Nexi from determining who was responsible, even if they had captured a praetorian alive. However, although the Nexi could not trace the attack back to a surviving Corvad cell, the Nexus One was now alert to the threat and would take appropriate actions. That included scouring Domus Valens for clues that might reveal the existence of Lijuan and her disciples in Domus Salus.

On multiple camera feeds on her video display, Lijuan followed the progress of the Nexi personnel as they foraged through Domus Valens. When a Nexus detachment entered the archives, her anxiety peaked.

Thirty-three years ago, before Lijuan had departed for Domus Salus, the three Corvad Placidia Tens had requested her presence, along with the Deinde Nine, who would accompany her. The plan to sequester them in Domus Salus had been explained, and then something even more important was revealed. There was a hidden repository in the archives, within which rested a container holding one of the Krystalis fragments.

Throughout the ages, each Corvad princeps and a minimum of two other Corvads were apprised of the container and its hidden location. Although the Nexi might prevail during their pending assault and temporarily occupy Domus Valens, the Corvad princeps was loath to move the container to Domus Salus because it was protected in its current location by a physical and psychic view shield projected by sophisticated technology that they did not understand and that not even their views could penetrate. The Corvad princeps feared that the container, if removed from its hidden location, would become visible to Nexus views. After all, the goal of the six true houses, professed on the eve the House War began, was to reclaim the Krystalis fragments.

Lijuan watched as the Nexi floated several hover-containers into the library and began stripping the shelves bare, loading the books into the containers for transport to Domus Praesidium. The Nexi would no doubt search the books for information—references that might reveal the existence of Domus Salus and the surviving Corvad contingent. When the Nexi approached the location of the hidden container, Lijuan's body tensed. Her breathing turned shallow as the Nexi shoved the books into the hover-containers and scanned the bookshelves and adjoining walls for hidden compartments. After a close examination, however, the Nexi moved past the alcove, hidden by an imaginary granite wall.

As the Nexi departed the barren library, Lijuan's thoughts turned to revenge. For three decades, the development of Corvad Nines and Tens had been hindered by a lack of experienced instructors and a limited pool of candidates, since they could not recruit publicly like the Nexi did. Even so, the Corvad House was finally on the verge of developing another Ten.

On her display panel, she selected the portal to Domus Salus, entering the password to the encrypted video feed. Nero Conde, her Primus Nine, appeared on the display.

"Yes, Princeps."

"What is the status of Gavin's development?"

"He still cannot view alternate timelines. He can split the timeline at will now, but he hasn't been able to deviate from the Prime."

"What about his talent?"

"He is making progress, but the Primus Talentum advises patience. He is not yet ready to engage in battle. I agree—we do not yet have sufficient strength to prevail against the Nexus House. We need more praetorians."

"Considering the outcome on Darian 3, we need more *capable* praetorians," Lijuan clarified, aiming her criticism at her Primus Nine.

"Our talent pool is limited," Nero replied. "I need better raw material."

"I cannot improve the pool of candidates. You will have to train them better. More intensely, longer hours. Whatever it takes. We must close the capability gap between Corvad and Nexus praetorians."

"Yes, Princeps. I will redouble my efforts."

24

Aboard the 2nd Fleet command ship, Lara lay beneath her bedcovers in the darkness, waiting for the nausea from the early morning jump to dissipate before beginning her day, when the control panel beside her stateroom door chimed.

"Who is it?" she called out.

"It's Jon."

"Lights on," Lara commanded as she slid from her bed. After the lights energized, she was about to order the door open when she realized she was wearing a silk nightgown that went down only to the top of her thighs. Plus, it was cold in the room, and the outline of her nipples was evident through the thin fabric. She reached for a robe, then stopped, reassessing the situation. Thus far, McCarthy hadn't made any romantic advances. Perhaps a nudge would help. She decided to skip the robe.

"Open door," Lara ordered.

Her door slid aside to reveal Admiral McCarthy, dressed for the day in his Fleet uniform.

As she approached him, she slid her hands through her disheveled hair, giving him a better look as the silk nightgown shifted over her curves.

Lara repressed a smile as McCarthy's eyes moved over her body in a way they hadn't done before.

"What's up?" Lara asked when she stopped before him.

McCarthy quickly raised his eyes to hers as he replied, "I have something to show you. Meet me on the command bridge as soon as possible."

"Something good or something bad?"

"I'll let you be the judge," he replied, adding a smile before he left.

Thirty minutes later, after showering and grabbing a bite to eat, Lara exited the elevator onto the command bridge. After only a few steps, she stopped to take in the view through the bridge windows. The command ship was in orbit around a planet in a triple-star system.

Each star was a different size and color. The largest and hottest star burned a brilliant blue-white, while its two sister stars were smaller and cooler. One radiated yellow, and the third glowed a reddish-orange hue. Two of the bridge monitors displayed the planets orbiting the stars in the distance. Both were gas giants, one with broad pastel swirls and the other with deep earth-tone eddies. Wide asteroid belts orbited the planets, with their broad swaths of debris illuminated in distinct bands of bright colors.

Lara spotted McCarthy conferring with Admiral Amani, who was seated in his command chair, and she joined them. After they greeted her, McCarthy motioned toward the bridge windows.

"This is the most beautiful spot in the galaxy," he said. "The Solarus system. I'm biased, of course."

Lara pondered McCarthy's comment, then remembered he was an off-worlder like her, born on Polermis, a planet in the Solarus system.

"We're orbiting Polermis?" She turned her attention to the nearby planet with white, wispy clouds swirling over deep blue water and purple-green continents.

McCarthy nodded. "I'm headed down to the planet. Want to join me?"

"I'd love to."

They headed to the spaceport and boarded McCarthy's shuttle, and it wasn't long before they were plummeting through the planet's atmosphere. The shuttle's thrusters kicked in, slowing the vehicle before it settled gently onto the planet's surface.

They stepped from the shuttle into a small clearing surrounded by lush green-and-purple vegetation on three sides and a tranquil lake on the other. She could see the lake bottom through the crystal-clear water as it lapped gently onto a white, sandy shore.

"Our timing is perfect," McCarthy said. "A rare triple-sunset."

Behind a mountain range rising before her, the blue-white sun was setting, with only half of the star visible over the jagged mountain peaks. The sun's two sister stars hovered a few degrees above and to the right of the setting sun, their yellow and reddish-orange hues illuminating the cirrus clouds high in the atmosphere in a stunning palette of colors. Small ripples spread across the lake's surface, reflecting the light from the three stars in a dazzling spectacle, radiating every color imaginable.

McCarthy interrupted the peaceful silence. "I was in orbit with First Fleet, tasked with delaying the Korilian advance long enough to evacuate Polermis. We paid heavily for the time we needed, losing almost one-third of the Fleet. When my battle group jumped away, I swore that I would return home."

He stared at the triple-sunset for a moment, then said, "Walk with me."

McCarthy led Lara to the lakeshore, where they slipped off their shoes and socks. Lara's feet sank into the soft sand, the cool water lapping over them as they walked along the edge of the tranquil water.

Lara suddenly realized that this was the vision she'd had aboard the 1st Fleet command ship while she was training with McCarthy for the Final Stand: walking along the shoreline, hand-in-hand. As she walked beside him, she tried to convince herself that she had received the vision for a reason. McCarthy had failed to make a romantic advance thus far; perhaps the onus was on her.

Preparing herself for rejection, she took his hand in hers. He turned to her and smiled as he gently squeezed her hand. Warmth spread through her body, and her pulse quickened from the physical contact.

They approached a trail that began at the edge of the lake, leading up into the dense green vegetation. After donning their socks and shoes again, McCarthy led her onto the path, which wound up toward a pass between two mountain peaks. Purple fir-like trees rose high above them, the underbrush populated with an array of flora sporting colorful flowers, their pleasant fragrances drifting by in the light breeze.

At the top of the pass, McCarthy stopped at the edge of a cliff. They stood overlooking a plain a half mile below them. All three stars were clearly visible, no longer blocked by the mountain peaks, burning brightly as they continued their descent. The sky above the horizon was bathed in a bright red hue, transitioning to orange, then pink, until the sky directly overhead shone a light, pastel blue.

On the center of the plain sprawled a large city, stunning both in its beauty and simplicity. It was built in a circular pattern, with main roads radiating out from the center. Tall spires rose in the center of the city, with the outer reaches filled with parks and lakes, and a river that wound its way lazily beneath arched bridges.

"Dialis," McCarthy said. "I was born and lived here until I was five, when I was inducted into the Nexus House." He gestured toward the left rim of the city. "My home when I was a kid."

He stood motionless as he stared at Dialis, and Lara reflected on the physical and emotional strain that McCarthy and the rest of humankind had been subjected to as they retreated from the Korilian assault for thirty years until there was nowhere left but Earth.

They stood silently in the mountain pass for a moment, and Lara took comfort in the warmth of McCarthy's hand in hers. Finally, McCarthy began moving again, leading the way down a trail toward the city.

They reached the outskirts of Dialis and traveled down a street lined on both sides with five-story structures that stretched as far as Lara could see, curving gently along the city's radius. The building exteriors were a smooth glass-and-cobalt-blue composite with flowering plant terraces and balconies along each level.

McCarthy eventually stopped at one of the entrances, then spoke into his wristlet, ordering his shuttle to rendezvous with them at this location. He released Lara's hand and headed up the walkway toward a glass-front lobby. As they approached, a wide glass door slid open. The city's main or backup power cells were still operating. He led Lara into the lobby, which had three circular elevator pods on each side.

After they stepped onto one of the pods, a woman's voice asked, "Which unit?"

"Three-zero-five," McCarthy answered.

A golden shimmering force field encompassed the pod up to shoulder height, then the pod began rising. After examining the translucent cylinder, Lara touched it gently with one finger, surprised that it felt like a solid surface.

The pod rose to the third level, then slid right along the building's circumference, finally stopping before a door displaying a blue digital 305. The force field disappeared, and they stepped from the pod.

Affixed beside the door was a retina scanner, blinking red. McCarthy scanned his right eye, and the door slid open, revealing a small foyer leading to a spacious living room with a retractable glass façade along the exterior, opening to a large open-air terrace that spanned the length of the unit. The terrace was enclosed with a railing overgrown with flowering vines and contained several lounge chairs around an infinity pool. The water was still flowing over the exterior edge, although dead leaves had collected on the pool's surface.

McCarthy entered the living room and surveyed the furnishings. A nine-section sofa formed a U facing a wall with a large video display built into it, and along another wall was a built-in desk and shelves filled with decorations, framed videographs, and other knickknacks. McCarthy closed his eyes, and Lara felt the chill from his view. He didn't explain, but Lara surmised he was viewing a future where he searched the apartment for something.

After a few seconds, McCarthy opened his eyes and moved toward the shelves, scanning each section until he found what he was looking for. He retrieved a thin box containing several dozen small disks, each about one inch in diameter, then selected one. He slid the disk into a slot in the video display and stepped back as the display energized.

It was a video recording of a man sitting at the desk across the room, manipulating icons on a touch screen display, his back to the camera. He wore a uniform similar to McCarthy's, and a large green duffel bag lay near him on the floor. A woman stood beside him, her hand on his shoulder, also looking at the display. She was dressed in a loose-fitting blue silk dress that fluttered about her feet, apparently in response to a light breeze that flowed into the room from the open terrace.

An infant's cry rose from a crib beside the couch, and the man and woman turned toward the sound. The man looked like Jon, only younger and with darker brown hair. The woman was tall and beautiful, with blonde hair and McCarthy's deep blue eyes. She walked over to the crib and picked up an infant about four months old. She propped him up against her chest, cradled in one arm.

"Is it on?" she asked.

"Yes," the man said.

The woman took one of the infant's small hands in hers and looked toward the camera. "Say hi to Grandma." She waved the baby's hand back and forth and turned sideways so the child's face was visible, its cheek resting on her shoulder. The baby looked at them with his mother's blue eyes.

The man swiveled his chair toward the camera. "Hi, Kristen."

"Hi, Mom," the woman said. "Just sending you a quick update. Trent's shipping off today for another deployment with the Space Exploration Corps. He'll be back in six months, we hear." She looked down at the child in her arms, then back toward the camera. "As you can see, Jon's grown quite a bit, and he's still got our eyes. I'm hoping they don't turn."

"There's nothing wrong with brown eyes, Claire," Trent said. "But I do hope they stay blue."

The baby began to fuss. Claire bounced him gently in her arm and patted his back. "Looks like it's feeding time," she said. "I'll send you another recording in a few weeks. We love you and miss you."

"Take care, Kristen," Trent said, then turned back toward the computer screen.

Claire walked toward Trent, then stopped abruptly and turned slowly around with a strange look on her face. She gently rubbed her child's back, scanning from right to left until she stopped, staring directly at Lara. Claire squinted for a moment. Then she smiled and gently kissed the baby on his cheek, never taking her eyes off Lara.

Trent walked up behind Claire and wrapped his arms around her waist. "What do you see?" he asked.

The man and woman froze, their final image captured in the last frame of the recording.

McCarthy looked at Lara. "My mom sent me several videos, including this one, after I was inducted into the Nexus House, something to remember them by. I've always wondered what my mom saw at the end of this video. It must be a coincidence, however. You must be standing in the right spot by accident."

Before she could respond, the shuttle landing outside the house caught their attention. But Lara noticed McCarthy running his fingers through his hair as he glanced at her from the corner of one eye.

25

A Nexus executive transport emerged from gray clouds as it descended, its navigation lights piercing a light snowfall in the darkness. It glided across the center of Rome, angling down toward an estate on the city's outskirts. The transport hovered over a shuttle pad adjacent to a three-level mansion faced with white marble, its engine exhaust blowing away a thin covering of snow until it landed, joining two dozen other shuttles whose occupants had already debarked.

The transport door slid open, and ten Nexus praetorians moved quickly down the ramp, assembling into a wedge-shaped formation aimed toward the mansion. After assessing the surroundings, the lead praetorian tapped his wristlet, and an eleventh Nexus emerged, her blue robe flowing behind her as she moved down the ramp. Upon taking her place at the head of the human phalanx, Rhea led the formation down a path toward the mansion entrance. Tall, black metal doors swung slowly inward as the Nexus One and her guard approached.

They passed through the entrance into a large foyer, which was barren but well decorated: marble floors, gilded walls, and an arched ceiling illuminated by an immense chandelier of crystal and gold. There was a fifteen-foot-wide circular design in the floor, containing several dozen house symbols arranged in a pattern spiraling out from the center.

The Nexus detachment stopped inside the circular design with The One in the center and her praetorians along the perimeter, facing outward. A few seconds later, a low rumble emanated throughout the foyer as the circle began sinking, granite walls appearing to rise as the platform descended.

After traveling several hundred feet, the platform ground to a halt, leveling off with an exit carved into the granite. The Nexus guard preceded this time, with The One following as they entered a large antechamber. Rhea removed and hung her robe on a wall hook, then left her guard behind as she traveled through an opening and entered the Regnandi Aethereum Thalamum—often referred to as simply the Thalamum—the chamber where the Concilium had met for the last twelve centuries.

The Concilium was the house version of the Colonial Council, which comprised the principes of every major and minor house. The Nexi were different from other houses in that they did not have a true princeps. While other houses were ruled by a single leader, Nexus Placidia Tens co-ruled. For Concilium meetings, any Nexus Placidia Ten could attend, although it was customary for the same Ten to participate for continuity purposes. With Rhea being the only Nexus Placidia Ten at the moment, she was technically the Nexus princeps as well.

Within the Concilium, the major houses ruled over the minors, with decisions made via majority vote by the major house principes. During the last few decades of the House War, with only two major houses remaining —the Nexi and Corvads—whose leaders often took differing positions, democratic rule was extended to the minor houses to break the majors' deadlock. Shortly after the Korilian War began, and with the House War fading into memory, Rhea—as the last major princeps—had suspended Concilium meetings.

It had been almost thirty years since Rhea's last trip to the Thalamum, and she was the last to arrive as was customary for the major principes. After entering the chamber from its upper entrance, she stopped before a crescent-shaped table with twelve chairs, which overlooked several rows of similarly shaped tables facing her. Seated at the opposing tables, amid fourteen vacant seats, were twenty-two minor house principes, who rose as she entered. She glanced at the eleven empty seats at the Concilium's ruling table, vacant due to the extermination of the eleven other major houses, then took her seat.

However, instead of the minor principes taking their seats as was customary, almost half of them remained standing.

"Yes?" Rhea asked.

Claude Verhofstadt, princeps of Devinctus House, responded. "After the Corvads were eliminated, you disbanded the Concilium because you no longer needed us. Now," he spread his arms apart, gesturing to those around him, "you suddenly find us useful again?"

"I did not convene the Concilium because I need your help. I called you here tonight to issue a warning. Two Nexi, one of whom is Admiral McCarthy, were attacked on Darian 3 by praetorians. That means—one of you gave the order to attack my House."

There was silence throughout the Concilium as the principes cast furtive glances among themselves.

Rhea continued, "However, I do not seek retribution tonight. I seek to communicate. I want to make it *very* clear that if any Nexi are attacked again, I will exterminate the offending house. Does anyone here not understand?"

There was a momentary silence before Verhofstadt spoke again. "You issue an empty threat. The Nexus House is a shell of its former power. You have barely a hundred praetorians."

"That is being rectified."

"You will be weak for years. Even a modest coalition of minor houses could defeat you. And rest assured, if you attack a minor house again, we will not stand by, paralyzed like we were in the past. If you make any attempt to exact retribution against a minor house, it is *we* who will destroy *you*."

"The House War is *over!*" Rhea said. "Combat is no longer an acceptable method of resolving our differences. Henceforth, we will resume our quarterly meetings, and all issues will be resolved diplomatically in this forum."

"You expect us to forget what the Nexus House did, annihilating entire houses? How many seats are vacant tonight because of Nexus aggression?"

"The Corvads slaughtered my people for three millennia. Did you expect us to do nothing? How many seats are vacant tonight because the

Corvads *and their allies* razed their domus and hunted them down until none were left?"

"The major houses used us as pawns in your wars. We were given no choice. Either align with a major house or be destroyed." Verhofstadt surveyed the other minor house principes, then returned his attention to Rhea. "The minor houses will no longer bow to the will of the majors. We demand equality."

"You are not equal," Rhea replied. "Viewing and shaping alternate futures is beyond you, and with that ability comes responsibility *and* authority. Concilium leadership is an acknowledgment of the burden the major houses have borne throughout history."

"The major houses have done nothing but threaten and extort the minor houses to their will. Tonight, it is the minor houses who issue the ultimatum to you. Equal rule within the Concilium, or the Nexus House will pay the price."

"Do not threaten my House, Verhofstadt. Nexus power is defined by more than the number of praetorians. We are the only house with Tens, and the talents possessed by Tens are far superior to anything manifested in Nines. I assure you, the Nexus House has the means to defend itself and exact retribution."

"Regarding your other Ten," Verhofstadt said, "Admiral McCarthy is preoccupied by the war, and any attack on your House would be orchestrated at a time when his support would not be available. As to you, your leadership is pathetic. You grovel before the Colonial Council, acquiescing to their demands instead of putting them in their place, exercising our power. As to your supposed talents, they are likely nothing more than fairy tales. Stories weaved to frighten us into submission. Not one of us here tonight has witnessed a single example of your supposed abilities."

Rhea clenched her teeth, controlling her anger as she assessed how best to respond. After a moment, she decided to ignore Verhofstadt's attempt to provoke her.

"Be seated," Rhea announced. "I bring the Concilium to order."

The minor house principes who were still standing ignored Rhea's command. After a quick survey, Rhea realized they were the leaders of the minor houses that had aligned with the Corvads. They had clearly discussed ahead of time a coordinated plan to challenge her leadership.

"I speak for all houses whose principes remain standing," Verhofstadt said. "We have decided that the Concilium needs new leadership, someone who has the best interest of all houses in mind instead of just their own. Not someone who calculates how best to take advantage of us."

"The major houses have ruled the Concilium for thousands of years," Rhea replied. "That will not change tonight."

"That isn't written anywhere in our charter. The major houses forced their will upon the minors, and we acquiesced. I propose a more civilized approach now that the House War, as you pointed out, is over. We should put the matter of Concilium leadership to a vote."

"There will be no vote."

"You cannot force your will upon us. We will vote."

Rhea paused again before replying. The attack against McCarthy and Lara on Darian 3 had emboldened Verhofstadt and other minor house principes. He was challenging her leadership of the Concilium, and if the situation wasn't properly addressed, the very existence of the Nexus House would be threatened. Although she had previously decided to ignore Verhofstadt's inflammatory words, she could do so no longer.

"I may not have your consensus to rule this Concilium. But I have the power to do so."

Rhea flexed her fingers, and Verhofstadt's chair slid toward him, hitting him behind the knees and knocking him down into his seat. But instead of acquiescing, Verhofstadt leaned forward, placing his hands on the edge of the table.

"How quaint. Your ability to move objects with your mind frightens no one."

Rhea stood, her patience with Verhofstadt finally exhausted. "Perhaps *this* will frighten you."

There was a hollowness to her voice as she invoked her power of command, freezing Verhofstadt's rib muscles. Without the ability to pull his ribs outward and expand his lungs, Verhofstadt could no longer breathe. He was startled at first, unsure of what was happening. Rhea descended from her Concilium table and stopped before him.

"Now, Verhofstadt, as you attempt to breathe, you realize it's my fairy-tale talent that is suffocating you. You realize that without the ability to breathe, you will be dead in a few minutes."

As Rhea stood patiently in front of him, she could see the terror in his eyes as his skin slowly turned a blue tint, his mind and body screaming for oxygen.

Verhofstadt began flailing about, trying to somehow undo what Rhea had done. She had purposely frozen only his chest and not his entire body so his desperate antics would produce a more dramatic effect than a man suffocating while frozen in place.

The minor house principes shifted their eyes between Verhofstadt and Rhea, wondering if she would actually kill him. His eyes bulged as he tried to breathe, then his face went slack, and he slumped in his chair.

Rhea spoke again. "I request you show proper respect in the *future*."

Verhofstadt suddenly gasped for air, gulping down huge breaths as the color of his skin slowly returned to normal.

Rhea scanned the Concilium chamber, meeting the eyes of every princeps. "Are there any other objections to continuing the Concilium tradition of major house rule?"

There was no response from the other principes, and Rhea dropped her gaze to Verhofstadt. He offered no further objections, but hatred simmered in his eyes.

26

Standing on *Controlador*'s command bridge beside McCarthy, Lara exited the jump darkness as 2nd Fleet rendezvoused with the 3rd Marine Expeditionary Force. She drew in a deep breath as she was hit by the now-familiar but gradually lessening nausea that accompanied each jump. As she rubbed her pounding temples, she peered through the bridge windows, examining their new location. Arrayed before 2nd Fleet were almost one hundred gray troop transports ferrying the 3rd MEF.

A bright white flash nearby caught Lara's attention, and the sensor supervisor announced, "Shuttle transport from Third Fleet, carrying Rear Admiral Rajhi and the Third Fleet guide."

Lara turned to McCarthy. "Nesrine Rajhi?"

McCarthy nodded.

Lara recalled the tense standoff between McCarthy and Rajhi on the bridge of her battleship *Athens* during the Final Stand. Rajhi had defied McCarthy's order to sacrifice *Athens*'s sister ship *Sparta*, and Lara had held a pulse-pistol to Rajhi's head to force her to comply. As far as Lara was concerned, Rajhi should have been court-martialed after the battle instead of promoted, and she didn't understand what McCarthy or Fleet Admiral Fitzgerald saw in her. Rajhi had shown her true colors when she disobeyed McCarthy aboard *Athens*. She couldn't be trusted.

The communications supervisor added, "The Third Fleet shuttle will drop off Admiral Rajhi on the cruiser *Aiguillon*, then rendezvous with *Controlador* for the fleet guide swap."

Lara turned to Carson Lieu, the 2nd Fleet guide, whose face was turning slightly red. For the critical mission to Hellios, he was being replaced by a more capable guide. Lara knew the swap would sting the young man's pride.

Admiral Amani shook McCarthy's hand. "Good luck, Jon. We'll have a drink afterward."

McCarthy and Lara would complete the rest of their journey to the Hellios system with the 3rd MEF, which would jump into the system only after 2nd Fleet had eliminated the Korilian warship contingent.

Lara bid farewell to Amani and Lieu, then accompanied McCarthy to the spaceport, where they were met by aides with their prepacked duffel bags. The 3rd Fleet shuttle landed, and Angeline Del Rio, the 3rd Fleet guide, debarked. Lara greeted her former mentor with a hug, then boarded the shuttle with McCarthy for the short trip to their troop transport.

During the transit, McCarthy answered Lara's questions about their destination. *Artemis V* was a standard troop transport, capable of carrying one brigade of ten thousand combat troops and support staff. The 3rd MEF was the equivalent of an Army corps, comprising ten Combined Arms Divisions of one hundred thousand troops each when at full strength, plus one Heavy Air Support Division and one Heavy Ground Armor Division, although the Ground Armor Division was currently undergoing refit and wouldn't be employed on Hellios due to the short duration of the operation.

As the shuttle approached the troop transport, its spaceport doors opened, and the pilot guided the shuttle to its berth, settling onto the spaceport deck. McCarthy and Lara exited the shuttle and were greeted by Captain Tom Bradner, commanding officer of *Artemis V*, Major General Vern Hutton, commanding officer of the 3rd MEF, plus a Marine Corps major and a civilian.

"Good to see you again, Admiral," Hutton said. "And it's a pleasure to meet you, Miss Anderson." He gestured to the Marine Corps officer beside him. "This is Major Drew Harkins, who will be your platoon leader.

Normally you'd have a first lieutenant, but we put the best we've got in charge of your platoon, and we also handpicked the two squad leaders and other platoon members."

Hutton motioned to the civilian. "This is Winston Albright, who will accompany you into the Korilian complex."

"What's your task?" Lara asked.

"I'm from SID—Special Intelligence Division. We've determined how to read Korilian software. I'll download the code from the Korilian intelligence center for analysis so we can determine what algorithms they're using and hopefully reverse engineer them for our use."

Harkins addressed McCarthy, Lara, and Winston. "Dinner is in an hour. Why don't I introduce you to our platoon?"

"Some other time, Major," Winston replied. "I'm scheduled for a data feed from Star Base Two."

"I'll go," Lara said, then turned to McCarthy.

"I'll pass for now," McCarthy said. "I have a few things I'd like to discuss with General Hutton. I'll meet the platoon later tonight or tomorrow." McCarthy grinned, then added, "Have fun."

27

Major Harkins escorted Lara through the maze of passageways, finally stopping beside the entrance to one of the troop transport's recreation rooms. There were two dozen Marines in the room gathered around a few tables, some playing cards and others playing a game with holograms displayed from their wristlets. Half of the Marines were women, and all of them were in their late teens except for two older sergeant majors, one male and one female, who sat together at a table drinking by themselves. The Marines were all clean-cut with short-cropped hair, even the women, and they wore green T-shirts tucked into fatigue pants.

Harkins and Lara stood by the doorway, unnoticed, as one of the Marines, with *Tony Rodriguez* embroidered on his uniform, began complaining about the long transit. He was sitting at a table with five other Marines, and he looked to be about eighteen or nineteen.

"Why do we have to wait so long between jumps?" he asked. "We've got eighteen more to go. That's over a week aboard this flying guana."

A Marine sitting across the table from him said, "I'm with you, Tony. All this talk about what happens if you jump too soon is a bunch of malarkey. I bet they need time to recalibrate their nav system and juice the jump drive. They probably make up these stories to frighten fleet non-quals like us."

"You two don't know what you're talking about," a woman beside

Rodriguez said. She was an attractive blonde with an Australian accent. "Hey, Sergeant Jankowski," she called to one of the two older Marines. "We got two unbelievers here. They think this jump stuff's a bunch of crap."

The male sergeant major turned his chair around, facing the six Marines. He looked to be near forty, with flecks of gray hair in his sideburns. A thin scar ran down the right side of his face, and he wore a pair of dark glasses. He was tall and muscular and spoke with a deep, resonating voice.

"Them aren't stories," Jankowski said, looking at the Marines at the table. "I can vouch for that."

"How would you know, Sarge?" Rodriguez asked.

"Because I was aboard the *Argonaut*, eighteen years ago."

"The *Argonaut*?" another Marine asked. "When it jumped five times in a single day?"

"It wasn't five jumps in one day. It was five jumps in two hours." He adjusted his dark glasses before continuing. "We were on our way to Darian 3 when we received the order to accelerate the jumps. The Korilians had launched a major offensive, and we needed to arrive before the supply corridor collapsed.

"There were one hundred troop transports that began the trip that day. We felt the normal nausea after the first jump. Then we jumped two more times only a few minutes apart. The entire brigade started puking, and we were so dizzy that only half of us could stand. An hour later, we jumped again. That's when our eyes started bleeding. All of us, crying blood tears as the whites of our eyes hemorrhaged and turned solid red."

Jankowski gazed at each Marine at the table, their eyes widening.

"Then it was time for the fifth jump. Only a dozen transports had made the fourth jump, and the other ship captains decided they'd had enough. But not our captain. The old man must've had two glass eyes, because at the one-hour point, he ordered the fifth jump.

"I'll never forget it," Jankowski said as he leaned toward the six Marines. They listened intently as he continued his tale. "I was holding one of my buddies, Aaron was his name, as he sat on his knees spewing yellow bile from his gut into a jump bag. I was looking at 'em when we made the jump, and when I felt the jump wave pass, his eyes exploded."

Jankowski grabbed one of the Marines at the table as he said *exploded*, and the young corporal nearly jumped out of his chair.

The corporal laughed and said, "Nice one, Sarge. You had us going there for a minute."

"It ain't no tale," Jankowski replied.

"You expect us to believe you?" Rodriguez asked. "Five jumps in two hours? And nothing happened to you when your buddy's eyes exploded?"

"I never said nothing happened to me, kid." Jankowski lifted his dark glasses and stared at Rodriguez with one blue eye and one brown. "I was one of the lucky ones, losing only one eye. We limped our way to the nearest star base, but by the time they got to me, they had only brown eyes left."

Jankowski lowered his glasses. "So shut yer trap and enjoy the next few days of downtime."

Harkins cleared his throat loudly as he stepped into the room, joined by Lara. The female sergeant major noticed them and called out, "Attention on deck!"

The Marines snapped to attention as Harkins said, "At ease. Be seated."

All except the two sergeant majors settled back into their chairs.

"I'd like to introduce you to Lara Anderson," Harkins said. "She's one of the civilians who will be accompanying us into the Korilian facility."

The two older Marines approached and introduced themselves.

"Welcome to the team," the female said. "I'm Sergeant Major Narra Geisinger."

"I'm Sergeant Major Edward Jankowski," the other Marine said. "But my friends call me Eddie."

"Hey, Sarge, can we call you Eddie too?" a Marine at one of the other tables asked.

Jankowski glared at the Marine while a few others chuckled.

Both sergeant majors towered over Lara. Jankowski was at least six feet, six inches tall and well over two hundred pounds, with a lean, muscular body. Geisinger was also over six feet tall, with broad shoulders.

They grow 'em big in the Marines, Lara thought. *Or maybe it's survival of the fittest.*

Lara surveyed the scar on Jankowski's face, and a thin scar on

Geisinger's left arm that ran the circumference of her forearm. They'd obviously engaged in close combat, with Geisinger having her left arm severed, then reattached.

"So, what're you supposed to do while we're in the facility?" Rodriguez asked. "Are you gonna analyze the dead bugs while their bodies are still warm?"

The Australian woman beside Rodriguez said, "Korilians are cold-blooded, you idiot."

"I know that," Rodriguez replied. "I was just tryin' to have a conversation with our new friend."

"Actually, no," Harkins said. "Lara is one of our guides. Once we're inside the facility, she'll give us directions to the intelligence center."

"You've been there before?" Rodriguez asked.

"No," Harkins answered. "Miss Anderson is a Nexus."

"Get out!" one of the Marines said. "I've never actually met one. I've only heard stories about how they can see the future."

"Not all of us can," Lara replied. "It depends on what level we are. I'm a level-eight Nexus, which means I have glimpses of the future."

Rodriguez put his arm around the Australian Marine. "So, tell me, Miss Anderson, with your powers and such. Am I gonna get lucky with Deanna tonight?"

Before Lara could reply, Deanna wrapped her arms around Rodriguez's neck and kissed his cheek. With her lips only an inch away from his face, she said, "Only in your dreams."

Then she bit Rodriguez's ear, digging her teeth into his flesh. His face contorted in pain, and he pulled Deanna's hair. When she didn't release him, he punched her in the chest.

Deanna let go, and Rodriguez rubbed his ear. He pulled his hand away, his fingers covered with blood.

A redhead on Rodriguez's other side leaned over and locked her arms around his neck. "Sleep with me tonight," she said in a Russian accent. "I will give you more pleasure than you have ever imagined."

"Oh, I can imagine a lot," he replied.

"Be careful, Tony," one of the Marines at another table said. "Liza is the Black Widow."

All eyes turned toward Liza.

Lara whispered to Harkins, "What does he mean by *Black Widow*?"

Harkins replied, "The Black Widow has more Korilian kills than any other Marine."

Rodriguez pulled back to get a better look at Liza, her arms still locked around his neck. "You're the Black Widow? I thought you'd be older."

"You do not need to be old to kill bugs. You just need to be good. And I'm *very* good, in more ways than one."

The other Marine added, "Killing bugs isn't why she's called the Black Widow. We nicknamed her that because everyone she sleeps with gets bagged during the next battle."

"This is true," Liza said. "They all die horrible deaths. But each one has told me with his dying words that it was worth it."

Geisinger, still standing beside Lara, spoke loudly. "All right, children, give it a rest."

Liza released Rodriguez, and he leaned back, eyeing both women beside him warily.

Harkins said, "I'll let you get back to your activities. Enjoy your downtime, Corporal," he added, aiming his comment at Rodriguez.

"It was a pleasure meeting you all," Lara said.

"The pleasure's all mine," Rodriguez replied as he surveyed Lara in her form-fitting Nexus uniform, his eyes moving slowly across her body.

Deanna punched him in his chest. "Mind your manners!"

Lara felt her cheeks warming and hoped her embarrassment didn't show.

Harkins acknowledged the two squad leaders. "Sergeants." Then he turned toward the recreation room door, waiting for Lara to depart first.

As Harkins and Lara walked down the passageway, Harkins said, "They're really a good bunch of Marines. Very competent, and very professional when the time comes. They've been in combat almost continuously for the last three years. They're just letting their hair down. I hope you weren't offended by their behavior."

"I understand," Lara said as she thought about the young Marines. "Are they really the best in the Third MEF?"

"Absolutely. We selected two Marines from each division, plus each squad leader handpicked one additional Marine."

"Who did they pick?"

"Jankowski selected Deanna, and Geisinger tabbed Liza—the Black Widow. Liza would have been my choice as well. She's the best there is. She's been assigned as your personal bodyguard, and she'll serve you well."

"Okay, Major. I'll take your word that they're good. But what I don't understand is why they're so young. Except for the two sergeant majors, they're all teenagers."

"It's a result of our war strategy. During the first twenty-five years of the war, as the Korilians advanced toward Earth, we built up our planetary defenses and amassed a sizable army, with the goal of defending every inch of soil on Earth. We had over four billion soldiers and Marines digging in for the inevitable Korilian invasion. Twenty-five years of continuous defeat conditioned us to expect the worst—that the Fleet would eventually be destroyed and a Korilian invasion would follow.

"But Fleet Admiral Fitzgerald changed all that. She convinced the Council that the Fleet was the most important resource we had. That if the Fleet were destroyed, our armies, no matter how large and prepared, would eventually be defeated. As long as Korilian warships were in orbit, pounding our positions on Earth mercilessly, we could never win. She insisted that we needed to deploy our armies to our remaining colonies, bogging down the Korilians to gain us time to assemble additional construction yards and build more starships. Admiral Fitzgerald's premise was that we needed to sacrifice the ground forces to buy enough time to build a Fleet strong enough to defeat the Korilians.

"The Council agreed, and we transported our armies to our remaining colonies, then abandoned them. The Fleet avoided major confrontations whenever possible during the five years before the Final Stand, which meant little to no resupply to our troops, and in most cases, no evacuation. We marooned our entire force of four billion soldiers and Marines, plus another two hundred million recruits every year, on distant planets with no hope of survival.

"By the time we defeated the Korilians at the Final Stand, our armies were expended, with nothing remaining but a handful of veterans and millions of teenagers fresh out of boot camp. But the last three years have been different. With the Korilian armada retreating and the Colonial Fleet in orbit providing fire support, we've consistently defeated the Korilians and rapidly reclaimed our planets. In the process, we've gained valuable experience. I can't tell you how much easier it is going into battle with seasoned troops instead of raw recruits.

"So yes, they're young, and that's because they're all we've got. But don't let their age fool you. They're very good at what they do. You'll see, soon enough."

Harkins grew quiet after his soliloquy, and they soon reached the officers' quarters on O-Deck. When they arrived at Lara's stateroom, they stopped at her door.

"Liza will escort you to the armory tomorrow morning at zero-eight-hundred for your fitting."

"Fitting?" Lara asked.

"You'll be wearing an armored suit during the assault on Hellios. If you encounter a Korilian without armor, you won't have a chance."

"Eight o'clock will work," Lara replied, then added, "Thank you, Major. For everything."

A quizzical look formed on his face.

"I'm sorry...," Lara said, "for everything you and your Marines have gone through. I can only imagine how difficult it's been."

"You've got nothing to be sorry for, Lara. It's not your fault. It's the Korilians', no one else's. With your help in a few days, we'll deal them a blow that will make our jobs easier, saving millions of lives in the future."

Yes, the future, Lara thought. She wished she was more capable than just an Eight. She'd had only one vision related to Hellios thus far—Major Harkins leading the platoon into a dark opening in the side of a Korilian facility. Unfortunately, she couldn't see what else the future held in store for them.

The next day, precisely at eight a.m. as Major Harkins had mentioned the night before, Lara's stateroom door tone chimed. She opened the door to find Sergeant Liza Kalinin standing in the corridor. A short distance down the passageway, Corporal Chris Travis was waiting outside McCarthy's stateroom. Lara and McCarthy joined the two Marines, who escorted them to the armory for their equipment fitting.

Along the way, Travis asked McCarthy if he'd ever worn armor.

"I have," McCarthy replied, "but it was over twenty years ago while I was training as a Nexus Nine, before I was assigned to the Fleet."

"Armor has advanced quite a bit in the last two decades," Travis replied. "Or so I'm told. I'm only seventeen. Liza, on the other hand, is practically ancient by Corps standards. She's almost twenty."

"Watch it, Travis," Liza replied, "or you won't make it to eighteen."

They arrived at the armory, and after passing hundreds of weapon racks stacked a dozen tiers high on automated retrievers, they reached the armor fitting rooms. Travis took McCarthy into one room while Liza escorted Lara into another.

Inside the fitting room, equipment bins lined two bulkheads from floor to ceiling, while built into the third wall was a lighted chamber large enough to hold one person.

After the door slid shut behind them, Liza said, "Strip to your skivvies."

Lara gave her a quizzical look, and Liza added, "You need to step into the chamber and get measured for your armored suit."

Lara stripped down, then stepped into the cold chamber. Red lasers activated, scanning her body from head to toe. When the lasers deactivated, Liza motioned for her to step from the chamber.

The bins along the two walls—each column containing a different article of clothing or equipment—began moving, each column shifting up or down until they eventually stopped. The bins along a single row, about chest high, lit up in a soft blue glow.

"Your equipment," Liza said, "based on your measurements."

Liza started on one end of the row, pulling out the contents, which she tossed into a pile on the floor. Lara did the same, starting on the other end of the row. Socks, a micromesh full-body suit, thin gloves, a utility belt, and a dozen armored suit components, all black.

"Put the undergarments on, then I'll demonstrate how to don the armored suit."

As Lara pulled on her new clothes, Liza tapped her wristlet and said, "Liza Kalinin, 851051."

The bins repositioned, and Liza stripped down to her panties, then retrieved equipment in her size. Liza was even more impressive physically, once out of her uniform. She was six feet tall, and muscles rippled in her arms and legs as she moved. She had a circular scar around her right elbow.

Liza noticed her stare. "The Korilians aim for the joints in the armor. They have razor-sharp limbs that can take an arm or leg off if they get a clean hit." Liza flexed her arm. "It's mine—no bionics. The Fleet hospital ships are pretty good at reattaching limbs. But most important, protect your neck and waist seams. There's no reattaching your head or putting you back together if you get cut in half. The best strategy if you want to survive, however, is don't let a Korilian get close."

As Liza flexed her arm, explaining it was her own instead of a bionic one, Lara noticed a three-dimensional tattoo on the Marine's shoulder: a skull on fire with a snake slithering from each eye socket. The snakes moved as Liza donned her equipment, the serpents shifting their heads and keeping their eyes focused on Lara, their forked tongues flicking occasionally. Inside the skull's open mouth, flames flickered around the number 21.

Liza followed Lara's eyes and explained. "It's the emblem for the Twenty-First Marine Combined Arms Division. Every enlisted Marine in the division has this tattoo."

Once they donned their undergarments, Liza demonstrated how to attach the armored components. She began with the heavy boots, working her way up. Lara mimicked Liza, with the Marine assisting her on occasion. Each segment automatically attached to the adjacent ones when placed in proximity, and they continued until only the armored gloves and helmet remained.

The suit was made of a composite material—tougher and lighter than metal, Liza explained—but it was still heavy and stiff once assembled. Lara could barely move and wondered what good the extra protection was if she could only shuffle across the floor while wearing it.

"Give me your left forearm," Liza said.

Lara lifted her arm as the Marine added, "Watch what I do."

Liza tapped two indentations on Lara's armored wrist, and her suit activated. She felt the armored segments adjust slightly, and when she withdrew her arm, it moved almost effortlessly, as if she were wearing nothing at all.

"I've set your suit to neutral," Liza said, "which will allow you to move as if you were wearing normal clothes. The suits can also augment your strength and speed, but it takes a bit of training to learn how to handle hyper strength and speed. For example, if you were to throw a punch with augmented strength and speed, you'd likely fall over because you don't know how to properly counterbalance the faster and more powerful thrust. We don't want you falling down on the job on Hellios," Liza added with a smile, "so it's the neutral setting for you."

The armored gloves were a funky contraption, with the top flayed open. She followed Liza's example and placed a hand, palm down, inside it, and the edges immediately clamped around her hand, sealing it inside. She felt her armored suit with a finger and was surprised that it felt like she was touching her suit with her bare skin.

Liza reached toward the floor, retrieving Lara's last armored suit component—her helmet—which was split open along a seam that ran from the temple down to the neck on both sides. Liza slid it slowly onto Lara's head. Once it locked into place, Liza said, "Tap your helmet by either ear twice, quickly."

Lara tapped her helmet twice with an armored finger, and the helmet slowly closed, then sealed itself to the armored neck seam. The helmet facepiece lit up with an array of indications on one side while data scrolled down the other. Liza explained the indications, starting with life-support status: air quality, hours of oxygen remaining, heart and breathing rates, blood pressure, and suit temperature.

The Marine then explained the additional settings that could be changed by simply talking to the suit, such as strength, reflex, and speed settings; low light, infrared, and magnified vision; augmented hearing and communication channels, plus an explanation of the data available: facility schematics, a map that displayed the location of all Marines in their unit, and myriad other data feeds Lara could tap into.

As Liza walked Lara through the suit settings and features, Lara studied the young Marine. It was hard to believe a nineteen-year-old was a seasoned veteran, the best in the Corps.

Lara spoke, her voice emanating from her suit speaker. "Have you really killed more Korilians than any other Marine?"

"So they tell me," Liza replied.

"You must be very good at what you do."

"Yeah, I'm pretty good," Liza said. "But more important, I'm lucky. There's a saying in the Corps—*it's better to be lucky than good.*"

"Nexi don't believe in fate or luck."

Liza laughed. "You *clearly* have never fought Korilians."

The Marine finished explaining the suit controls, and after Lara figured she had a handle on things, she said, "I'm ready for my weapon and shield." She was half joking but figured that since she now had an armored suit, a weapon and shield would go nicely.

"No weapon for you," Liza replied. "Major Harkins decided not to issue you or Admiral McCarthy a weapon. The last thing we need is two non-quals behind us wielding assault carbines. You're probably just as likely to shoot a Korilian as one of us in the back. Regarding shields, they mess with our physiology too much. An encapsulating full-body shield strong enough to stop a Korilian pulse would have you puking in five seconds. We have flat energy shields we can deploy in front of us, but it quickly incapacitates whoever wields them. We carry them but use them only in an emergency and for a short duration.

"A type of Korilian called a slayer, on the other hand, can be encapsulated by a spherical energy shield indefinitely."

"Slayer?"

"Slayers are extremely rare versions of your standard combat Korilian—about fifty percent bigger and much nastier, as if your standard Korilian isn't unpleasant enough."

Liza explained that Korilians were hive creatures, like Earth's bees, with different variants performing different functions. There were your standard Korilians, akin to human civilians, then those bred for combat, then slayers—which were so rare and potent that a single slayer would typically lead an entire Korilian army into battle—and then there was a royalty version that formed the Korilian diplomatic and ruling classes. Additionally, Korilians were asexual—there were no males or females—just different variants.

"You seem to know a lot about Korilians," Lara said.

Liza shrugged. "I meet Korilians, I kill Korilians. We've learned to identify the different types; each poses a different threat level. It helps us prioritize our opponents."

The Marine picked up the last piece of equipment, a utility belt, and had Lara fasten it around her waist.

"What's in here?"

"Nothing of much use if we're in and out in a few hours like the op brief said. Some rations, first aid, and an enviro-mask in case you have suit failure. You'd take your helmet off and slip the mask on. But even if your life support fails, you shouldn't need the enviro-mask for this mission. The planet is a class four-delta. The air will be cold but breathable."

The fitting room door intercom beeped, and Liza answered. McCarthy had finished his armored suit fitting, and he and Travis were waiting outside.

Liza slipped out of her suit and helped Lara from hers, then they dressed and joined McCarthy and Travis in the passageway. The two

Marines escorted Lara and McCarthy back to their staterooms, then departed. McCarthy seemed to hesitate outside his door for a moment for some reason, then bid Lara farewell and entered his stateroom.

Lara entered her room, and as she pondered how to spend the rest of the day, the temperature of her stateroom plummeted. Fog began seeping into her room from the passageway door seams, descending to the floor, then snaking toward the far corner of her stateroom, where it collected, rising upward. The fog became denser, taking the shape of a human. It suddenly disappeared, and Lara stared at her mother standing in the corner. It had been eighteen years since she had last seen her.

Lara was an only child, born on the planet Altaria, evacuated to Ritalis at the age of seventeen as the Korilian Empire advanced toward the Pleiades star cluster. By then she was an orphan; her dad had been tasked to the Colonial Fleet and was killed during the fierce battles attempting to keep the supply lines open to Darian 3. Lara was twelve when her mother, Cheryl, died in an accident at the starship shield generator factory where she worked.

Cheryl opened her arms, offering an embrace. Even though Lara knew she was an apparition, she couldn't resist. She hugged her mom, surprised that the apparition had substance—Cheryl felt firm in her grasp and warm in her embrace. She rested her head on her mom's shoulder while Cheryl stroked her hair.

After a long moment, Lara released her mom and stepped back, although Cheryl kept her hands on her daughter's shoulders.

"Why are you here?" Lara asked.

"Things are about to change," Cheryl replied, "and you could end up in a vulnerable position."

"What do you mean? What's about to change?"

"I can't provide specifics, but you will understand when it happens."

"Why can't you provide specifics?"

Cheryl smiled. "You should know by now that when I appear, whether in the form of your mom, Regina, or Admiral Rajhi, I am limited in what I can say."

Lara recalled the apparition she had seen aboard the battleship *Atlantis* during the mission to capture a Korilian cruiser, which had taken the form of McCarthy's dead former guide, Regina. Another apparition had appeared aboard the 1st Fleet command ship during the Final Stand, impersonating Nesrine Rajhi. Each time, the apparition had offered vague but helpful advice. Now, it had taken the form of her mother. But what was the source of the apparitions?

"Who—or what—*are* you?" Lara asked.

Cheryl smiled again. "You will understand at the appropriate time. Until then, be careful."

The stateroom door chimed, and the apparition vanished.

Lara stood there for a moment, trying to make sense of her mother's words. When the stateroom door chimed again, Lara answered.

"Open."

The door slid aside to reveal Admiral McCarthy. Lara immediately sensed that something was amiss. Instead of emanating his usual air of confidence, indecision played across his face.

"Is something wrong?" she asked as McCarthy entered her stateroom, the door sliding shut behind him.

"No, nothing's wrong," McCarthy said as he stopped before her.

"What is it?"

McCarthy considered her question for a moment, then replied, "It's your line. Or lack thereof."

"You can't see my future and you're worried about what's going to happen to me on Hellios?"

"No, it's not that," he said. Then he quickly added, "Well, yes, of course I'm worried. I can't follow my line or yours into the future, and that's worrisome. But that's not what I'm here to discuss."

McCarthy's eyes searched hers as Lara waited for him to continue.

"It's that you have no line to follow," he said again. "I'm accustomed to being able to predict the outcome of critical or sensitive issues. As a Ten, I can view the situation and postulate alternate courses of action, then select the one that produces the optimal outcome. With you, I'm in the dark, like a blind man fumbling around. And since I can't foresee the future on Hellios, the thought that one or both of us might not make it…"

He paused again, then added, "There's something I've been struggling with, and I don't want to have any regrets."

Lara replied, "I'm sorry, Jon. I'm not really following you."

McCarthy stepped closer and placed his hands on her waist, then kissed her.

Lara accepted his kiss, wrapping her arms around his neck, letting their embrace linger. After a while, he began to pull back but she kept him close, offering a kiss of her own. His hands began to wander, and she felt a heat building in her body, but it was a different kind of warmth than what she had felt on Darian 3.

Lara spotted Cheryl as she appeared in the corner of her stateroom again, shaking her head in exasperation. But then she smiled before disappearing.

29

Lara stretched beneath the bedsheets in the darkness, then felt beside her for McCarthy. He was gone, but the sheets where he'd lain were still warm. His stateroom was faintly lit, and a thin strip of light leaked beneath the bathroom door. Not fully awake yet, she rolled onto her side as her thoughts dwelled on how much things had changed in the last three days.

Although the first segment of the journey to Hellios had passed slowly, the last three days had sped by. She had spent most of that time with McCarthy, in either her stateroom or his, exploring their new relationship. During their long talks into the night, with Lara resting her head on McCarthy's chest and his arm wrapped around her, he had explained the fragmented comments he made before their first kiss.

He had been attracted to her since they met on the Fleet hospital ship *Mercy*, but he'd been fighting it. His relationship with his former fiancée, Teresa Davis, his chief of staff when he was in command of the Normandy battle group, had been the main issue. After what he had done to save her when her ship became disabled—sacrificing five battleships and thousands of lives in the process—he realized the danger emotion posed to a Ten: that emotion could lead you astray, making you do what you *want* to do instead of what you *should* do. After Teresa's death a few months later, McCarthy had vowed to not enter another relationship until the war was over.

When he met Lara aboard *Mercy*, he had initially pushed her away, insisting he didn't need a replacement guide after Regina's death at Ritalis. He could already feel the attraction and decided the best path was to ensure there was no opportunity for a relationship to develop. However, The One had forced his hand and he had relented, accepting Lara as his new guide.

Fortunately, there had been little time for romance during the hectic weeks preparing for the Final Stand, and after the battle, The One had assigned Lara to Domus Praesidium to continue her prescient training. It was an arrangement that suited McCarthy's desire well, although he was still drawn to Lara and couldn't help but spend a few minutes with her whenever he visited the Praesidium.

During their trip to Darian 3 to search for Elena's remains, he'd been forced to deal with emotions he had buried for twenty years—his relationship with Elena and the sacrifice she had made for him. In the interim, his feelings for Lara grew stronger, and his resolve to refrain from another relationship until the war was over began to waver. As they journeyed toward Hellios, his inability to predict the future—whether he or Lara would survive—had been the breaking point. He had finally decided to reveal his feelings for her and hope for reciprocation, even if their relationship might last only a few days, depending on the outcome on Hellios.

McCarthy stepped from the bathroom dressed for the day in his Fleet uniform. He stopped beside the bed as Lara rolled into her back.

"We jump to the staging area in an hour," he said. He leaned over and kissed her. "Meet me in the combat information center for the assault brief."

An hour later, Lara entered the troop transport's command information center, an oval compartment in the center of the ship, with an outer row of control consoles surrounding a data fusion table. Video displays populated the outer rim, upon which were the faces of ten brigadier generals—the commanding officers of the 3rd MEF's 21st through 30th Divisions.

Assembled in the combat information center were the senior personnel aboard *Artemis V*, which included Admiral McCarthy, Major General Hutton, in command of the 3rd MEF, and Colonel Demi Kavanagh, in charge of 21st Division's 1st Brigade, whose ten thousand troops were embarked aboard *Artemis V*. Major Harkins was also present, seated by the fusion table, and Lara took a vacant seat beside him as five deep tones reverberated throughout the ship. A minute later, they made the jump to the Telac system.

Shortly after the dark, swirling journey through space ended, Lara's skin tingled as the starship's shields were energized. One of the video displays showed 2nd Fleet, which had split into two formations during the jump: sixteen cruiser squadrons in one group, with the sixteen battleship squadrons and sixteen carriers in the other. Assembled in the Telac system was a formidable task force: a Marine Expeditionary Force of almost one million troops, a cruiser detachment of 192 starships, and the rest of 2nd Fleet—192 battleships and sixteen carriers loaded with eight thousand single-pilot vipers.

One of the vacant displays energized, and the image of Rear Admiral Rajhi, in command of the cruiser task group, appeared. Two more displays energized, with Fleet Admiral Fitzgerald and Marine Corps Commandant Narendra Modi appearing from their respective command centers on Earth. A third monitor flicked on, displaying Admiral Amani with his new guide, Angeline, standing over his shoulder. Now that the key players were online, the assault briefing began, although there were slight delays as the communication jump-pods relayed the discussions between the Hellios task force and Earth.

Fleet Admiral Fitzgerald was the first to speak. "Recon probes indicate your approach hasn't been detected. There has been no change in the number of Korilian warships stationed in the Hellios system, their operational schedule, or alert level. Additionally, the Rignao system is clear of Korilian warships and probes, so your double jump via Rignao into the Hellios system can proceed as planned. From a Fleet perspective, the mission is a go."

The brief then shifted to Admiral Amani, who provided more details: 2nd Fleet and the 3rd MEF would jump together into the Rignao system. As soon as the cruiser jump drives recharged, they would make a successive jump to Hellios and engage the one hundred non-alert warships docked at the Korilian star base. Thirty seconds after the cruisers arrived at Hellios, the battleships and carriers would join them, engaging the one hundred Korilian warships on alert, which should be in the middle of a pulse-generator recharge after attacking the Colonial cruisers. The 3rd MEF would wait in the Rignao system until the Hellios system was secured, which would likely take several hours.

Admiral Amani wrapped up his portion of the brief with, "The Hellios task force is ready to proceed. D-Hour is set for two-one-hundred at the completion of our twelve-hour hold, with L-Hour set for zero-six-hundred the following morning."

Lara leaned toward Major Harkins. "What's D-Hour and L-Hour?"

"D-Hour is Departure Hour—when the task force begins the two-jump sequence to Hellios. The MEF cares more about L-Hour, which is Load Hour—when the MEF units board the surface assault vehicles for the planetary assault.

"Liza and Travis will escort you and Admiral McCarthy to the armory at zero-five-hundred, where you'll don your armored suits. I recommend you skip breakfast. Between the jump and the descent through the atmosphere, it'll be rough on your stomach. Our platoon will be in the last SAV down, launching after the surface perimeter is secure and all air-defense artillery has been eliminated. We want to minimize the risk to Admiral McCarthy." Then he quickly added, "You too, of course."

Lara smiled. "That's quite all right. I realize McCarthy is far more important than I am."

Harkins returned the smile. "We'll do everything we can to keep both of you safe."

30

Krajik lumbered into the Korilian Fleet command compound, the black fibrous floor giving slightly with each step of its six-hundred-pound body. After reaching a vertical shaft and clambering down several levels using all six limbs, Krajik reached the command center supervising the war against the humans. Krajik stopped beside Pracep Mrayev, commanding all fleet and ground forces assigned to the campaign.

It has revealed its plan, Krajik thought to Mrayev, conveying its words telepathically instead of using crude sounds like the humans. *The trap has been set.*

Finally, Mrayev thought. *I told you it would tell us when it was ready. Where is it setting the trap?*

The Hellios system.

Hellios? Mrayev's thoughts were infused with surprise, quickly supplanted by humor. *Outstanding. The humans cannot resist the bait. What is the human force composition?*

One full fleet, accompanied by almost one million troops.

Only one million?

They intend only to harvest algorithms from our main facility there, not gain control of the entire planet.

When will they reach Hellios?

They are two jumps away. It believes they will double jump to Hellios after completing a six-quign hold, which has just begun.

Mrayev glanced at the far wall, where one of the screens displayed the sector in question. The pracep conveyed a thought, and the display shifted to the Hellios system. On one side of the screen, various symbols represented the Korilian warships in orbit—those on alert and those docked at the star base—along with the number of combat units on the planet and their strength.

Krajik also surveyed the data, then thought to Mrayev, *The human fleet will outnumber our warships two to one. Should we warn our ships?*

No, Mrayev responded. *We cannot risk alerting the humans. We must let them believe their assault will succeed. After the humans engage, I will route additional forces to replace our losses and gain the advantage.* Mrayev's gaze shifted to another screen, which reported available warship reserves. Krajik sensed Mrayev's irritation after the assessment.

We do not have sufficient reserves to overwhelm an entire human fleet. I have only one battle group available.

It said to request resources from Pracep Meorbi.

Pracep Meorbi will not be receptive. We have received more than our fair share of replacement warships for the last three years, to more quickly replenish the losses we sustained in Earth's solar system.

Krajik waited for Mrayev to finish assessing the situation, accepting the fact that there were no alternatives. After a moment, Mrayev relented and conveyed a thought. A hologram of Pracep Meorbi appeared, hovering over Mrayev's console. Mrayev explained the situation, then made the request for a temporary reallocation of warships from Meorbi's campaign to Mrayev's.

Krajik sensed Meorbi's irritation, which was infused into the pracep's response. *For three years, half of my replacement warships have been redirected to your campaign against the humans, forcing me to make do with less. I suggest you do the same.*

Mrayev pressed the issue, making its case. *I have the opportunity to eliminate an entire human fleet, almost twenty percent of their strength in a single blow. All I need are adequate resources. If the situation were reversed, you know I would support you as best possible.*

Krajik waited while Meorbi absorbed the honesty in Mrayev's thoughts. Finally, Meorbi replied, *What do you need and when?*

Mrayev analyzed the pending assault: twelve Earth hours before the human fleet jumped to Hellios, then the time required to eliminate two hundred Korilian warships on station, after which the ground assault would commence, lasting long enough to gain control of most of the main complex on Hellios 4.

I need four battle groups, Mrayev thought, *able to reach the Hellios system within nine quign.*

Meorbi replied, *I have three battle groups in reserve within range of Hellios in the required time, which I can temporarily assign to your campaign.*

Krajik followed Mrayev's thoughts as the pracep calculated the battle losses. It would take longer than Mrayev preferred, but four battle groups— three from Meorbi plus the one Mrayev had available—combined with superior Korilian command and control due to their ability to coordinate their efforts telepathically should be enough to annihilate the human fleet.

Agreed, Mrayev thought, infusing its response with gratitude.

After Pracep Meorbi's hologram disappeared, Mrayev turned to Krajik. *Prepare the fleet and ground counterattack in the Hellios system.*

31

Twelve hours after their arrival in the Telac system, Lara found herself back in *Artemis V*'s combat information center with Admiral McCarthy as he monitored the displays. Although there was nothing for McCarthy to do at the moment, it was obvious that the task force's imminent jump into the Hellios system weighed heavily on his mind. She could tell he wanted to be on the 2nd Fleet command ship assisting Admiral Amani, using his prescient ability to guide the task force to victory. If there was any consolation, it was that Amani's guide for the battle was Angeline, the most capable of the six fleet guides.

Amani was having a final discussion with Rear Admiral Rajhi and General Hutton, with the two Fleet officers on video screens and General Hutton in the combat information center. Recon probes in the Hellios system continued to report no change in Korilian warship strength or alert level. Lara listened as Amani reviewed the critical details, her eyes shifting to Rajhi's image when the cruiser mission was discussed. The cruisers would jump to within weapon range of the one hundred Korilian warships docked at the star base and immediately fire, hopefully destroying or disabling those ships. The alert Korilian warships, however, would be able to fire before the cruisers brought up their shields. Rajhi estimated that seventy-five of her cruisers would be heavily damaged or outright destroyed before shields could be raised.

Lara asked McCarthy, "Why was Admiral Rajhi assigned to lead the cruiser attack?"

"She volunteered," McCarthy said.

Rear Admiral Rajhi's face displayed no emotion as she prepared to lead the cruisers on what would likely be a suicide mission for over one-third of her task force. Lara recalled the confrontation she'd had with Rajhi during the Final Stand, when Lara held a pulse pistol to Rajhi's head, trying to force her to follow McCarthy's order. Instead of complying, Rajhi had pulled the pulse-pistol against her forehead, then pried Lara's fingers from the gun one by one, daring Lara to pull the trigger. Now, she had volunteered to lead the cruiser suicide mission.

It figures. The bitch has a death wish.

Finally, Admiral Amani gave the order. "Admiral Rajhi, commence the double jump to the Hellios system at time two-one-hundred. General Hutton, accompany 2nd Fleet to Rignao and hold there until directed to join us at Hellios. I'll provide an updated L-Hour if it appears the battle will take longer or conclude earlier than expected."

After Rajhi and Hutton acknowledged, their videos went dark, leaving only the main display in the combat information center energized, showing the cruiser detachment and the rest of 2nd Fleet arranged in front of the MEF transports. A moment later, five deep tones reverberated throughout the troop transport, followed by an announcement over the ship's intercom system.

"One minute to the jump."

Thirty seconds later, bright white flashes lit up one of the video displays as the cruiser detachment made the jump to Rignao. Shortly thereafter, five deep tones reverberated throughout *Artemis V* again. When the time reached zero, Lara's vision went black as the rest of 2nd Fleet and the MEF commenced the final leg of their journey.

32

Rear Admiral Rajhi sat in her command chair aboard the cruiser *Aiguillon* as the 192 cruisers in her detachment materialized in the Rignao system. After over a thousand jumps in her career, Rajhi paid no attention to the physical effects of the jump as she waited for the starship drives to recharge for the subsequent jump to Hellios. She put the two-minute wait to good use, scanning the bridge displays and control consoles, reviewing the data being relayed from reconnaissance probes embedded in asteroids in the Hellios system.

The cruiser bridge was much smaller than what she was used to after five years in command of the battleship *Athens* and several more commanding the Excalibur battle group, but the sensor and communication systems were adequate for her task. After jumping to Hellios and engaging the Korilian warships docked at the star base, the decision she'd face would be straightforward—assess the damage to her cruiser task group and either stay and fight with 2nd Fleet or jump away to regroup, returning to battle once enough of the damaged cruisers had repaired their affected shields and pulse generators.

As Rajhi waited for the cruiser jump drives to recharge, her thoughts shifted to the upcoming battle: seventy-five of her cruisers would take a direct hit before they could bring their shields up—each of the fifty

Korilian dreadnoughts would target a Colonial warship, while the less powerful Korilian cruisers would team together, firing dual-pulses at another twenty-five Colonial cruisers—and all of those ships would be significantly damaged or destroyed. Her heart went out to the men and women aboard those cruisers, but she had no concern for her own fate. As far as Rajhi was concerned, she was already dead.

With thirty seconds remaining to the jump, Rajhi tried to focus on the pending carnage, but instead, her thoughts drifted back to when she was a ten-year-old girl.

She stood on the edge of a cliff on the eastern shore of Tunisia as white frothy waves crashed into jagged boulders six hundred feet below. Tears streamed down her dust-coated cheeks and her body trembled as she extended her arms out to her sides, level with her shoulders. Both parents had been killed in the Korilian War, leaving her an orphan; there was no one left to care for her. As she contemplated her future, the raw emotions—rage, hate, and despair—consumed her.

Rajhi leaned forward and took a step to her death, but a blast of hot air rising up the cliff buffeted her body, knocking her backward. It was as if the hand of God had intervened. As she teetered on the cliff edge, trying to make sense of what happened, she looked toward heaven. A container shuttle was streaking upward in the distance, delivering a starship section to one of the construction yards in orbit. She studied the ascending spaceship until the red-hot exhaust faded into the clouds, and considered the signs. God had intervened, showing her the path he had chosen for her—an opportunity for revenge.

She stepped back and breathed the warm air deeply, attempting to calm her trembling body. Her resolve hardened at that moment. She would not plunge to her death—she would have revenge instead. She wasn't sure how, but was confident that God had chosen her because she wasn't afraid of death. As far as she was concerned, she had died that day. She was now living on borrowed time, and God would decide when that time was up.

Five deep tones reverberated on the cruiser's bridge, bringing Rajhi's thoughts back to the present. As the last ten seconds to the jump counted down, she smiled.

Another opportunity for revenge.

33

Rear Admiral Rajhi exited the dark void of jump-space as her starship materialized in the Hellios planetary system. Her eyes went to the sensor display as she surveyed the status of the Korilian warships in orbit around Hellios 4. Everything was as reported by the reconnaissance probes just before the jump: one hundred warships on alert, their shields up and pulse generators charged, with another one hundred starships docked at the star base, shields down.

The Korilian warships on alert fired first as expected, before Rajhi's cruisers were able to bring up their shields. Red pulses carved through the vulnerable Colonial warships, and almost two dozen starships disintegrated in bright orange or blue flashes as damaged jump drives or pulse generators imploded. The surviving cruisers ignored the warships attacking them, counterfiring instead at the Korilian starships docked at the star base, focusing on the fifty dreadnoughts. Blue pulses melted through the unprotected warships.

The exchange took only a few seconds, and Rajhi assessed the situation during the fifty-seven seconds while Korilian and Colonial pulse generators recharged. Her cruiser, *Aiguillon*, hadn't been hit, but twenty Colonial cruisers had been destroyed. Another fifty-five were heavily damaged—some with down shields, others with inoperable pulse generators, and some with damage to both systems. Regarding the Korilian dreadnoughts docked at the star base, seven had been destroyed, and the remaining forty-three hadn't energized shields thus far.

At this point in the battle, Rajhi had full discretion as to how to proceed. She could jump away with the entire cruiser detachment, order all of them to stay and fight, or direct some to jump and others to stay. The battle plan she had formulated prior to the engagement remained sound: she ordered all damaged cruisers to jump to the Rignao system, where the 3rd MEF awaited, then return to Hellios if full shields and pulse generators were restored. In the meantime, Rajhi would remain with 117 Colonial cruisers.

A flash of white light announced the arrival of the rest of 2nd Fleet. The sixteen battleship squadrons brought up their shields before the Korilian warships completed their recharge, then fired at the Korilian ships with missing shields docked at the star base. Instead of the less powerful cruiser pulses, almost two hundred battleship pulses tore through the unshielded dreadnoughts. The bright orange flashes almost blinded Rajhi as all forty-three dreadnoughts disintegrated.

Rajhi's cruisers completed their pulse-generator recharge, unleashing another barrage toward the star base, this time targeting the fifty Korilian cruisers that were just now beginning to bring up shields. After 117 blue pulses bore down on their enemy, all fifty Korilian cruisers were damaged or destroyed.

34

Angeline Del Rio stood beside Admiral Amani on *Controlador*'s command bridge, assessing the battle. As 2nd Fleet engaged the remaining Korilian warships, she didn't bother analyzing the data filling the screens or pay attention to the flashes illuminating the bridge through the starship windows. Instead, she closed her eyes and studied the colored mosaic in her mind.

In addition to being a Nexus Eight, able to obtain glimpses of the future, Angeline, like all fleet guides, was a synesthesian, able to translate her premonitions into a common format. Specifically, Angeline was a color synesthesian. No matter what type of premonition she received, it always had a color scheme, letting her interpret the colors rather than require her to understand the premonition. This was particularly important in battle, since fleet guides usually didn't have time to digest the meaning of each premonition—they were almost always different—and they didn't always interpret them correctly. The synesthesia was critical.

The battle was just beginning, and the color scheme in Angeline's mind was thus far limited to the Colonial starships. Most were green, but over half of the cruisers were yellow or red, indicating the extent of their damage. Regarding the entire 2nd Fleet formation, there was no defensive front or flank to analyze, since Admiral Amani had a significant numerical starship advantage and was on the offensive, coordinating his ships to amass overwhelming superiority against as many Korilian dreadnoughts as possible. Overall, the battle had begun as expected, except...

Angeline's eyes were drawn to the Korilian star base. Thousands of marauders streamed from openings in the central hub, then a shimmering spherical shield materialized around the star base. But what caught Angeline's attention was that the star base was glowing red in her mind. She focused on the immense star base, attempting to ascertain the reason for the foreboding premonition.

In addition to being much larger than any other Korilian star base discovered up to now, it was of an unusual design, with only five docking arms along a flat plane instead of the dozen or more that would have been possible had the star base been the usual spherical design with arms radiating in multiple directions. After the shield formed, the star base began to spin on its axis, slowly increasing speed, and gradually twisted its rotating arms toward 2nd Fleet. That's when it dawned on Angeline.

She turned to Admiral Amani. "It's not a star base. It's a star fortress!"

Only the Colonial Fleet had employed star fortresses up to this point in the war, with the last Colonial star fortresses being destroyed when the Korilians gained control of Telemantic.

Admiral Amani's eyes shot to the star fortress, which was considerably larger than anything the Colonial Navy had built. Angeline could tell he was trying to assess the strength of the impending pulses once the fortress completed its alignment and fired. The arms were twenty times as long as a Korilian dreadnought, with warship size driven by the long tyranium coils that generated the destructive pulses. The star fortress would be capable of generating enormously powerful pulses, maybe even strong enough to penetrate a starship shield and its armor with a single shot.

One arm of the star fortress aligned with 2nd Fleet, and a thick red pulse fired from the end. The pulse sped toward the nearest Colonial battleship, collapsing the impacted shield. After the shield disintegrated, the pulse melted through the starship's amor and interior compartments, setting off a series of rippling explosions within the damaged vessel.

The star fortress's speed steadied, bringing one arm into firing position every twelve seconds. Admiral Amani issued an urgent order to his operations officer. "To all battleships, engage the star fortress as first priority! Orient bow shields toward the fortress, and shift power to the forward shields."

The Colonial battleships turned toward the star fortress, but not before it fired again, and a red pulse carved through another battleship. Just before the third arm fired, the Colonial battleships completed their maneuvers, and the entire group of battleships fired at the star fortress in unison. Unbelievably, the star fortress shield held, although Angeline could tell the shield had been weakened. The report from the sensor supervisor confirmed her assessment.

"Star fortress shield strength reduced to forty-four percent."

The critical question was—could the star fortress regenerate its shield to one hundred percent between Colonial pulses, or would the battleships be able to gradually weaken and then collapse the shield?

The fifty-seven seconds between pulse recharges passed, with the Colonial battleships enduring four more star fortress pulses. Shifting power to the forward shields helped, but the star fortress pulse still collapsed the battleship shields with enough energy bleeding through to inflict significant damage. The Colonial battleships completed their pulse recharges and fired in unison again, and the report from the sensor supervisor was welcome news.

"Star fortress shield strength now at thirty-eight percent." The shield was weakening.

The outcome of the engagement with the star fortress was clear, but it was still imperative to destroy the star fortress as quickly as possible, minimizing the number of destroyed or damaged Colonial battleships.

Angeline turned her attention to the rest of the battle, where the Colonial cruisers were outmatched by the mix of Korilian cruisers and dreadnoughts, now that Amani had directed all battleships to engage the star fortress. Angeline focused on one interaction in particular, where two Colonial cruisers were being engaged by two dreadnoughts. One of the cruisers had lost a shield, and the other cruiser—Admiral Rajhi's flagship, *Aiguillon* —had maneuvered nearby to block both dreadnoughts from obtaining a clear shot through the missing shield. Unfortunately, that left Rajhi's cruiser in the unenviable situation of being pounded by two dreadnoughts.

An unaided cruiser wouldn't last long against two dreadnoughts, and Admiral Amani evaluated whether to divert battleships to help Admiral Rajhi, then decided otherwise. With the star fortress heavily damaging or destroying a battleship every twelve seconds, destroying the star fortress was the highest priority.

Rajhi's crew fought tenaciously, rotating the starship after each dreadnought pulse to bring other shields into play while the impacted one recharged, but the cruiser shields gradually weakened. Finally, one of *Aiguillon*'s shields collapsed, and the Korilian pulse continued through the starship. Internal explosions rippled through the cruiser, and several other shields collapsed. Seconds later, *Aiguillon* and the other cruiser disappeared in bright white flashes as they jumped away.

With Admiral Rajhi departing the battle in her damaged cruiser, command of the cruiser task group shifted to Admiral Amani. Angeline settled in for a longer than expected battle. Amani had similar thoughts, because he sent an update to the 3rd MEF, delaying the ground assault by several hours.

35

Dressed in her Nexus uniform, Lara sat on the edge of her bed, her right knee jittering nervously as she waited for Liza to escort her to the armory. She had skipped breakfast as Major Harkins had advised, although his recommendation wasn't necessary. She had no appetite. She checked the time on her wristlet: almost eight a.m. One hour until L-Hour, which had been pushed back to nine a.m.

The previous evening, she'd been in the troop transport's combat information center monitoring the battle with Admiral McCarthy, who had been surprised that the Korilian star base was also a star fortress. He had commented on the issue, mumbling more to himself than to Lara beside him, that he should have seen it in his view. There were no difficult decisions related to the employment of a star fortress—it was an event that would occur with one hundred percent certainty—and was therefore something he should have seen in any of the prime timeline or alternate views of the battle. The absence of the star fortress in his views put McCarthy in a dark mood for the rest of the evening, and he had stayed glued to the video and data screens late into the night as the battle progressed.

It was well past midnight when exhaustion began to set in, and Lara had retired to her stateroom, leaving McCarthy in the combat information center. But sleep hadn't come easily. She tossed and turned all night, her sleep interrupted frequently by images of Korilians rearing up before her, their razor-sharp limbs pulled back, preparing to slice her in half.

The stateroom intercom activated, and Liza's voice emanated from the speaker, announcing the Marine's presence outside the stateroom. Lara took a deep breath, attempting to calm herself as she rose from the bed, then joined Liza in the corridor. McCarthy exited his stateroom at the same time, joining Corporal Travis and Winston Albright, the computer software engineer who would download the Korilian algorithms from the intelligence center. Uncharacteristically, McCarthy offered Lara no greeting; he seemed lost in his thoughts.

The Marines escorted Lara, McCarthy, and Albright to the armory instead of the fitting rooms, joining one of several long lines of Marines that quickly progressed through armory portals. Liza explained that the process was essentially an assembly line, where Lara's armor components would be selected based on her fitting. She'd stand on a platform that progressed through the armory, where robotic arms would assemble the suit around her and provide the weapons and other components prescribed for the assault.

Upon entering the armory, Lara followed Liza's example and stripped to her underwear and donned her suit undergarments, then stepped onto a platform that whisked her through the armory at a surprising speed. Her armored suit was quickly assembled around her, and the helmet went on last. Her suit electronics activated, with life-support statistics appearing on the right side of her helmet visor. Everything was as she had experienced during her outfitting, except life support was currently configured to bring in fresh air instead of consuming the oxygen supply and expending the carbon dioxide filter in her suit.

After donning her armored suit, Lara received no weapon but watched as Liza was outfitted with an assault carbine—a large heavy-duty rifle with a short barrel—which she slung over one shoulder, pulse-pistol, grenades, small reconnaissance drones, communication relay pods, and a thin three-foot-long shield rod that she slung over her other shoulder, where the rod slid into an indentation in the back plate of her armored suit.

When she exited the armory, Lara noticed that every Marine was similarly outfitted. Liza explained that their brigade would enter the Korilian complex with only small arms due to the confined spaces, while the other nine divisions in the MEF would be outfitted with heavier weapon systems, since they would be operating on the planet's surface, forming a perimeter defense during the assault. The other nine brigades in 21st Division would be held as a reserve, able to reinforce either the perimeter or 1st Brigade's assault into the Korilian facility.

Waiting for them at the armory exit was Major Harkins. As he approached, an alarm reverberated throughout the troop transport—a series of alternating high and low tones—followed by an announcement by the ship's computer.

"Attention. All Twenty-First Division, First Brigade personnel, commence load operations. Infantry report to forward flight decks. Support personnel report to aft flight decks."

The alarm and announcement repeated itself, and at the end of the instructions, Harkins led the group through a set of air lock doors onto a platform overlooking the ship's forward flight deck.

The flight deck spanned the width of the ship and was split down the middle into two halves, with three levels per side and the center section open. Almost one hundred surface assault vehicles sat on the flight deck, each SAV mounted onto ejection rails facing large doors in both sides of the troop transport. Several cranes atop the center section were lifting the last dozen SAVs from openings in the hangar deck below to their launch positions on the third level.

Thousands of Marines poured from openings in the flight deck and surged toward the SAVs, each vehicle with its rear ramp lowered onto the deck. From Lara's vantage point, the Marines looked like an ant colony swarming toward its prey—the SAVs—on both sides and all three levels of the flight deck.

Harkins led Lara and the others into an elevator that descended to the bottom level of the flight deck, then escorted them into one of the SAVs. The rest of the platoon was already inside, with most of the one hundred seats vacant. The inside of the SAV was otherwise bare, aside from a weapon stowage rack beside each seat for the assault carbines and a bank of green lights at the rear of the vehicle above the ramp opening.

Sergeant Major Geisinger sat in the first seat on one side while

Jankowski occupied the first one on the other side, with the other Marines in each squad in adjacent seats. Lara sat with Liza at the end of one squad, while McCarthy, Travis, and Albright sat at the back of the other. Albright's face was faintly lit and visible through his helmet visor. His skin was pale, and his armored hands seemed glued to his seat armrests. He had a thin backpack strapped to his armored suit, which Lara presumed carried the computer he needed to download the data from the Korilian intelligence center.

A low rumble emanated from the back of the SAV as the ramp rose. Light inside the vehicle faded until the ramp closed with a heavy clank, then thin strips of blue light energized above each seat and on the deck. Lara's apprehension began to mount as she sat silently, while the Marines chatted quietly and occasionally broke into laughter.

A few minutes later, the green lights at the rear of the SAV began flashing. Shortly thereafter, Lara felt the jump wave pass through her and was temporarily enveloped in darkness as *Artemis V* made the transit to the Hellios system. When she found herself in the SAV again, she looked at the time displayed in her helmet visor.

0900. The assault was occurring precisely on schedule.

She closed her eyes and breathed deeply until the nausea subsided.

A moment later, Lara felt the SAV shudder as the ninety-nine other SAVs were ejected from the troop transport's flight deck. But their SAV didn't move. As Lara wondered why, she recalled that they wouldn't head down to the planet until the ground perimeter had been secured and all Korilian air-defense artillery had been eliminated.

About an hour later, the lights above the ramp turned from green to yellow. Conversation ceased, and Liza reached over and touched a control button on Lara's armrest. Curved flaps in her seat rotated inward and clamped themselves around Lara's waist and head. Liza then tapped the controls on the left forearm of Lara's suit, shifting life support to the suit's internal resources. Travis did the same for McCarthy and Albright.

Lara's muscles tensed, realizing they were moments away from descending to the planet's surface. A deep thud on the SAV's deck startled Lara, and it was followed by several more. She spotted Jankowski, who had retrieved his heavy assault carbine and was pounding its butt onto the deck in a steady rhythm. She wondered what he was doing when the Marines began humming a low tune, which gradually increased in volume until surprisingly, they began singing. Lara listened intently to the words. It was an ancient hymn, it seemed, about battles in strange places and distant shores, on land and on the sea.

After the song drew to a close, Jankowski's squad shouted, "We are!" and Geisinger's squad responded, "The Third MEF!"

The lights above the ramp turned solid red, and a few seconds later, Lara felt a jolt as the SAV was ejected from *Artemis V*.

36

After the initial jolt from the SAV launch, the transit was smooth, with no indication the assault vehicle was moving at all. Lara felt light, as if she were floating in her seat, then realized the SAV didn't have the gravity generators she took for granted on the Fleet warships and troop transports. The smooth transit was short-lived, however, as she felt tremors in the SAV's deck. Then the vehicle began pitching and bucking as it plummeted through the planet's atmosphere, twisting and tilting as it descended.

An alarm in Lara's suit went off, and she noticed flashing numbers in the life-support section of her visor. Her heart and respiration rates had doubled. She focused on her breathing, taking deeper and more deliberate breaths. She tried to relax but had little success as she involuntarily tensed at every jolt and shudder during the SAV's descent.

She looked across the SAV at McCarthy and Albright. McCarthy seemed unfazed, but Albright had his eyes closed, and his face seemed even paler than before. The Marines' faces were expressionless as they stared straight ahead, not seeming to notice the rough descent, as if they were seated on a transit pod on their way to work in the morning.

The volatile descent subsided, and the red lights above the ramp began blinking yellow. Liza reached over and pressed a control on Lara's armrest, and the restraints around her head and waist retracted back into her seat.

Travis did the same for McCarthy and Albright, and the Marines retrieved their carbines from their stows. Lara felt a sudden thud, then the SAV was still. The lights at the rear of the vehicle turned green, and the ramp lowered quickly onto the planet's surface. However, instead of charging out of the SAV as Lara had imagined, the Marines simply walked down the ramp in two columns.

A stark landscape greeted Lara as she exited the SAV, her suit sensors reporting a bitterly cold temperature on the planet's surface. Dark gray clouds hung low overhead, and a brisk wind blew a light, swirling snowfall across the planet's bleak, flat horizon. An occasional small plant clung to life on the otherwise barren ground, its roots digging tenaciously into thin cracks in the planet's surface. Explosions dotted the horizon, forming a circle of fire around them about a mile away. Black smoke billowed up from the explosions toward the menacing sky, and the low rumbling of detonations in the distance rolled across the inhospitable landscape.

A sonic boom blasted Lara's ears as forty large drone aircraft, loaded with ordnance, swept past them a hundred feet above their heads. Components of the Heavy Air Division, Liza explained, as they streaked toward the MEF's protective perimeter. On the platoon's right side, a dozen large blue pulses jetted down from the sky. Tremors rumbled through the ground as the horizon erupted in fiery explosions roiling up toward the dark clouds.

There were hundreds of SAVs nearby, each one empty with its ramp down. Not far away was a large gray complex that sprawled outward on both sides as far as Lara could see. Lara counted ten breaches in the side of the complex at ground level, one for each of the brigade's battalions, she surmised, spaced a few hundred yards apart. Each opening was about twenty feet in diameter, its edges blackened and tattered.

Harkins led the platoon toward an MEF command center and stopped to talk to General Hutton, who stood beside a data fusion table. Harkins beckoned for McCarthy and Lara to join them.

"The Korilian facility has standard wireless jamming," General Hutton informed Harkins, "which means you won't have any remote sensors or weapons. You'll have to rely on eyes-on-target and the weapons you're carrying.

"The entire First Brigade of Twenty-First Division is inside the Korilian complex now," Hutton said. "We're pushing forward on all ten levels, with one battalion per level, meeting varying levels of resistance."

Hutton pointed to a three-dimensional holographic projection above the fusion table, with thousands of green and red symbols displayed on a ten-level schematic of the complex. The green symbols were arranged in semicircles on each level, expanding down and outward from the openings in the complex. Red symbols opposed each green semicircle, with most of the red symbols concentrated on the seventh level.

Hutton turned to McCarthy and Lara. "We need to know where the intel center is so we can reinforce the correct area and push forward."

McCarthy shrugged his shoulders. "I can't follow any line past when we enter the complex." He turned to Lara. "Can you help?"

Lara examined the green and red symbols, then attempted to invoke a vision. As she concentrated, a light fog rose from the edges of the fusion table, growing denser until it obscured the holographic projection. A small gap in the mist appeared, showing only the seventh level of the Korilian complex, then the fog vanished.

Lara pointed at the seventh level, which had the heaviest concentration of red symbols.

"Figures," Hutton said. He entered several commands into the fusion panel beneath the display. "I'll reinforce the seventh level and push forward. Inform me if you discern a more precise location for the intel center." Turning to Harkins, Hutton added, "Good luck, Major."

Harkins saluted, then returned to the front of his platoon. Lara and McCarthy took their place near the end of the Marine columns, with Liza and Travis behind them. Harkins began moving again, leading the two columns toward the nearest opening in the Korilian facility.

As the platoon entered the complex, darkness enveloped each pair of Marines as they passed through the opening. As Lara approached the entrance, she heard a faint echo of laughter. She looked around for the source, but only Liza and Travis were behind her, their faces emotionless, assault carbines in their hands. She turned to McCarthy, walking beside her, but he gave no indication he had heard anything. Lara decided she must have imagined it, then pushed it from her mind as she and McCarthy were swallowed by the darkness.

37

When Lara entered the facility, her suit automatically shifted to low-light vision, and the Marines reappeared. The platoon halted for a moment, and Lara surveyed the strange surroundings.

They were in a twenty-foot-wide corridor with the walls, ceiling, and floor constructed of black fibers woven tightly together. There weren't any distinct joints where the walls met the floor or ceiling—the fibers simply curved up from the floor to create the walls and then inward at the top to form the ceiling. A faint blue light leaked through the wall fibers, and a magenta illumination pulsed through the ceiling—four flashes followed by a few seconds of darkness. A low throbbing sound accompanied each magenta pulse as the sequence of light and sound repeated continuously.

"Alarm system," Liza said, after she noticed Lara examining the pulsing light.

At the front of the platoon, Harkins issued an order, and two Marines launched tiny reconnaissance probes from their utility belts. The drones flew down the corridor, then smashed into the wall where the passageway turned to the right.

"That's expected," Liza explained. "Most Korilian facilities have anti-drone technology that corrupts automated units."

The platoon began moving again, with the two columns walking on separate sides of the passageway, while Harkins walked between the two squads. After a short trek, they arrived at what appeared to be a dead end. Harkins stopped beside a set of colored symbols embedded in the wall and touched them in a specific sequence. The wall fibers wriggled as if they were alive, pulling back to create an opening. Lara shuddered as she watched the fibers move like the tentacles of a hidden organism.

Harkins stepped through the opening into an adjoining passageway, then led the platoon past the remnants of close combat: dozens of dead Marines and Korilians strewn across the corridor floor. The Korilian bodies were riddled with pulse holes, while the dead Marines were dismembered in various ways: missing arms and legs, severed necks, or sliced in half at the waist.

Lara picked her way through the corridor, her armored boots slipping somewhat on the blood-drenched floor. Albright began fumbling frantically with his helmet, yanking it from his head just before he vomited. The platoon halted, waiting for him to finish heaving.

As Albright replaced his helmet, a nearby Marine said, "Suck it up, Doc. This is nothing. It's gonna get a lot worse."

The platoon began moving again, traveling deeper into the Korilian complex, passing several other areas where Korilians and Marines had battled. At each encounter, the ratio of dead Marines to dead Korilians rose, evidence of increasing Korilian resistance. They soon reached another dead end, but this time there were two sets of Korilian symbols on the corridor walls, one on each side. Harkins examined a display on his forearm armor, then pressed the symbols on the right side of the passageway in the required sequence. The black fibers began curling back, creating an opening into a darker passageway.

After a quick examination, Harkins announced, "Hyperbaric sleep chamber. Don't touch anything."

He stepped through the opening, and the two Marine columns followed. Connected to the new passageway were dozens of corridors on both sides. Harkins led the platoon into the nearest corridor on the left, and as they moved through the dimly lit passageway, Lara realized it was different from the ones they had traveled along thus far: the walls and ceiling weren't illuminated like the previous portion of the Korilian complex. Instead, orange symbols were embedded in the walls, chest-high at eight-foot intervals. Between each set of symbols, the black fibers converged toward a thin, ten-foot-tall vertical seam.

The platoon halted when they reached the end of the corridor, and Harkins checked his forearm display again. While they waited, Albright examined one of the orange symbols. It was a few inches in diameter, made of a viscous substance held in place by a thin transparent membrane. Albright gently pressed the clear film covering the Korilian symbol, his finger sinking slightly into the gelatinous substance.

Black fibers leapt from the wall, enveloping Albright's hand and arm. He tried to pull away and cried out for help, but before any of the Marines could react, thousands of fibers wrapped around Albright's body. The vertical seam separated, and Albright screamed for help as the fibers pulled him toward the opening. As he was dragged inside, the Marines refrained from touching him. His outstretched arm was the last to disappear as the wall grew back together and met in a thin seam again.

Geisinger moved toward the seam and stopped before the Marine who had been behind Albright, responsible for keeping him out of trouble. She glared at the Marine, then backhanded him across his head, her armored glove clanking off his helmet. The Marine avoided Geisinger's gaze as the platoon waited in silence.

As Lara wondered what happened to Albright, the seam split apart, and he was ejected from the opening. He hit the wall on the other side of the corridor, then fell to the floor. His entire armored suit was covered with black fuzz. Geisinger walked over and placed the muzzle of her carbine against his helmet.

"The next time you're given directions, you damn well better follow them, or I'll blast a hole through your head. Understand?"

Albright nodded quickly, his eyes wide with fright. Geisinger returned to the front of her squad, and the Marine she disciplined helped Albright to his feet.

Harkins began moving again, leading the platoon down another passageway, passing dozens of similar corridors. They eventually reached another dead end with Korilian symbols on the wall. Harkins pressed the controls in the required sequence again, then stepped through the opening created by the wriggling black fibers.

After several turns down this new passageway, the platoon rounded a corner to find more than a hundred dead Marines and Korilians littering the length of a long corridor. Pulse blast holes pocketed the passageway walls and ceiling, with frayed ends of black fibers hanging from the blast holes' ragged edges. Medics were tending to a dozen injured Marines, some of them lying on the floor while others sat with their backs against the corridor walls. As Harkins's platoon passed by, the injured Marines stared at them with glazed looks in their eyes.

The platoon picked their way through the bodies, so numerous and closely spaced that Lara sometimes had to step on them. They eventually reached the end of the corridor—a dead end with red, blue, and yellow symbols pulsing on the wall before them. This time, the black fibers met on the floor instead of the wall. Embedded in the ceiling above the converging fibers were several metal spikes with thin strands attached and hanging down to the floor, where the ends were sheared off. Harkins talked with one of the medics, then issued an order.

Two Marines from each squad stepped to the front of the platoon and took up firing positions in a circle, pointing their carbines at the floor where the fibers converged. Harkins pressed the Korilian symbols on the wall in the same sequence as before, and the fibers began wriggling back toward the walls, creating a large opening in the floor.

The four Marines peered down through the hole.

"All clear," one of the Marines reported.

The four Marines shouldered their carbines and each retrieved a rappel-pistol—a device that looked like a pistol with a large barrel—from their utility belts. A spike protruded from the end of each barrel, which the Marines pointed at the ceiling. The spikes shot from the pistols, embedding themselves in the fibers. Attached to each spike was a thin strand leading back to the pistol.

"Saddle up," Harkins ordered.

The Marines assembled into four lines, then the first Marine in each line, holding the rappel-pistol, jumped through the opening and disappeared into the darkness. The following Marines attached themselves to the thin line with two hooks from their utility belt, wrapping the line around their waist. In sets of four, the Marines followed the first set. Soon only Harkins remained, along with Lara, McCarthy, Albright, and their two Marine escorts. The three Marines likewise attached themselves to the thin strands with two hooks.

"Put your arms around my neck," Liza said to Lara, "and hold tight."

Lara wrapped her arms around the Marine. Leaning back over the opening, Liza pushed off from the edge, and they descended through the Korilian facility.

38

They rappelled to the seventh level, where Liza swung side to side once before gaining a foothold, and two Marines pulled her and Lara into a large chamber. A moment later, they were joined by Harkins and Travis descending with McCarthy and Albright. The first four Marines pressed a button on each rappel-pistol, retracting the spike edges, and the rappel line snaked back into the pistol until the spike re-mated with the muzzle.

The other Marines in the chamber had formed a semicircle around the entrance, facing outward with their carbines, examining the carnage: several dozen slain Marines and dead Korilians were scattered across the floor, their bodies fading into the darkness. Throughout the chamber were large cylindrical vats, with one end attached to the floor and the other end to the ceiling. Each vat was about twenty feet in diameter with a transparent outer shell. Inside the vats, a mottled red-and-yellow substance rippled as black shapes slithered about, occasionally approaching the clear outer membrane.

Harkins ordered the platoon into two columns again, then led them through the chamber. As they proceeded, Harkins and the platoon leaders shouldered their carbines and drew their pulse-pistols, examining the Korilians they passed. As they approached one of the cylindrical vats, Lara noticed hundreds of small black objects with spidery appendages moving randomly inside. After studying them for a moment, she realized they were miniature Korilians.

"Korilian hatchery," Liza said. "If Second Fleet wasn't going to destroy this place in a few hours, we'd set charges in this place."

As the platoon traversed the chamber, Lara noticed that some vats contained larger Korilians, although fewer in quantity. She wondered what happened to the others as the Korilians grew within their embryonic pouch, and her question was answered as three Korilians flittered near a vat outer membrane. The Korilian in the center was suddenly attacked by the ones beside it and savagely torn to pieces, then devoured by the other two. Lara shrank back in revulsion.

Built-in food supply.

As the platoon worked its way past the dead Korilians and Marines, McCarthy announced, "Sergeant Geisinger. Live Korilian to your left."

"Got it," Geisinger said as she picked her way through the bodies.

Seconds later, a Korilian near Geisinger, seemingly dead until this moment, rose up and lunged toward the Marine. The Korilian was injured, with three of its six appendages severed, but its two upper limbs were intact and both swung toward Geisinger in a pincher movement. Geisinger fired her pulse-pistol twice, severing the appendages at the shoulders, then spun to her right, dodging the Korilian's razor-sharp fangs by barely a foot, and fired again. She blasted a hole through the Korilian's head, and it fell to the chamber floor.

Geisinger examined the Korilian, ensuring it was dead this time. As the platoon resumed its journey through the chamber, Lara picked her way even more carefully through the Marine and Korilian bodies. They reached the end of the hatchery and stopped by a wall seam with the colored Korilian symbols nearby. Harkins ordered four Marines to the front of the platoon again as the rest of the Marines held their carbines ready. Harkins pressed the Korilian symbols, and an opening appeared in the wall.

To Lara's relief, the opening revealed an empty passageway. But as she stepped into the adjoining corridor, Harkins issued an urgent order.

"Quick time!"

The platoon sprinted down the corridor with Harkins in the lead. Lara, McCarthy, and Albright fell behind, with Liza and Travis matching their pace.

"Faster!" Liza shouted. "We must keep up!"

39

As the platoon surged down the passageway, Lara ran as fast as she could, but the Marines continued to pull away. The faint sound of pulse blasts soon reached Lara's ears, followed by the din of battle: jumbled orders and reports from another Marine unit streamed into her suit audio. Pulses began illuminating the passageway ahead of them, the intensity growing as they sped down the corridor.

A video appeared on the left side of Lara's visor, apparently relayed from the Marines ahead. The Marine unit was in a large circular intersection, about two hundred feet wide and fifty feet high, with ten openings along the perimeter, plus a half dozen passageways in the ceiling and several more in the floor. A formation of about forty Marines was surrounded in the center of the hub, with hundreds of Korilians streaming toward them from every direction, including several dozen Korilians crawling along the ceiling. Hundreds of dead Marines and Korilians were strewn across the hub floor, with the advancing Korilians clambering over them.

The Marines fired at the closest Korilians, trying to prevent them from reaching their formation. But every few seconds, one of the Korilians broke through, wreaking havoc among the Marines until it was killed. More and more Korilians reached the Marine formation as the number of Marines dwindled, and eventually several Korilians on the ceiling reached a point directly above the Marine formation. They released their grip, dropping onto the Marines below. The Marine formation disintegrated as the Korilians overwhelmed them, just before Harkins's platoon was able to assist.

"Halt," Liza said, stopping twenty feet from the end of the corridor, ensuring Lara did the same. Travis similarly instructed McCarthy and Albright.

The Korilians finished off the Marines in the hub center, then focused on Harkins's platoon, emerging from the corridor. Additional Korilians poured from the hub passageways and swarmed toward the Marines on every surface. Harkins ordered the platoon into a semicircular formation just inside the hub, framing the passageway opening. He gave another order, and Corporal Travis raced forward and joined the formation, leaving Liza safeguarding the two Nexi and Albright.

The Marines organized into two rows, the first row kneeling and the second one standing, with Harkins behind both rows. Harkins issued a command, and his Marines opened fire on the advancing Korilians. Lara listened to a continuous stream of orders and reports flowing through her helmet as the platoon coordinated its fire.

There were only twenty-four Marines in the formation compared to the forty Marines in the hub a moment ago, yet Harkins's platoon was much more efficient at killing the advancing Korilians. The lead Korilians made it to within ten feet of the Marines on several occasions, but the platoon never wavered. Each time, the Korilians were beaten back by the steady stream of blue pulses leaping from the assault carbines. The dead Korilians stacked up in front of the Marines, three and four bodies high.

Harkins issued an order, and the front row fell back fifteen feet, then the other row did the same. The Marines returned to their original formation, the front row kneeling and back row standing, except it was closer to the corridor entrance.

As Lara wondered why Harkins pulled the Marines back, a wave of Korilians used the pile of bodies as a ramp and launched themselves into the air toward the formation. Fortunately, the Marines had retreated far enough to give themselves sufficient time to react. The front row fired in a single volley and the back row followed, targeting any Korilian that escaped the initial barrage. Every Korilian was dead or mortally wounded by the time it landed among the Marine formation. Harkins quickly examined each carcass, blasting a hole in the head of any surviving Korilian.

Several more Korilian waves launched themselves at the Marine formation, but the platoon coordinated its fire, ensuring all Korilians were dead or severely injured by the time they landed. However, on the fifth wave, one of the Korilians was only slightly wounded and impaled three Marines through their armored suit neck seams with its appendages as it landed. The other Marines successfully dodged the Korilian's dangerous limbs, and Harkins dispatched the Korilian with a head shot.

The Korilians ceased pouring from the hub's passageways, and the number opposing the Marines thinned out. A few minutes later, every Korilian in the hub was either dead or severely injured. The Marines ceased fire and lowered their carbines, their muzzles glowing dull red. Harkins examined the three impaled Marines. They were dead, their necks almost completely severed. The Korilian limbs were indeed razor sharp, able to pierce the soft armor seam.

After verifying their suit beacons were activated, marking them for retrieval, Harkins spoke, but Lara couldn't hear him; he was communicating on a different channel than the platoon.

A moment later, Lara heard his voice emanating in her suit. "Sharpen up, boys," he said. "We're at the front line now. There's no one between us and the bugs, and no reinforcements on the way. They're pressing the surface perimeter hard, and we've been given one hour to get the job done and extract."

Harkins looked at the two sergeant majors. "Set point."

Each squad leader called out one name.

"DelGreco!"

"Tanaka!"

Their voices had an edge Lara hadn't noticed before, and the Marines carried themselves differently now. There was a new vigilance in their eyes as they scanned their surroundings.

Two Marines headed to the front of the platoon as the others formed back into two columns. The lead Marines picked the lowest spot in the pile of Korilians and carefully climbed the corpses, firing their pistols occasion-

ally, putting a pulse through the head of any Korilian still alive. The
Marines slowly climbed over the dead Korilians, and Lara did the same.
The platoon soon reached the center of the hub, where they stopped amid
the dead Marines who'd been trapped there.

Harkins turned to Lara. "Which way?"

Lara examined the large hub. There were ten openings along the outer
rim, like spokes on a wheel, with six more in the ceiling and another six in
the floor. Lara breathed deeply, trying to relax and force a premonition,
then looked at the dark holes. She scrutinized each, looking for a sign that
would show her the way.

A dense black fog began pouring from one of the passageways along the
perimeter, drifting along the floor toward the platoon. It flowed through the
center of the Marine formation, caressing each Marine's legs as it continued
toward Lara. As the black mist approached, white, wispy fog collected at
Lara's feet, coalescing into a human form. The white fog vanished, leaving
Lara's mom standing before her.

Cheryl smiled warmly, as she had done aboard *Artemis V*, and looked at
Lara with loving eyes. "Go back, my child," she said. "You must turn
around."

"Why?" Lara asked.

McCarthy and the Marines stared at Lara as she spoke.

Cheryl replied, "You are not ready for what awaits you—the outcome is
unpredictable."

"We have to reach the intelligence center," Lara replied. "Which way is
the safest route?"

Cheryl's smile faded, and her voice hardened. "There is no safe route,
Lara. You cannot continue."

Lara hesitated before responding again. Up to now, these unusual
apparitions had offered sage advice. Whether it was her mom, informing
her a few days ago that things with McCarthy were about to change, or the
images of Admiral Rajhi and McCarthy's dead guide, Regina, providing
crucial clues during the Final Stand, they all seemed genuine in their intent
to help her. However, her mom's current advice meant abandoning their
quest to reach the Korilian intelligence center to download the software
algorithms.

Thousands, if not tens of thousands, of Marines had given their lives clearing a path for Lara and McCarthy's platoon, not to mention the crews of over a hundred starships destroyed in the battle above the planet. Turning back now meant those lives had been sacrificed for nothing. Additionally, obtaining the software algorithms would likely save millions more.

Turning around and leaving the complex was not an option. If that meant risking her life, so be it.

"No," she told her mom. "We're not stopping."

A brisk wind blew Cheryl's hair back from her face, and her features turned harsh.

"You will do as I say. Turn around, now."

"We're not turning around. Do you have any guidance that would be *helpful*?"

The wind increased in intensity, and her mom's voice became hollow, menacing.

"Do not disobey me. Turn around, now!"

"No!"

Cheryl's skin began to fester, sores spreading across her face. Her skin began to burn, blackening and cracking from unseen heat. The wind increased in force until a ferocious gale began ripping the charred flesh from Cheryl's face. Soon only a skull remained, red orbs burning within eye sockets. Then the skull grew in size, expanding above Lara to ten feet in diameter.

"You will turn around, or suffer the consequences!"

"No!"

The apparition opened its mouth, revealing a fiery inferno within, then lunged toward her. Lara brought her arms up to protect herself from the specter's attack as it enveloped her in a cauldron of fire. The blazing heat melted through her armored suit seams, burning her hair away and scorching her skin. Lara screamed for help, but the intense heat seared her lungs, suffocating her desperate plea. The temperature inside her suit raced past two hundred degrees, and her skin started bubbling as her bodily fluids began boiling. She writhed in pain as she desperately searched for a solution, then strange words tumbled from her mouth.

"Intellegitur consilium tuum!"

The apparition disappeared, and the suit's cool air replaced the heat that had scorched her body a second before. McCarthy and the others were staring at her as she held her arms in front of her face, her upper body bent backward as she had tried to avoid the ghoulish attack. She seemed unharmed by the apparition, although alarms were flashing on the right side of her helmet visor—her pulse rate had doubled.

Lara looked around the hub; the white fog was gone. Only the black fog remained, retreating into the passageway from whence it came.

"Are you okay?" McCarthy asked.

Lara dropped her arms and stood erect, making a concerted effort to calm herself, taking slow, deep breaths.

"I'm okay. Just an unusual vision." She paused for a moment as she gathered herself, attempting to decide whether to heed the apparition's warning. Finally, she pointed toward the opening across the hub as the last remnant of fog disappeared. "That corridor."

Harkins directed another deployment of reconnaissance probes from one of the Marines, but the drones fell to the floor again after flying only a few feet toward the passageway. The recon drones were still inoperable.

Harkins then ordered the two lead Marines forward, and as they moved into position, Lara asked her suit, "Translate 'Intellegitur consilium tuum' into Colonial language."

Her suit replied, "Your advice is understood."

As Lara pondered how she had known what to say to dispel the vision, the platoon began moving forward again, into the dark corridor.

40

The platoon delved deeper into the Korilian complex, cautiously making its way down the new passageway as Harkins communicated with the point Marines ahead. The platoon caught up to them several times, when the point Marines reached intersections and waited for guidance on which way to go. Each time, the path was clear to Lara. The fog beckoned her, dark tentacles flowing toward her from one of the corridors, growing thicker at each intersection.

After the third juncture, the platoon had traveled a short distance down the passageway when Lara heard one of the point Marines report, "We've got a double-shielded slayer. Two hundred feet ahead, around the corner to the right."

Harkins ordered the platoon to halt while he assessed the situation, examining a map of the facility on a display embedded in his armored forearm.

Deanna lowered her carbine muzzle toward the ground. "There must be another way." She approached Lara. Deanna's eyes were wide and her lips trembled as she spoke. "Find another path to the intel center. We can't go this way!"

Lara wasn't sure how to respond. There was only one way to the intelligence center as far as she could tell.

Jankowski moved toward the two women. When he reached them, he grabbed Deanna by the neck and slammed her against the passageway wall.

"It's only one Korilian. In a few minutes, it'll be a dead Korilian. Understand?"

Deanna shook her head from side to side, her eyes tightly closed. Jankowski kept her pinned against the wall, a firm grip around her neck.

"We've been through this before," he said through gritted teeth.

"Not against a double-shielded slayer! We'll need an entire company to defeat it!"

Jankowski replied, "This platoon was handpicked. We're the best Marines in this MEF. We *will* kill it. The same way as before. Understand?"

Deanna opened her eyes and stared at Jankowski. Then she nodded her head and rotated one of her assault carbine controls fully clockwise. The other Marines did the same. Then she glanced toward the thin rod hanging over her shoulder.

"That's right," Jankowski said.

Deanna's breathing slowly returned to normal, then Jankowski released his grip. Deanna stood with her back against the wall, her eyes still wide with fright. Then her eyes narrowed, determination replacing the fear in her eyes.

"That's my girl," Jankowski said.

Deanna punched him in the chest.

Jankowski grinned. "Get back in formation."

Deanna returned to her place in his squad.

"You know the drill," Harkins said. "Four by fives. Travis and Kalinin, stay behind with our guests. Points on video."

Geisinger and Jankowski called out names, and the platoon formed up into four columns. The largest Marine in each column moved to the front, then shouldered his assault carbine and removed the thin rod slung over the other shoulder, holding it in both hands.

"We'll halt in two hundred feet, just before the right turn, then deploy on my command," Harkins said. "Kalinin, keep Admiral McCarthy and the others a safe distance behind. Any questions?"

No one replied, and Harkins ordered the platoon forward.

"We wait here a moment," Liza directed Lara, McCarthy, Albright, and Travis.

After the other Marines had treaded quietly down the long corridor about twenty feet, Liza moved forward, matching the platoon's pace. Lara and the others followed.

The platoon soon reached a ninety-degree bend to the right. Both point Marines were at the corner, their backs pressed against the corridor wall. One held a thin, snakelike probe in one hand. After receiving an order from Harkins, the Marine fed the tip of the probe around the corner. A video image appeared on the left side of Lara's facepiece, and the passageway around the bend rotated into view.

The corridor ran another hundred feet, then ended with another passageway door. In front of the entrance stood the slayer—a type of Korilian Lara hadn't seen before. It was about fifty percent larger, its body encased in fibrous black plates that looked more like a natural part of its body than armor. Its head was likewise encased, its eyes protected by translucent panes. The slayer's limb armor tapered to sharp edges that glowed bright red.

Two shimmering spheres enveloped the slayer, one slightly inside the other, with the slayer in the center of the two energy globes. It stood there, holding a firearm in each of its four upper appendages.

Harkins holstered his pistol and unshouldered his carbine. He joined one of the columns and ordered the point Marines to join two others, creating four columns of five Marines each. Harkins began counting down from five to zero. The platoon crouched down, with the Marines in the front of each column gripping the thin rods.

When Harkins's count reached zero, the four columns surged around the corner, stopping just around the bend. The slayer immediately raised all four appendages to fire at the Marines. But Harkins shot first, lighting up the outer sphere surrounding the slayer in sizzling electrical sparks, delaying it from firing for just a second.

The delay was long enough. The Marines at the head of each column jammed their rods into the ground, and each rod expanded into a thin, shimmering energy shield about four feet in diameter. The lead Marines planted their feet and leaned into their shields while the other Marines hid behind the shields in single file.

The slayer fired, his orange pulses hitting the four shields. They flashed bright white, with sparks of electricity sizzling across each shield's surface.

The Marine holding the shield in the farthest left column began counting down from five. After reaching one, he announced, "Fire!"

The other four Marines in his column popped out from behind the shield—two over the top and one to each side—and fired simultaneously, then immediately dropped behind their protective shield. However, instead of the usual blue pulses, bright green pulses shot from their carbines. The four pulses hit the slayer's outer shield, lighting it up with electrical arcs.

The Marines in the other three columns attacked the slayer in a similar manner, each column firing two seconds after the previous one. After the fourth column fired, the slayer's outer shield collapsed in a bright flash, the inner one arcing and sparking as its companion had a few seconds earlier.

After each column fired, the Marines huddled behind their shields, waiting for their carbines to recharge. After the fourth column fired, the first was ready to go again. The four Marines popped up and fired, the four pulses impacting the slayer's remaining shield. But this time the slayer was ready.

It fired all four weapons when the Marines emerged from behind their shield, with the four pulses converging on the Marine to the right, severing his right arm from his shoulder. The Marine fell to the floor beside his arm as he screamed in agony. Blood gushed from his shoulder as he writhed in pain, and he stopped moving after a few seconds. The four green pulses from the Marines lit up the slayer's remaining shield, but it held.

The next column of Marines fired, and the slayer scored another hit with its counterfire, vaporizing one of the Marines above the shoulders. The headless Marine collapsed beside her fellow platoon members. The third and fourth columns of Marines fired next, eliminating the slayer's remaining shield, with the loss of a Marine in each column as well.

The slayer suddenly released its weapons and dropped down onto all six appendages, then surged toward the Marines at a ferocious speed. It crashed through their shields, its limbs slashing outward, sending bodies flying through the air. Two Marines hit the passageway walls and slumped to the floor while a third Marine flew up, crashing against the ceiling. A fourth Marine soared past the passageway intersection where Lara waited, his body sliced in half. Blood sprayed across Lara's visor as the upper half of the Marine went spinning past her.

It was chaos in the corridor, filled with green pulses and flying Marines, sometimes whole bodies and sometimes just limbs. Screams and commands filled Lara's ears as the Marines tried to coordinate their response. But in less than a minute, not a single Marine was standing aside from Liza and Travis, hiding with Lara, McCarthy, and Albright around the passageway corner.

The slayer raised two limbs and prepared to drive them through two Marines crawling on the ground. Liza gave an order, and she and Travis stepped into the passageway around the corner and fired at the slayer, their green pulses blasting two pits in its chest armor. It looked at the two Marines, then dropped down on all six limbs and sped toward them.

Liza and Travis braced themselves for the impact, and just before the slayer reached them, a green pulse hit the slayer's left rear appendage from behind. The limb detached from its body, and the slayer lurched to its left and ground to a halt. The pulse came from Sergeant Jankowski, sitting against the passageway wall, his legs splayed out in front of him, a wide gash in his chest armor. He dropped his carbine onto his lap, no longer able to hold it at shoulder level. The slayer examined Jankowski, then turned back toward Liza and Travis just as it was hit by another green pulse, this one severing its right rear appendage.

Geisinger knelt on one knee across the corridor from Jankowski, her carbine at shoulder height, and fired again. But the slayer tilted its body just as she fired, and the green pulse hit the slayer's armor, blowing chunks of black material into the air. The remaining four appendages partially withdrew into its armor, shielding the vulnerable joints.

Liza and Travis rotated the controls on their rifles back to their original positions and began firing rapidly at the slayer, the blue pulses creating craters near the seam between its chest and head armor. Several other Marines behind the slayer regained their feet and fired, their pulses blasting pits in its back armor.

The slayer focused again on Liza and Travis, advancing slowly toward them on its four remaining limbs, no longer able to travel quickly with its joints protected inside its armor. It reached Liza and Travis and raised itself up on its two middle limbs, pulling back its two upper appendages as it prepared to slice through the two Marines.

The slayer slashed with both upper limbs simultaneously, and Liza and Travis turned their carbines sideways at the last second, using them to block the slayer's razor-sharp appendages. Travis and Liza slammed into the passageway wall on opposite sides, where they slumped to the ground. The slayer then turned the corner and prepared to attack the three persons still standing: Lara, McCarthy, and Albright.

McCarthy dove toward Lara, knocking her off her feet just before one of the slayer's limbs swung past Lara, barely missing her head.

After she and McCarthy rolled to a stop, Lara spotted Albright standing with his mouth agape, frozen in fear, as the slayer turned toward him. It pulled back one of its limbs and thrust it through Albright's stomach. Ragged flesh and blood spurted from Albright's back along with the end of the slayer's appendage. It tilted its limb downward, and Albright slid off onto the ground.

The slayer advanced toward Travis, still lying on the corridor floor, and lifted one of its appendages to impale him. But Liza recovered and pushed herself to one knee, aiming her carbine. She fired, her pulse hitting the side of the slayer's head, distracting it. Liza kept firing as she moved to the center of the passageway, her pulses eating away at the seam between the slayer's head and chest armor.

Travis regained his feet and joined Liza as the slayer swung at them with two limbs. Liza blocked the blow with her carbine, but it snapped in half as the force of the blow knocked her to her knees. The slayer aimed low at Travis, and he partially deflected the thrust with his carbine, but the limb hit Travis on the side of his knee, jamming the joint. Unable to move nimbly with a frozen armored knee joint, he couldn't avoid the next slayer limb, which slashed into his chest armor and flung him down the corridor, where he landed on his back, dazed.

Liza was still on her knees as the slayer pulled back both appendages, preparing to slice her into pieces. She brought her forearms up beside her face, attempting to protect her neck from the powerful limbs. She activated her helmet speaker and screamed in defiance as she prepared for the slicing blows.

Suddenly, the slayer reared backward and twisted from side to side. As it swiveled, Lara spotted Deanna on its back, her hand clinging to a seam between the slayer's head and shoulder plates. She jammed her pistol muzzle into the joint above the slayer's right shoulder and fired. Its upper right appendage fell lifeless to its side.

The slayer howled and reached over its shoulder with its other upper limb, grabbing Deanna in its claw. It pried her from its back and held her high in the air, then impaled her through the chest with another appendage. It threw Deanna down the corridor, where she skidded to a halt. She lay motionless, blood pouring from the holes in her armored suit.

The slayer looked back at Liza, but she was no longer kneeling. She stood in front of it, an arm's length away. She had her pulse-pistol in her hand, which she shoved into a small gap that she and Travis had blown in the seam between the slayer's head and chest plate.

"Eat this," Liza said, then pulled the trigger.

A bright blue light flashed out from the seam between the slayer's head and chest armor, and the translucent shields in front of the Korilian's eyes lit up briefly. The slayer fell forward on top of Liza, who collapsed to the ground beneath it.

41

McCarthy helped Lara to her feet while several Marines pulled the dead slayer off Liza. She appeared unharmed, holstering her pistol as she stood. She surveyed McCarthy, then Lara, confirming neither Nexus was injured.

Geisinger knelt beside Jankowski, tending to his wound. She removed his helmet and damaged breast plate, revealing a deep gash across his chest. Jankowski was in pain, a grimace on his face. Geisinger opened one of Jankowski's utility belt compartments, retrieved a vial with an applicator tip, and injected the contents into his shoulder. He relaxed, his eyes glazing over. She pulled a packet from another compartment in his belt, ripped it open, and poured a powdery substance into the wound across his chest. The powder turned into a gelatinous substance as it mixed with his blood, and Geisinger smeared it around until the wound was sealed.

"You'll be okay," Geisinger said as she replaced Jankowski's chest plate. "It's just a scratch." Jankowski laughed, his response cut short by a spasm of pain that wracked his body. Geisinger pressed a control on Jankowski's suit, activating the medical aid beacon.

"Help will be here soon," she said, "or we'll get you on the way out."

She found a pistol lying nearby and gave it to Jankowski, then placed her hand on his shoulder. Jankowski nodded.

After checking on McCarthy and Lara, Liza scanned the carnage around them, then knelt beside the upper half of one of the Marines. Lara recognized him as Tony Rodriguez, who had tried to talk Deanna into spending the night with him, then declined Liza's offer after he learned that she was the Black Widow.

Liza turned to Lara. "He should have slept with me first."

She then approached Albright and flipped him onto his stomach, then took his backpack, which contained the computer tablet needed to download the Korilian algorithms, and slung it over one shoulder. She turned to McCarthy as she picked up an assault carbine, replacing her broken one.

"Will you be able to download the algorithms in the intelligence center, sir?"

McCarthy nodded. "I should be able to figure it out."

Beside Liza, another Marine was helping Travis. The Korilian blow had cut a gash through his chest plate, but he'd been luckier than Jankowski—there was only a surface cut across his chest. However, Travis's armored knee joint was damaged, so they removed his left leg armor.

Harkins assessed the status of his platoon. Only five ambulatory Marines remained besides himself: Geisinger, Liza, Travis, and two others. Jankowski had also survived but was too injured to continue. After examining the sealed door to the intelligence center, Harkins approached McCarthy.

"There are no reinforcements on the way. Do we continue on, with the possibility there could be hundreds of Korilians in the intel center?"

Lara felt McCarthy's view again, then he turned to her. "The line ends when we pass through the opening. Something's blocking me. Do you have anything?"

Lara stared at the door and inhaled deeply. She let her breath out slowly, trying to relax, hoping to force a premonition. Nothing materialized.

"I've got nothing."

McCarthy turned to Harkins. "We keep going."

Harkins ordered Liza to take charge of both McCarthy and Lara, freeing Travis up for normal duties. He approached the door controls, then directed the other Marines to form up for a standard entrance. Geisinger and three Marines took station beside the door, while Liza hung back with McCarthy and Lara. After verifying his Marines were in position, weapons ready, Harkins pressed the open sequence on the Korilian symbols.

The black fibers wriggled back, creating an opening. But instead of revealing an intelligence center crammed with equipment and Korilians, a dark chamber greeted them, its dimensions and contents unknown. Geisinger and the three other Marines slipped into the chamber, two ducking left and the other two right, with Harkins close behind.

As the fibers wriggled open, revealing the dark chamber, Lara was hit with a blast of emotion. She felt several intertwined feelings, with the most dominant being hatred—a simmering, decades-long resentment. Lara and McCarthy waited with Liza outside the chamber for the report that it was safe to proceed, but before they received the all clear from Harkins, McCarthy suddenly stepped through the opening.

Liza immediately followed McCarthy inside, leaving Lara alone in the corridor. Lara hesitated, then passed through the entrance to find McCarthy and Liza a few feet inside the chamber, which was faintly lit in dull gray light, the source unknown. Moisture clung to black walls that extended up until they were lost in the darkness. The chamber appeared barren, and instead of the springy black fiber surface throughout the rest of the facility, the floor was a crimson color that felt smooth and slick beneath her boots.

As she tried to locate the source of the emotions she had detected, she sensed something else, which took her a moment to discern. She had no idea how she knew what it was, but was positive she detected—*power*.

Immense power.

There was something pleasant to the feeling yet sickening at the same time, as if a power meant for good had been perverted into something evil.

Before Lara could explain what she had detected, McCarthy moved forward. Liza matched his pace, and Lara followed them deeper into the darkness. As they advanced, something slimy dripped onto her face shield. She looked up but couldn't see its source in the darkness. She quickly wiped it away with her armored hand.

McCarthy kept walking, his eyes fixed on the far end of the chamber. Harkins suddenly materialized before them, standing still with his weapon aimed ahead. He joined McCarthy, Lara, and Liza as they advanced, passing several dead Korilians on the floor. They were in various stages of decay, with some of the remains consisting of only the outer shell.

Lara spotted movement ahead. A small, slender humanoid, about five feet tall, was feeding on one of the Korilian carcasses. It looked up and stared at them as they approached, wiping its mouth with the back of its hand. Then the creature scampered toward a small alcove in the base of the chamber wall, disappearing into the darkness.

McCarthy kept moving toward the alcove, and the others followed. As they approached, an object became visible within the shallow recess. It was the humanoid, squatting on its haunches, its back hunched over and head down. Brown matted and tangled hair hung in front of its face, and its head swung from side to side in a slow rhythmic movement.

They stopped a few paces from the humanoid, and Lara examined it more closely. It was wrapped in a filthy garment that clung to its torso and fell loosely over its thighs. It was emaciated, its legs barely the thickness of Lara's arms, the ripples of its sinews visible beneath pale white skin.

The creature gave no indication it noticed them this time. It sat there, bent over, its head swaying back and forth. Lara looked at McCarthy and was surprised by the expression on his face. His lips were drawn thin, and he had a look in his eyes that she hadn't seen before—*uncertainty*.

The creature's head stopped moving.

It sat there, motionless.

McCarthy stood there, waiting, and Lara wondered what he was thinking or planning. Geisinger and the other three Marines appeared on the periphery. The six Marines were arranged in a semicircle around the creature, with three Marines on each side of Lara and McCarthy.

Lara considered talking to the creature when it suddenly spoke. The creature's voice was gravelly, as if it hadn't talked in years.

"You've finally come for me," it said. "I've been waiting for you."

A chill went down Lara's spine. Intertwined in the creature's words was a hatred so intense it made her shudder.

The creature's head swiveled toward Lara. It stared at her for a moment, sniffing the air. Then it pointed a bony finger at her.

"What is *that*?"

McCarthy activated his suit speaker. "She is not your concern."

The creature's gaze snapped back to McCarthy. "You brought it here, which makes it my concern."

"Leave her out of this," McCarthy said sternly.

"It is an abomination!"

The creature's head began swaying back and forth again, and it began speaking in a low voice. Lara couldn't make out the words and concluded the creature was talking to itself—or to something nearby. The creature continued on, seemingly oblivious to those around it while McCarthy waited.

The creature suddenly looked up at McCarthy and spoke, its voice strong again. "It matters not what it is. It will share the same fate as you and your task force."

Venom dripped from its voice.

"What are your intentions?" McCarthy asked.

"Perhaps you would like to view the future clearly?" The creature gestured slowly in the air with its hand, as if pushing back a curtain. Lara felt a subtle change in McCarthy's view.

"What have you done!" he asked.

The creature emitted a cackling laugh. "Yes, your vaunted Third MEF will be eliminated, and your fleet in orbit will be destroyed! You, however," the creature spread its arms toward the eight men and women surrounding it, "have been left to me to vanquish. It was a...special request of mine."

A grin broke across the creature's face, accompanied by a snicker. Then it pounded its fists into the ground. "But first, remove your helmet. I want to see your face, and I want you to look upon me with human eyes, not with armored suit sensors."

McCarthy hesitated.

"Look at me!"

As the creature spoke, Lara realized there was something odd about the interaction between McCarthy and the creature, as if McCarthy had encountered it before. But Lara's thoughts were interrupted as McCarthy reached up and pressed the release buttons on his helmet. It split open, and he lifted it slowly, then tossed it onto the chamber floor.

McCarthy stared at the humanoid.

The creature parted the hair from its eyes so it could see McCarthy clearly. Tangled hair fell across gaunt cheeks. Its lips were dry, cracked, and its eyes were sunk into dark recesses in its skull. Inside those black pits, green eyes looked upon him with a fiery intensity.

"I gave you clear instructions," it said. "I waited, year after year, and you left me here to *rot!*"

Lara absorbed the creature's words, then reconsidered her initial assessment. It wasn't just a humanoid; it was human. Someone enslaved by the Korilians years ago. As Lara examined the remnant of humanity that sat before them, the clues came together.

She sucked in a sharp breath.

Elena!

42

Elena hadn't been killed on Darian 3!

The Korilians had taken her prisoner. They must have detected her ability and brought her to Hellios. On Darian 3, Lara and McCarthy hadn't positively identified Elena's remains, assuming the decapitated skeleton was her.

After eighteen years of incarceration, Elena bore faint resemblance to the beautiful young woman in the video transmission from Darian 3. As Lara looked at what had become of her, a wave of pity and sadness overwhelmed her, along with anger and a desire for revenge.

Lara wondered why the Korilians had kept Elena alive, bringing her to this facility. Then the answer dawned on her.

Elena was the intelligence center!

She had been viewing for the Korilians. On that last day on Darian 3, Elena had known what would happen and gave instructions to destroy this facility—to destroy her—so that she couldn't be used as a weapon against humanity.

"Major Harkins," McCarthy said, "lower your weapons. Whatever happens, do not fire or interfere in any way."

Harkins gave the order, and the Marines lowered their weapons.

"I prayed for you to destroy this place," Elena said, "to stop me from betraying humanity. But you didn't. It's too late now. So many dead because of what I've done."

Elena started rocking back and forth. "I fought them, Jon. Believe me, I fought them. But you can't imagine what they've done to me." Tears began running down her face, then the tone of her voice changed. "It's your fault. If you had done what I told you to do, none of this would've happened." The speed of Elena's rocking increased, and her voice became agitated. "You abandoned me. Left me here to live in pain. To live in fear and shame. *You didn't care!*"

Elena pounded her fists into the floor again, this time so hard that Lara heard bones crack. Splintered bone shards protruded through Elena's hands as blood dripped onto the floor. Elena grimaced in pain as she examined her ruined hands, but then the bones began mending themselves. Lara watched in amazement as the bones rejoined and the wounds closed. In only a few seconds, Elena's hands were healed, leaving no indication of her wounds aside from the blood on the floor. Elena looked up, her eyes narrowing as they settled on McCarthy.

The scent in the room changed. Power still permeated the air, but hatred and fury were now dominant and growing stronger. Lara felt a change in McCarthy's view again, back to how it felt before Elena allowed him to see the future clearly—his view was being blocked again. Lara wondered why Elena would block his view again, then realized why.

To prevent him from viewing what she was about to do.

The information coalesced in Lara's mind a second too late. Elena launched herself at McCarthy with a speed and ferocity that belied her frail appearance. She clamped both hands around his neck and wrapped her legs behind his, like a spider clinging to its victim. The momentum of Elena's attack knocked McCarthy backward, and he lost his balance, falling onto the floor with Elena on top, her hands tight around his neck as she strangled him.

McCarthy tried to pry her hands away but couldn't break Elena's grip. Lara looked at the Marines, who kept their weapons down and didn't interfere, as McCarthy had directed. McCarthy's face turned pale as Elena choked him, her arms and face straining with the effort. Yet McCarthy seemed unable or unwilling to resist. If no one acted, Elena would kill

McCarthy. Lara recalled his words, directing the Marines to refrain from interfering.

But not her.

Lara approached the two Nexus Tens and kicked Elena as hard as she could, her armored boot impacting Elena's head with a heavy thud. Elena shrieked as the force of Lara's kick broke her grip on McCarthy and sent her rolling across the floor. She propped herself up on her forearms, shaking her head from side to side. Then she scrambled back into her alcove and curled into a fetal position against the damp wall, whimpering as she wrapped her arms around her legs.

McCarthy stood, rubbing his neck, then moved toward Elena, who flinched and turned away as he approached. He knelt beside her.

"I didn't know you were here," he said softly. "I didn't receive your message until a few weeks ago. Your message from Darian 3 was incomplete, and the communication center didn't forward it to Army command."

McCarthy removed one of his armored gloves, then gently caressed the side of her face.

Elena suddenly reached toward him, wrapping her arms tightly around his neck, burying her face against his chest. She began crying and sobbing, tears streaming down her cheeks. McCarthy held her close, and Elena eventually relaxed her grip. But her crying didn't subside. She finally spoke, revealing the reason why.

"It's a trap. The mission to Hellios is an ambush. Korilian combat troops are hidden on the planet's surface and inside this complex, and a Korilian fleet will arrive soon. No one will make it off the planet's surface.

"You will die here."

43

Upon hearing Elena's confession, Major Harkins attempted to contact 3rd MEF headquarters to inform them of the pending ambush. He received nothing but static, combined with a high-pitched squealing sound.

"I'm being jammed," he announced.

He directed the other five Marines to contact headquarters, and all five had the same result.

"We can't get through from this deep in the facility," he added. "We need to get closer to the surface."

McCarthy replied, "If Elena is correct, we aren't going to make it to the surface."

As Elena clung to McCarthy while he knelt beside her, Lara vacillated between sympathy and rage. Looking at what had become of Elena, she could only imagine what the Korilians had done to her. At the same time, Lara was furious. It was obvious Elena had capitulated, using her talents against humanity, constructing a trap about to be sprung on 2nd Fleet and the 3rd MEF.

McCarthy must have concluded the same and more because he asked Elena, "You've developed the ability to block timelines, haven't you?"

Elena nodded, her face pressed against McCarthy's chest armor.

"I need you to unblock those lines," McCarthy said, "so we can warn Second Fleet and the Third MEF."

When Elena didn't respond, McCarthy asked softly, "Can you do that for me?"

After a moment, Elena nodded again, and Lara felt the same subtle change in McCarthy's view that she had experienced a few minutes earlier.

44

Angeline Del Rio stood beside Admiral Amani on *Controlador*'s bridge as 2nd Fleet orbited above the Korilian complex. Not far away, the dark and gutted remnant of the Korilian star fortress spiraled slowly, with three of its five arms sheared off. Scattered in the distance, the hulks of destroyed Korilian and Colonial warships were illuminated by Hellios's reddish-orange star. It was quiet aboard the fleet command ship, now that the starship battle was over.

For the last few hours, it had been quiet on the planet's surface as well, while they waited for 21st Division to gain control of the complex and locate the Korilian intelligence center. Everything had gone as planned, aside from the star base being a star fortress, but an uneasy feeling permeated Angeline's thoughts. She had received no premonitions concerning 2nd Fleet for the last few hours. It seemed like whatever had been blocking the Nexus views was blocking her premonitions as well.

Her knees suddenly went weak as her vision was bathed in a red hue. She steadied herself on a nearby console, attempting to make sense of the premonition. She closed her eyes, hoping for something more specific, and she received the most vivid premonition she had experienced in her decade-long assignment as a fleet guide. Bright red flashes peppered her vision, appearing around the 2nd Fleet formation; hundreds upon hundreds, announcing the arrival of Korilian warships. On the planet's surface, the perimeter glowed bright red, accompanied by a blotch of red in the Korilian complex, growing larger as it spread outward.

Angeline opened her eyes and turned to Admiral Amani. "It's a trap! Inbound Korilian warships! They're also launching a ground counterattack on the perimeter and from within the complex!"

Admiral Amani skimmed the command ship's displays, which thus far gave no indication of an impending Korilian assault. 2nd Fleet had launched thousands of reconnaissance probes, saturating the surrounding area out to a two-jump radius. There were no signs of Korilian warships. "Estimated strength of the Korilian armada?"

"Three to five battle groups."

"Are you sure?" Amani asked. "Where the hell did they get that many ships, on top of the two hundred we just destroyed?"

"Three to five battle groups," Angeline repeated, confident in her assessment.

Amani frowned. Even if there were only three incoming battle groups, the Korilians would hold the advantage due to their superior command and control. It was a question of *when*, not *if*, 2nd Fleet would be forced to evacuate the Hellios system. Before then, they needed to retrieve as much of the 3rd MEF as possible and especially McCarthy's platoon.

Amani informed General Hutton, in command of 3rd MEF, then sent orders to his fleet, transitioning it from a ground-support formation into a defensive bubble above the Korilian complex. They needed to protect the 3rd MEF while the SAVs evacuated the troops from the planet's surface to the awaiting troop transports.

"Korilian warships!" the sensor supervisor announced as recon probes two jumps away reported the detection. Three more announcements followed in succession as recon probes detected four incoming Korilian battle groups.

Angeline watched tensely during the two-minute-long jump-drive recharge, when the Korilian armada's intentions would become clear— hold two jumps away or continue onto Hellios—but she already knew the answer. Korilians weathered the jump effects better than humans, and although they tended to follow the same two-jump-limit-into-battle that

Colonial warships followed, in rare circumstances they would engage after a triple jump.

Two minutes after the Korilian battle groups had been detected by the recon probes, all four battle groups jumped again. They were now one jump away. Thankfully, Angeline had given Admiral Amani advance warning, and the 2nd Fleet starships were completing their maneuvers, forming a defensive bubble capable of temporarily withstanding a superior force.

As the seconds counted down for the Korilian jump into the Hellios system, Angeline steeled herself for battle.

45

McCarthy turned to Major Harkins. "We need to exit the complex as quickly as possible. Elena is correct. There are two million Korilian combat troops about to counterattack the perimeter and the Marines inside this facility."

McCarthy stood, but Elena remained huddled against the wall. "I'm not going with you," she said. "If you make it out, order Second Fleet to destroy this place."

"You're coming with us," McCarthy said.

"No. After what I've done, I deserve to die here."

"I'm not leaving without you."

Elena's head pivoted toward McCarthy. "Leave me!" she screamed, the veins in her neck bulging.

McCarthy bent down and lifted her up, cradling her in his arms. Instead of protesting or struggling to escape, Elena simply stared at him for a moment, then wrapped her arms around his neck and pressed her face against his chest as she started crying. McCarthy headed toward the chamber exit.

They stepped into the corridor to find Jankowski sitting where they had left him, leaning against the wall, a glazed look still in his eyes due to the pain medication Geisinger had administered. She helped him to his feet, explaining that they needed to evacuate the facility as quickly as possible. But Jankowski could barely walk and stumbled after a few steps, Geisinger catching him as he fell.

She removed his chest plate to examine his wound again. It had resumed bleeding, with small air bubbles reaching the blood's surface. Jankowski had at least one punctured lung. If they had any chance of reaching the surface, they'd have to hustle, and there was no way he could keep up. Lara saw the pain in Geisinger's eyes as she realized they would have to leave him behind.

Elena wiped the tears from her eyes, then spoke softly to McCarthy. "Bring me to him."

McCarthy knelt down beside Jankowski, and Elena placed a hand on his chest. Lara watched in fascination as the wound began healing, realizing that Elena had developed at least two talents: timeline blocking and the ability to heal herself and others.

The gash in Jankowski's chest quickly closed until there was no trace of the injury. Jankowski's eyes cleared and his strength returned. He stood, eyeing the woman in McCarthy's arms.

"Thank you," he said. But Elena just turned away and closed her eyes, pressing her face against McCarthy's chest again.

Geisinger replaced Jankowski's chest plate, then he retrieved his assault carbine. Harkins took the lead, shifting into a quick jog down the passageway. They soon reached the end of the corridor, entering the hub to find several dozen Korilians picking through the bodies, apparently searching for survivors. When they spotted the Marines, they charged toward them.

Harkins ordered a single-line formation facing the Korilians, taking the center position with the three Nexi behind the seven Marines. The Marines made short work of the Korilians, their bodies skidding to a halt on the hub floor not far away. The reprieve was short-lived, however, as more Korilians began streaming into the hub. Lara's pulse quickened when she realized they were emerging from the passageway that led back to the facility exit; their escape route had been cut off. Additionally, these Korilians were a different type.

Lara quickly concluded the Korilians racing across the hub toward them were combat troops. They were larger than the typical Korilians they had encountered, plus they were outfitted with armor, carried a weapon in each upper limb, and had a sheath over the sharp edges of their limbs that glowed bright red. The combat Korilians opened fire as they approached, and the Marines employed their shields, blocking the Korilian pulses.

"That way!" McCarthy pointed toward a nearby passageway.

They sprinted toward the opening, with the Marine shields blocking Korilian pulses along the way. After entering the corridor, they continued at full speed, but the Korilians gained on them. They soon reached a vertical shaft with closed portals above and below. Lara felt the chill of McCarthy's view, then he tapped the multicolored symbols on the wall. Six portals above opened in succession.

Harkins ordered three Marines to ascend with the Nexi. Jankowski, Liza, and Travis retrieved their rappel-pistols and shot upward, embedding their spikes in the top of the shaft. McCarthy handed Elena to Jankowski, while Travis took hold of McCarthy and Liza grabbed Lara. The three pairs lurched upward into the darkness just before the Korilians caught up to them. Harkins and the other Marines below opened fire, gunning down the lead Korilian, who was replaced by another, and another, as the Korilians closed on the four Marines left behind.

The three pairs of Marines and Nexi sped up through the portal until they stopped at the top level of the complex. The Marines swung from the center of the shaft onto a nearby ledge, then examined a corridor fading into the distance, their assault carbines ready, while they waited for the remaining four Marines. The shaft was lit up from the battle below, with blue and red pulses and shield flashes, as the four Marines backed up under the shaft, then quickly shifted to their rappel-pistols. The anchors shot up past Lara, embedding into the ceiling above her, and the four Marines began their ascent.

The Marines fired down with their pulse-pistols while they rose toward the first level. Korilian pulses filled the shaft, and the lowest Marine was hit twice. He lost his grip on his rappel-pistol and fell back to the seventh level, where he was swarmed by Korilians. The Korilian pulses that missed the rising Marines blasted chunks of debris from the ceiling, and one of the rappel anchors dislodged. Another Marine fell. Harkins and Geisinger made it to the top level, where they were hauled from the shaft onto the ledge by Liza and Travis.

Jankowski took the lead this time, sprinting down the passageway, which was narrower than previous ones, with Geisinger bringing up the rear. In the middle of the formation, Lara ran behind McCarthy, who carried Elena again. Glancing over her shoulder, Lara spotted Korilian combat troops climbing from the shaft onto their level, then speeding down the corridor toward them. The Marines and Nexi were running as fast as they could, but the Korilians were gaining.

Jankowski suddenly stopped. "Korilians ahead."

Harkins ordered Liza to join Jankowski in front and Travis to team with Geisinger behind, leaving Harkins in the middle with the Nexi. As the Korilians closed, Lara examined the corridor for escape routes.

There were none.

They were in a narrow passageway, wide enough for two Marines abreast to fight, with no side openings on either end in sight. Combat Korilians ahead of them appeared, barreling toward them while the Korilians behind closed in as well. There were only five Marines left now, with dozens of Korilians approaching from each end.

They were trapped and outnumbered.

46

On the planet's surface not far from the Korilian complex, General Hutton surveyed the displays in the 3rd MEF command center, assessing the deteriorating situation. Above the planet, 2nd Fleet was withering under the Korilian armada's onslaught, and he wondered how long they had before the Korilians breached the fleet's protective cone, placing his troop transports at risk. He would have ordered 3rd MEF's evacuation by now if it weren't for Admiral McCarthy, still somewhere inside the Korilian complex. His orders had been clear: ensure McCarthy's safety at all costs.

Hutton focused on the data reports from the Korilian facility. He had already directed 21st Division's 1st Brigade to exit the complex, but no units had emerged thus far. Additionally, data and voice transmissions were being jammed, and he had lost communications with all units inside the facility except for those on the first level, and those were pinned down by Korilian combat troops.

Before they lost communications, units on the seventh level reported that the perimeter had been breached, which painted a daunting scenario. McCarthy's platoon was likely fighting its way out and would almost assuredly need help, but Hutton was paralyzed. He had no idea where McCarthy's platoon was, and even if he did, he couldn't communicate with nearby units, directing them to assist.

"Sir," General Hutton's chief of staff said as he approached. "The Korilians have gained control of all complex entrances."

Hutton shifted his gaze to the holes they had blown into the facility, and seconds later, Korilian combat troops emerged from the breaches, speeding across the terrain toward the 3rd MEF command. Defense batteries positioned around the command center opened fire, as did the command post's security detachment. Orders were sent to the Heavy Air Division, and a moment later, drones swept down from the clouds and dropped bomb packets, devastating the advancing Korilian formation with a blanket of explosions.

An alarm went off in the command center, and one of the monitors, which displayed the perimeter formation of nine Marine divisions, began flashing. One section had turned red. Hutton's chief of staff relayed the grim news.

"Sir, the surface perimeter has been breached. We need to evacuate now, before we lose the entire MEF."

Hutton assessed the situation. Korilian troops had penetrated the perimeter and would begin enveloping nearby units. Immediate evacuation was the obvious response, except... He focused again on the Korilian complex.

McCarthy was still inside.

However, the Korilians now controlled all exits to the facility and likely the entire first level as well, which meant the outcome was clear. There was nothing more he could do.

Hutton pressed the communications override button, gaining access to all Marine channels.

"Evacuate Third MEF to the troop transports."

47

The two pairs of Marines—Jankowski and Liza on one end of the corridor and Geisinger and Travis on the other—fired their assault carbines at the lead Korilian on each end, scoring hits on their armored joints, hobbling and then killing each one. However, every dead Korilian was replaced by another, and the Korilians steadily moved forward. The Marines had used their shields for as long as possible, until nausea from the shield energy had almost incapacitated them, then had shifted to their carbines.

They took occasional counterfire, rocking backward as pulses impacted their armor. Harkins assisted, firing his pulse-pistol toward whichever Korilian had approached closest to the Marines.

The Korilians on both ends continued to advance, forcing both pairs of Marines backward until they could retreat no farther, with Harkins and the three Nexi sandwiched between. The lead Korilians on both sides approached to within striking distance with their limbs, which forced the Marines to shift tactics, as did the Korilians. Each lead Korilian holstered its pulse-pistols and employed all four upper limbs, the sheaths on the sharp edges glowing red, attempting to slash its opponents.

Fortunately, the corridor was wide enough for only one Korilian on each end to engage while providing enough room for two Marines, which gave them a fighting chance, having to block and dodge only two limbs instead of four. Lara was impressed by the Marines' prowess, evading some attacks while blocking others, but they were purely on the defensive now, warding off blows with their assault carbines instead of firing at the Korilians. Harkins assisted when possible, firing past the Marines on one end or the other.

Travis was fighting without his left leg armor, which didn't go unnoticed by his opponents. One of the Korilians eventually landed a blow, slicing Travis's leg off just below the knee. As he crumpled to the ground in agony, another limb severed his neck. Lara watched in horror as the Marine's head rolled to a stop a few feet away.

Harkins took Travis's place, but they were fighting a losing battle. There were at least a dozen Korilian combat troops lined up on each side of them, waiting to replace their comrade in front. It was only a matter of time before one of the four remaining Marines went down, and the single Marine on that side would soon be overwhelmed as well.

A swirling cloud of fog formed on the corridor floor a few feet from Lara, which rose rapidly, taking on human form. A few seconds later, Cheryl stood beside McCarthy, who still held Elena in his arms, cradled against his chest. The Nexus Ten's eyes were closed, and her face was pressed against his armor, her arms still wrapped around his neck.

"Ask Elena to assist!" Cheryl said.

It didn't seem like there was anything Elena could do, but this time Lara didn't argue with her mom.

"Jon!" Laura shouted over the din of the battle. "Ask Elena to help."

Laura felt McCarthy's view turn colder as he tried to foresee the type of assistance she could offer, then he spoke to Elena. "We need your help."

She was unresponsive, so he gently shook her. She looked up at him with dazed eyes.

"We need your help," he repeated.

Elena's eyes slowly focused, and she shifted her gaze to the Korilians on one end of the corridor, then the other. The Korilian combat troops on both sides suddenly collapsed to the ground, writhing in pain, their limbs flailing about. Twenty seconds later, they all lay still.

Elena then whispered, her voice weak with exhaustion, "I can't...do this...again. Not for...a few hours."

As Lara wondered what Elena had done to the Korilians, Harkins announced, "I've got a communication signal."

McCarthy approached the Marine. "Show me a map of the facility."

Harkins pulled up a map of the complex on the forearm display of his suit armor, and McCarthy pointed to a location along the facility's perimeter.

"Have a transport meet us at this location."

48

Harkins established a communication link with 3rd MEF command, requesting a transport at the location specified by McCarthy, then followed the Nexus Ten as McCarthy led the platoon through a maze of interconnecting corridors. Lara could tell they were working their way toward the complex's outer wall. When they reached the designated spot, Harkins ordered Liza to blow a hole in the side of the passageway. Liza fired her assault carbine, perforating the wall with blast holes in an oval pattern, outlining their exit. Liza kicked the center portion, and it fell away, providing access to the planet's surface.

After exiting the facility, Lara took in the scene. The 3rd MEF command post in the distance appeared abandoned, and the landscape was littered with destroyed SAVs and aerial drones, smoke rising from their remnants. The entire MEF perimeter was ringed with explosions and black smoke billowing toward the gray clouds, and SAVs were streaking skyward toward the troop transports. Korilian marauders swept beneath the protective Colonial warship bubble, then sped toward the rising assault vehicles while Colonial vipers descended from above. The sky above the complex was illuminated with a multitude of colored flashes: red and blue starship pulses, yellow flashes from starship shield impacts, and occasional orange and purple flares as jump drives or pulse generators imploded.

High above, an SAV plummeted toward them. Lara thought it had been shot down until its thrusters ignited, slowing the vehicle's descent before landing not far away. Korilian troops, stationed by the entrances the Marines had blown in the facility, spotted the descending SAV, along with the humans emerging from the complex. Several dozen Korilians raced across the terrain toward them, each proceeding at an amazing speed using all six limbs. The Marines and Nexi sprinted toward the SAV, and after closing most of the distance, some of the Korilians shifted to four-limb transit, unholstering and firing two pulse-pistols with their upper limbs.

The Marines used their shields to protect the three Nexi in front of them, and they reached the SAV seconds before the lead Korilians. Once the Marines and Nexi were aboard, the SAV lifted off. Two of the Korilians leapt toward the rising SAV, grabbing hold of the ramp as it rose to its shut position. The Marines fired at the Korilians, keeping them at bay until the ramp closed and sheared several limbs, which fell lifelessly inside the SAV.

Liza pushed Lara into a seat and locked her into place, as she had done before the SAV's descent to the planet's surface. She also locked McCarthy into his seat, but Elena, with no armored suit and emaciated, would have slid from the restraints, so McCarthy held her in his arms. Elena seemed oblivious to what was occurring, clinging to McCarthy with her eyes closed. Liza pressed controls on McCarthy's armrest, and a shimmering bubble appeared around his seat. Liza explained it was a life-support shield, activated when a Marine's suit was damaged during battle, since SAVs would travel to the troop transports high above the planet where there was no air. If the SAV sustained damage during its ascent, McCarthy, who was missing his helmet, as well as Elena, would need the life-support shield.

As the SAV streaked upward, Harkins informed 2nd Fleet of their status, then selected a video feed from the SAV's external cameras, which he relayed to the other armored suits. Korilian marauders were heading toward the SAV, and a squadron of vipers were vectored toward the SAV as well.

The vipers engaged just before the Korilians were within firing range of the SAV, but a few marauders made it through. The SAV swerved sideways and pitched up and down, but the bulky assault vehicle could do little to avoid the nimble marauders. Korilian pulses blew several holes in the SAV, but thankfully, no Marines or Nexi were hit. Additional Colonial vipers arrived, engaging the stray Korilian craft.

With the marauders occupied, the SAV headed toward the nearest troop transport, which had several flight deck bays still open and vacant. However, the Korilian armada punched a hole in 2nd Fleet's protective bubble and several cruisers passed through, targeting the nearest troop transports. Several pulses tore through the transport they were heading toward, and the starship began tilting and falling toward the planet's surface. The SAV changed direction, heading to the next nearest troop transport as three Korilian cruisers spotted the ascending SAV.

The three cruisers attempted to gain a firing position on the SAV, while the SAV tried to stay out of each pulse generator's firing arc. The cruisers herded the SAV into a narrowing cone as they maneuvered, and the SAV eventually entered the firing arc of one of the Korilian warships. Lara tensed as she watched the pulse generator doors in the cruiser's bow open. A bright red ring around the pulse portal illuminated, increasing quickly in brightness. Then a bright white flash almost blinded Lara, lighting up the inside of the SAV through the holes blown by the marauders.

To Lara's amazement, she was still alive, and she tried to make sense of things through the holes in the SAV. A Colonial cruiser—*Aiguillon*—had jumped into the battle, positioning itself between the SAV and Korilian cruiser. However, *Aiguillon* was missing several shields, and the three Korilian warships began maneuvering into a firing position. The cruiser's name was familiar, and Lara realized it was Rear Admiral Rajhi's command ship.

The Colonial cruiser had its mid-port shield down and its spaceport doors open, and McCarthy ordered the SAV pilot to enter the cruiser's spaceport. The SAV swerved toward the cruiser, racing toward its spaceport as the three Korilian cruisers attempted to bracket *Aiguillon*, so that one of them would have a clear shot through its missing shields regardless of which way *Aiguillon* turned or rolled. One of the Korilian cruisers slid into position, firing its pulse generator just as the SAV entered *Aiguillon's* spaceport. Explosions rippled through the cruiser, and seconds later, Lara felt the jump wave as *Aiguillon* departed the Hellios system.

The jump affected Lara more than usual, with this being the third jump in less than twelve hours. But Lara's attention shifted from her nausea to the deteriorating situation in *Aiguillon*'s spaceport. Explosions continued inside the wounded cruiser, and shock waves buffeted the SAV as it searched for a place to land. The spaceport's lights began flickering, with electrical sparks shooting through the air, and Lara heard McCarthy shout to the SAV pilot.

"Exit the spaceport. Now!"

The pilot banked the SAV in a tight turn before accelerating toward the spaceport exit. The SAV shot from the spaceport just before the cruiser shuddered from bow to stern, then exploded in a brilliant fireball, sending debris streaking in every direction.

49

The SAV coasted to a halt while Lara's heart rate slowly returned to normal. It was dark and quiet in the Rignao system, absent the multicolored illuminations from the furious battle above Hellios 4. Through the holes blown in the SAV, Lara noticed several dozen damaged cruisers lying in formation not far away. Suddenly, almost two hundred white flashes lit up the surrounding space as what was left of 2nd Fleet joined the damaged cruisers at Rignao.

McCarthy directed the SAV pilot to take them to the 2nd Fleet command ship, and Lara felt the thrusters kick in as the SAV accelerated toward *Controlador*. As they sped toward the command ship, Lara surveyed what was left of the twenty-five-strong Marine platoon that had entered the Korilian facility. Only four Marines had made it out: Harkins, Jankowski, Geisinger, and Liza. They sat in silence, along with the three Nexi, until the SAV entered *Controlador*'s spaceport, passing through the life-support shield. The starship's gravity generators took effect, pressing Lara into her seat.

Liza turned to Major Harkins. "How many made it to the troop transports?"

Harkins didn't immediately reply, but Lara could tell he was searching for the information on his data feeds. Finally, his voice emanated from his helmet speaker.

"We lost over half of the MEF."

"What about Twenty-First Division, First Brigade?" Liza asked.

Harkins hesitated for a moment, then replied, "You're the only one left."

Liza removed her helmet and threw it to the deck. She bent over and covered her face with her hands, and Lara felt waves of pain and anguish wash over her.

After a long moment, Liza sat up. There were no tears, but her face was flush with emotion. As Jankowski unlatched McCarthy's seat restraints, Liza's eyes locked onto Elena, still cradled in McCarthy's arms, and Lara felt Liza's emotion transition from anguish to rage.

The Marine disengaged her seat restraints and headed across the SAV toward Elena, and Lara got the distinct impression Liza wanted to rip Elena's limbs from her body. The Marine was still in her armored suit, and with its augmented strength, she could probably do so.

McCarthy spotted Liza approaching and placed Elena in the seat beside him, then stood and blocked the Marine's path. She stopped only a few inches from him, and the six-foot-tall Marine engaged McCarthy in a low conversation Lara couldn't overhear. McCarthy, only two inches taller than Liza, remained calm while they talked.

Suddenly, Liza tried to step around him toward Elena, but McCarthy blocked her again. Lara shifted her gaze to Major Harkins, who sat watching the altercation closely but made no move to intervene. Lara wondered if he, too, wanted to make Elena pay for what she had done.

McCarthy and Liza continued their conversation, and this time, McCarthy gently placed his hands on the sides of Liza's shoulders, then pulled her close and whispered into one ear. Lara felt the Marine's rage slowly dissipate until it faded altogether, replaced by the pain and anguish Lara felt earlier.

Liza returned to her seat as the SAV headed toward a docking station on the highest level of the spaceport. Lara turned to her and asked, "What did McCarthy say?"

Liza answered without looking at Lara, staring straight ahead. "He said, 'Elena will make amends for what she has done.'"

The SAV landed on the spaceport deck, and the ramp lowered, flooding the SAV with the spaceport's bright lights. The Marines kicked aside the severed Korilian limbs on the SAV's deck as they exited. The three Nexi followed, with McCarthy cradling Elena in his arms again. Waiting to greet them were several Colonial Fleet, Medical Corps, and Marine Corps personnel: Admiral Amani's aide, several nurses, and a captain in charge of *Controlador*'s Marine Corps security detachment.

McCarthy placed Elena gently onto one of the floating gurneys beside the nurses, then spoke softly to her. Elena nodded, then the nurses began their transit to the starship's medical bay, with Elena's gurney floating before them. McCarthy then turned to what remained of the Marine platoon, thanking them for their protection during their mission into the Korilian complex.

The captain in charge of *Controlador*'s Marine detachment greeted Harkins and the other three Marines, then inquired if they wanted to stay aboard *Controlador* or return to *Artemis V*. Harkins declined the opportunity to return to the troop transport. *Artemis V* had carried 21st Division, 1st Brigade during their transit to the Hellios system. With the entire brigade eliminated aside from Liza, *Artemis V* would be a literal ghost ship. The captain agreed it would be best if they stayed aboard *Controlador* with fellow Marines, then escorted them to the command ship's armory, which was small in comparison to a troop transport's but would suffice for armor removal and weapon stowage.

After the Marines departed the spaceport, Lara accompanied McCarthy to the starship command bridge. As Lara exited the elevator, she registered the tension in the air. Admiral Amani was seated in his command chair with Angeline beside him, studying the video displays. Technicians and supervisors were scrutinizing their consoles, evaluating starship damage throughout the 2nd Fleet and 3rd MEF task force, while others scanned the sensor displays. Amani and Angeline rose to greet the two Nexi.

McCarthy addressed Admiral Amani. "I want to thank you for sending Admiral Rajhi back to Hellios for us. That was a brilliant idea, using her starship to jump our SAV out of danger."

"I'd like to take credit," Amani said, "but I didn't give the order. Rajhi was monitoring the situation from Rignao while they tried to repair her cruiser's shield generators, then decided on her own to jump to Hellios without full shields.

"But I have good news," Amani added. "We recovered *Aiguillon*'s bridge capsule intact. It's being towed into *Controlador*'s spaceport. We haven't been able to establish communications with the bridge, but there's hope that some of the bridge crew survived."

"That's good news, indeed," McCarthy said.

He spent the next few minutes viewing the future and explaining what would happen next, the options available, as well as his recommendations. McCarthy focused on selecting jump locations that resulted in the longest rest times before they were located by Korilian recon probes again.

The bridge elevator door opened, and Rear Admiral Rajhi emerged, her uniform marred with soot and grime. Rajhi joined them, acknowledging the two admirals and Angeline, but not Lara. Lara wondered if it was because she wasn't assigned to 2nd Fleet in an official capacity, but figured it was probably a personal issue. After the pulse-pistol incident on *Athens*'s bridge, Lara didn't like Rajhi, and the feelings were probably mutual. However, after Rajhi had returned to the Hellios system with a cruiser missing several shields, inviting almost certain destruction, Lara reassessed her opinion. Rajhi had saved their lives while risking hers.

McCarthy thanked Rajhi for their rescue, but if she appreciated his gratitude, it didn't show. Her face remained expressionless as she replied, "A thank-you isn't necessary, Admiral."

Admiral Amani spoke next, addressing Rajhi. "I've lost the Tarawa battle group commander. Proceed to the battleship *Endeavor* and take command of Tarawa." Turning to McCarthy, Amani asked, "Is there enough time for Rajhi to take a shuttle before the Korilians arrive?"

McCarthy nodded, so Rajhi acknowledged Amani's order and turned to head to *Controlador*'s spaceport. As she stepped away, Lara pulled her aside.

"Admiral Rajhi," Lara began, "I also want to thank you for what you did at Hellios. You risked your life for us and—"

Rajhi cut Lara off. "I didn't risk my life for you. I risked it for McCarthy."

Lara was taken aback by Rajhi's brusque response, then quickly gathered her thoughts and continued. "I realize McCarthy is far more important than me or anyone else on the SAV, but I wanted to thank you anyway. I also realize that I misjudged you after what happened on *Athens*, and I want to apologize for putting a pulse-pistol to your head."

There was no visible reaction on Rajhi's face as she stared at Lara.

Rajhi finally replied, "Unless you have something important to say, don't talk to me again."

Without waiting for Lara's response, Rajhi headed toward the elevator.

Well, Lara thought, *Rajhi is clearly not the forgiving type.*

Amani and McCarthy turned their attention to the displays as Rajhi's shuttle headed toward *Endeavor*. Shortly after Rajhi boarded the battleship, the sensor supervisor announced, "Korilian recon probe, sector two-seven-nine!"

One of the 2nd Fleet cruisers fired, destroying the probe, but the response was too late. Less than a minute later, a cluster of bright white flashes illuminated the darkness.

"Korilian warships, just over three hundred. Four minutes to weapon range."

After being trained as McCarthy's guide for the Final Stand, Lara knew where to look for the information she wanted next, her eyes shifting to the order-of-battle display. 2nd Fleet comprised less than two hundred starships—over half of the fleet had been destroyed thus far—and of the surviving warships, twenty-one percent had damaged shields or pulse generators. They were in no condition to engage three hundred Korilian warships.

There was only one viable option, but the eventual outcome wasn't favorable. They were deep in Korilian-controlled territory, outnumbered, and on the run.

Admiral Amani gave the order. "All ships in the task force, jump at the mark."

50

Inside the Colonial Defense Force command center in Brussels, Fleet Admiral Fitzgerald monitored the nine Fleet battles in progress. Similar to the Fleet command center, the defense compound was deep underground and heavily fortified. The CDF command center was different, however, designed to accommodate the simultaneous command of a multiforce campaign.

The CDF compound comprised three adjacent command centers—a semicircle divided into three segments—with Fleet command in the middle and the Army and Marine Corps centers on either side. Illusory walls that could be made transparent or opaque, which personnel could walk through, separated the three command centers, allowing each military service to either focus on their units without distraction or communicate in person and otherwise monitor the status of a coordinated assault or defense. At the back of the Navy command center, Fleet Admiral Fitzgerald focused on the only campaign that really mattered—the mission to Hellios 4.

The information was slightly time-late, being relayed by a series of communication jump-pods stretching to the Hellios planetary system, deep in the Korilian Empire. The 2nd Fleet task force was currently in the

Rignao system, its status updated every few seconds as each data transmission rippled through the communication pods back to Earth.

The display suddenly filled with red symbols. The Korilian armada had followed 2nd Fleet from Hellios. Fitzgerald's worst fear had been confirmed. The Korilians weren't content with a victory. They intended to hunt down and destroy every ship in the 2nd Fleet task force. In a few jumps, as the physiological effects of the jumps accumulated without adequate rest between them, Admiral Amani would have no choice but to stand and fight.

When that battle occurred would depend on how quickly the Korilians located the task force after each jump. However, facing three hundred Korilian warships, the outcome was not in doubt. Without reinforcements, the task force would be destroyed.

Fitzgerald examined the available resources. Two fleets were in Earth's orbit and could not be dispatched for fear of a Korilian attack on Earth, plus they were too far away. Two other fleets were tied down in campaigns, supporting planetary assaults by Army and Marine Corps troops. That left 3rd Fleet, currently in reserve and being resupplied in the Pleaides star cluster. Fitzgerald tapped her wristlet and requested a communication link to 3rd Fleet. A few seconds later, Admiral Natalia Goergen appeared on Fitzgerald's screen.

"Admiral Goergen," Fitzgerald began, "terminate resupply and rendezvous with Second Fleet as rapidly as possible."

Goergen turned her head to examine a nearby display, then addressed Fitzgerald. "Second Fleet is deep in the Korilian Empire. It's extremely unlikely that my fleet will arrive before Second Fleet is destroyed, and you'll end up with an exhausted Third Fleet in Korilian territory, easy prey for fresh Korilian forces. You could end up losing both fleets."

"I'm aware of the risk, Admiral. Proceed at maximum speed. Push your crews to the absolute limit of their endurance."

"Yes, ma'am," Goergen replied. "I've been monitoring the situation at Hellios and have already terminated resupply. Third Fleet will begin transit momentarily."

As Goergen's display went dark, Fitzgerald felt fortunate that 3rd Fleet was available. If anyone could reach 2nd Fleet in time, it was Admiral Goergen.

51

Scattered throughout an asteroid field, 2nd Fleet and the 3rd MEF transports rested in a darkened ship status, hoping to avoid detection from the Korilian recon probes that had found them at Rignao. Starship shields were down, main engines off, and all communications terminated until further notice from Admiral Amani. Even the starship bridge shield doors were closed to prevent light from leaking into space through the bridge windows.

On *Controlador*'s command bridge, supervisors were busy reviewing the status of 2nd Fleet warships, evaluating repair projections for ships with damaged shields or pulse generators. Standing by his control console, Admiral Amani was discussing the way forward with McCarthy and Angeline. Lara wasn't the 2nd Fleet guide but had nothing better to do, so she joined them, hoping for a useful vision.

The asteroid field had come in handy. It'd been a stretch jump, barely in range of the Colonial starships. The last twelve hours hiding among the asteroids had provided a welcome reprieve, helping to alleviate the effects of four jumps in a fifteen-hour period for the Colonial starship crews.

Lara checked the clock. They were approaching the time that McCarthy predicted Korilian recon probes would arrive.

Not long thereafter, the sensor supervisor announced, "Korilian recon probe!"

On the sensor display, a recon probe appeared just outside the asteroid belt. A minute later, a dozen more probes appeared, scattered inside the asteroid belt, some not far from the 2nd Fleet warships and troop transports.

McCarthy turned to Admiral Amani. "They've detected us."

Amani announced, "All ships, jump at the mark."

Lara braced herself on a nearby console, preparing for the nauseating effects of the jump. She hadn't fully recovered from the previous four, and the next several jumps would likely come quicker than this one had. As they threaded their way through Korilian-controlled territory, there were few good hiding places.

52

Lara exited the jump darkness, with this being the sixth jump from Hellios and the third in the last ten hours. She emerged on a spinning starship bridge as her legs gave way. McCarthy caught her and lowered her slowly to the deck, resting her head in his lap as his face swam above her. Although McCarthy had jumped hundreds, if not thousands of times, his face was pale.

A migraine pounded in Lara's temples, and the pressure was so intense she thought her head might explode. With every heartbeat, pain shot through her body. The nausea increased in intensity until she could no longer keep the contents of her stomach down. She turned her head to the side and vomited into a jump bag McCarthy had ready.

The spinning bridge eventually stabilized enough for Lara to assess her surroundings. Everyone was suffering from the multiple jumps; many rested their heads in their hands as they sat at their workstations, and several watchstanders were slumped atop their consoles. Other crew members replaced them while medics attended to the incapacitated personnel.

A ship's medic was soon by Lara's side, and he gave her a shot in her arm. The pain throbbing throughout her body faded, but the pressure inside her head and nausea remained.

McCarthy helped Lara to a sitting position and she examined the displays. They were in an obscure planetary system known only by its number, with a blue-white sun illuminating a rocky planet not far away. Lara's nausea slowly faded, and McCarthy helped her to her feet.

Admiral Amani was seated in his command chair with Angeline sitting beside him, reviewing the status of 2nd Fleet and 3rd MEF starships. Most of the crew members could still function, and Amani's assessment was that his fleet was still battle-ready, but their condition was rapidly deteriorating. If they didn't jump to locations that provided longer rest periods between the jumps, they would soon reach the point where not only would the crews be too incapacitated for combat, but a portion of the crew would die after each successive jump.

One of the displays on Amani's console shifted to the medical bay, and an officer wearing the Medical Corps' purple uniform appeared on the screen. The man addressed Admiral Amani quickly.

"That woman you brought back from Hellios 4—she's gone berserk. She's killed two nurses and attacked others. I've got her sealed in one of the medical wards, and I've called for Marine security. I need guidance on how to deal with her."

McCarthy strode toward Amani's command chair. "Do not harm her," he said.

The medical officer shifted his gaze between McCarthy and Amani. Technically, this was Amani's command ship, and he took his orders from him.

"Do not harm her," Amani repeated. "We'll figure out how to deal with her and inform you momentarily."

Amani turned to McCarthy for guidance. Lara felt the chill as McCarthy viewed.

"I'll handle it," McCarthy said, then headed for the elevator.

"Can I come?" Lara asked as he passed by.

McCarthy nodded, and she joined him in the elevator, which dropped and slid aft, then opened to the medical bay. Waiting to greet them was the officer on the video: Commander Greg Vandiver by the name tag embroidered on his uniform. He escorted McCarthy and Lara through the medical bay, updating them along the way.

"She was resting comfortably at first, but became more agitated after each jump. She'd been mumbling to herself incoherently, then she flipped out after the last jump, killing the two nearest nurses and going after others in the ward, who were able to escape before she reached them. This woman is clearly abnormal," he added. "What the hell *is* she?"

Lara couldn't quite follow Vandiver's question about *what* Elena was. McCarthy seemed to understand, but didn't answer. When they reached the sealed medical ward, where four Marines from the starship's security detachment were standing by, Lara looked through the door window. Elena was in a fit of rage, knocking medical supplies from their tables and bins and throwing objects across the room at imaginary enemies.

Sprawled on the deck were the two dead nurses, their bodies emaciated —not much more than skeletons with thin, leathery skin stretched taut over their bones. Lara realized that Elena was not only a healer, healing Jankowski's wound in the Korilian complex, but she could use her power in reverse, sucking the life force from her victims. It dawned on her—that was what Elena had been doing to McCarthy in her chamber as she sat atop him with her hands clamped around his neck, with McCarthy unable to pry her off.

The lunacy of McCarthy's behavior suddenly hit Lara. He must have known what she was capable of as he carried her from the facility, and he let her wrap her arms around his neck while he cradled her in his arms. Lara didn't know whether she should be furious at McCarthy or just jealous that he was willing to place his life in her hands.

McCarthy stood at the door, and Lara wondered what he was contemplating while Elena rampaged through the ward. Eventually, Elena spent her rage, then dropped onto all fours and scampered into a corner, where she huddled with her knees drawn to her chest.

"Open the door," McCarthy ordered, "then shut it behind me."

Vandiver complied, and the door whisked aside. Elena's eyes locked onto McCarthy as he entered. He moved toward Elena at a steady pace while she seemed to study him. He stopped a few feet away from her, and Lara watched as several emotions played across Elena's face: anger, hatred, fear, and shame.

McCarthy sat beside Elena, his back against the wall, resting his forearms on his knees. He said nothing, and Elena's eyes went from McCarthy to Lara, then back to McCarthy. Elena slowly reached toward McCarthy with one hand, poking his shoulder with her index finger, as if testing to see if he was real. McCarthy smiled and spoke. Unfortunately, with the ward door closed, Lara couldn't hear what he said.

They talked for a few minutes. Rather, McCarthy spoke, and Elena nodded every so often, keeping her eyes fixed on him. After a while, McCarthy stood and spoke again, and Elena nodded. He picked her up in his arms and laid her on a nearby bed, then tapped his wristlet. Vandiver's wristlet activated in response.

"You can enter the ward now," McCarthy said. "Leave the Marines outside. Medical personnel only."

Then McCarthy typed a message. *Sedate and restrain her.*

Vandiver opened the door and ordered a doctor and four nurses inside after relaying McCarthy's instructions. McCarthy stood beside Elena's bed with his hand on her shoulder as the nurses approached. The doctor grabbed a cartridge and injector, shielding his actions with his body, then turned quickly and pressed the injector against Elena's arm.

Elena bolted upright and grabbed the man's forearm. His face turned pale, and he fell to his knees. McCarthy grabbed Elena's wrist and began prying her fingers from the man's arm while repeatedly saying, "No, Elena."

McCarthy finally pulled Elena's hand from the doctor, and he crawled away as the four nurses pounced on Elena, attaching straps to her wrists and ankles, then fastening the restraints to her bed. Elena's face lit up in fury, and she struggled against the straps as she launched into a tirade directed at McCarthy. Spittle flew from her mouth as she screamed at him, and she yanked and bucked against her restraints so violently it looked like she was having a convulsion. From across the ward, Lara felt the intensity of Elena's emotions: betrayal and rage.

The medication kicked in, and Elena's struggle began to subside. She soon lay still, her eyes growing heavy. McCarthy leaned close and spoke quietly. Lara couldn't hear what he said, but Elena shook her head from side to side repeatedly. Finally, Elena's eyes closed, and her breathing slowed.

McCarthy left the ward, stopping outside the entrance where Lara waited, and leaned back against the wall. The anguish on his face was unmistakable.

"She's unstable," he said.

"That's an understatement," Lara replied. "You just now figured that out?"

McCarthy didn't reply, but the look on his face said it all. Even though he was excellent at controlling his emotions, he couldn't hide them completely, and Lara knew her words had hurt.

She took McCarthy in her arms. "I'm sorry, Jon. I know it's hard seeing what's become of her. Worrying that we might not be able to undo what the Korilians have done." McCarthy nodded as he wrapped his arms around her.

The starship's jump alarm sounded—five deep tones reverberating throughout the ship, followed by the ship's computerized announcement. Not long thereafter, the jump wave passed over Lara, and her knees went weak. She collapsed, and McCarthy tried to catch her, but this time they both fell to the deck.

53

Lara was on her hands and knees on the starship's deck, puking into a jump bag while she waited for the bridge to stop spinning. They had endured three more jumps since Elena was restrained in medical, with insufficient rest time in the intervals. By now, Lara's stomach was empty, and the only thing coming out as she retched was a thin stream of yellow bile. She didn't want to look at herself in a mirror. Her eyes had begun hemorrhaging, turning the whites of her eyes solid red. It wouldn't be long before they burst, like Jankowski's friend's had aboard *Argonaut* during its journey to Darian 3.

Her eyes wouldn't last another jump, Lara figured. Some crew members had already lost one or both eyes and had been transported to the medical bay or 2nd Fleet's hospital ship, while other personnel had been rendered unconscious. They were approaching the limit of what a human body could endure. *Controlador's* medical ward was overflowing—no vacant beds —and some of the starship's crew remained slumped over their bridge consoles.

Lara had remained on the bridge with McCarthy during the last several jumps. It was the best place; at least she'd have advance notice of the jump when Amani gave the order. McCarthy knelt beside Amani's command chair, while Amani and Angeline slumped forward in their seats and emptied the bile that had collected in their stomachs since the last jump. For the last eight hours, they had been too nauseated to eat or drink. Anything that went down came right back up.

The spinning bridge slowly stabilized, and Lara looked up to assess their new location. Through the bridge windows, a red dwarf star swam in her vision. There didn't seem to be anywhere to hide nearby—no planets or asteroid fields.

As Lara wondered why McCarthy had chosen this planetary system for the last jump, the display updated and the sensor supervisor called out, her voice weak from the multi-jump transit. "Korilian recon probe. Bearing three-four-seven, two-four degrees down from fleet axis."

A nearby cruiser fired, destroying the probe, but it took longer to respond than normal, and Lara wondered what the point was, anyway. No matter how quickly they destroyed arriving recon probes, they always seemed to transmit the critical data back to the Korilian armada before they were destroyed. If history was any precedent, they'd have less than a minute before Korilian warships jumped to their location, appearing four minutes from weapon range.

Admiral Amani sat up in his chair, evaluating the situation. He tapped a control on his console, and the ship's medical officer appeared on a display. Commander Vandiver wore a patch over one eye as blood trickled down his cheek.

"Assessment?" Amani asked.

"We cannot jump again for at least four hours," Vandiver replied. "Anything sooner and brain hemorrhaging will begin."

"A recon probe has already located us, and the Korilian armada will arrive within minutes. We're in no condition to engage three hundred Korilian warships. We won't last four hours."

"I can only offer my medical opinion," Vandiver replied. "A four-hour rest period is required to avoid deaths. If we jump now, you'll lose about twenty percent of your crews, and many of the survivors will be unconscious."

"I understand," Amani replied as he terminated the video feed, and the display went dark. Turning to McCarthy, he asked, "Recommendation?"

"Stay and fight," McCarthy said, his head still sagging toward the deck. "Four-layer sphere."

The sensor supervisor announced, "Korilian warships! Three hundred strong. Four minutes from weapon range."

Amani decided to follow McCarthy's advice. "Operations officer, form the fleet into a four-layer spherical defense formation, with the carriers, troop transports, and fleet command ship in the center."

The operations officer acknowledged and sent the orders, and the 2nd Fleet task force, which was currently in a two-layer spherical formation, shifted to four layers, alternating between battleships and cruisers. During her training to be McCarthy's fleet guide during the Final Stand, Lara had learned that the extra two layers would provide additional time to destroy Korilian warships that attempted to penetrate the spherical formation toward the vulnerable ships in the center. However, with four layers instead of two, there'd be less firepower in the outer two layers. It would be easier for the Korilians to eat away at the formation, like biting into an apple, but it would take longer to penetrate. They were trading starships for time.

The quadruple-layer spherical formation was a solid move, but Lara wondered about the effectiveness of the Colonial starships in battle. She looked around the bridge. Normally, unconscious personnel were quickly transported to medical and replaced with new watchstanders. However, almost a dozen of the fifty men and women manning the consoles were slumped over their workstations. There were no more replacement watch-standers available. Amani, like other starship captains, would have to wait for them to regain consciousness, and even then, they'd be disoriented and unfit for combat for an hour or more.

Lara's hope, early on, was that the Korilians would suffer just as much from the multiple jumps and give up. However, McCarthy had explained that Korilians can jump with shorter hold times, so the Korilian crews would be in better shape than the Colonial crews.

"Two minutes to engagement range," the sensor supervisor reported.

McCarthy stood, then helped Lara to her feet as the Korilian armada approached. As the seconds counted down, Lara wondered if she'd have a vision that would somehow help. But she held little hope. McCarthy had been viewing the prime timeline and alternate futures and had selected the best option. At least she was by his side again, and they prepared for another Final Stand.

Bright white flashes lit up the darkness, forcing Lara to cover her eyes. As the light faded, *Controlador*'s sensor displays updated, showing four hundred additional Colonial starships arranged into two additional layers around 2nd Fleet's sphere. Through the bridge windows, Lara watched as the starship shields formed. A wave of relief swept over Lara as she realized —3rd Fleet had arrived.

The Korilian armada halted its advance just outside effective weapon range. There were now almost six hundred Colonial warships against just three hundred Korilian starships. How effective the Colonial crews would be in combat was a critical question, one Lara couldn't answer.

It appeared the Korilians couldn't answer that question either, or decided the Colonial crews were sufficiently battle-ready. After resting in space for a few minutes, the Korilian armada disappeared in a blinding white flash.

54

Shortly after the Korilian armada departed, Admiral Natalia Goergen's image appeared on Amani's display. The whites of her eyes were solid red, and blood trickled from both nostrils. Beside her, Nexus guide Carson Lieu, who had swapped positions with Angeline, sat slumped in his chair, unconscious, his face covered in blood. Where his eyes used to be, the orbs were filled with gelatinous goo. Lara turned away from the display. If there had been anything left in her stomach, it would have come up now.

"Admiral...Amani." Goergen spoke slowly, her words slurred. "Request you...or McCarthy...take command...of Third Fleet." She paused for a moment, then continued. "I cannot..." Her voice trailed off.

McCarthy answered, "I'll take command." He turned to Lara. "You'll be my guide. Carson is incapacitated."

Lara joined McCarthy as he headed to *Controlador*'s spaceport, proceeding slowly since both were still wobbly on their feet. Upon reaching the spaceport, they boarded McCarthy's Nexus shuttle. As they settled into their seats, McCarthy spoke to the shuttle's autopilot. "Take us to the Third Fleet command ship."

"Yes, Jon," the shuttle replied in Elena's voice, as it had been programmed per the direction of the Nexus One. The shuttle's voice jarred Lara, realizing that The One had ordered it programmed as a tribute to

Elena, to honor the sacrifice she had made on Darian 3. But Elena was alive, and Lara found her voice emanating from the shuttle somewhat... creepy.

The shuttle rose from the deck and passed through the shimmering life-support shield lining the spaceport's entrance, then accelerated toward *Surveillant*, the 3rd Fleet command ship, which was nearby in the center of the spherical defense formation. *Surveillant* dropped its mid-port shield and its spaceport doors opened as they approached, and the shuttle landed on the upper tier of the command ship's spaceport. There was no activity in the spaceport and no one there to greet them.

They took the elevator to the bridge, passing no crew members along the way, and exited to find *Surveillant*'s crew in worse shape than *Controlador*'s. Over half of the fifty men and women manning the bridge were unconscious, collapsed atop their workstation consoles, and many had blood trickling from their ears. A medic was on his knees beside Admiral Goergen's command chair as he tended to her, although he wasn't in much better shape than the admiral. He gave her a shot in her neck, then paused to gather himself before moving on to another crew member. Lieu was still unconscious. Thankfully so, Lara thought. He was going to need replacement eyes.

McCarthy scanned the operations consoles, then turned to Goergen. "Where is your fleet hospital ship?"

"In the Laconious system," Goergen said, her voice becoming stronger. "Two jumps away. I left it there so the medical staff would be well enough to care for the warship crews after our double jump here."

She added, "I was going to halt at Laconious. It was as far as I could push my fleet and still be combat-ready. But you and Second Fleet were only two jumps away as you prepared to engage the Korilians. Two jumps. I couldn't just sit there and watch Second Fleet be destroyed. I programmed both jumps before we left Laconious and set the shields for auto-generation after the second jump. I knew we'd be in bad shape once we arrived, but the Korilians wouldn't know. I took a gamble."

"It worked," McCarthy said as he placed his hand on her shoulder. "You did well."

Goergen smiled weakly. "What now?"

"We're going to hold here for the next twenty-four hours. I'll have your hospital ship join us as soon as they can endure the two jumps without impairment. In the meantime, we'll begin transferring your most seriously injured crew members to the Second Fleet hospital ship."

"Are we going to make it back?" Goergen asked.

McCarthy nodded. "The Korilians have no additional ships in the area, and the armada crews chasing us are exhausted as well. Their decision not to engage an adversary twice as large will hold." McCarthy paused, then asked, "Do you have anything else important to relay?"

Goergen shook her head.

"I relieve you of command of Third Fleet," McCarthy said.

Goergen closed her eyes. "I stand relieved."

55

As Lara sat beside McCarthy and Ronan across from The One's desk in Domus Praesidium, she listened as they discussed the mission to Hellios and the attack on McCarthy and Lara on Darian 3. The whites of Lara's eyes were still solid red; it would take a few weeks for the blood to be absorbed into her eyes. In the meantime, she and McCarthy, whose eyes had also hemorrhaged, sported a devilish look. Luckily, neither of them had required an eye replacement.

The discussion focused first on the Hellios mission. The combined 2nd and 3rd Fleet task force made it back to Colonial-controlled territory without further incident. The Korilians didn't appear to have additional reserves aside from the three hundred warships chasing 2nd Fleet as it retreated from Hellios, although Fleet Intelligence was perplexed as to how the Korilians had built so many warships so fast, or perhaps had held so many ships back in reserve status for the last three years. Fleet Intelligence was reassessing their Korilian starship construction model, but nothing was adding up, which was creating consternation among Fleet leadership.

The current discussion was focused on Elena. She had remained sedated during her transit to Earth, then was transported to a mental health facility. When Lara asked why Elena wasn't cared for at Domus Praesidium, Rhea explained that the Nexus House had a section of the complex dedicated to caring for the Lost Ones—Nexus Nines who failed the level-ten Test and became trapped in an alternate reality. Elena's condition, however, wasn't something Nexus physicians were trained to deal with. Elena required specialized care and had been admitted to a sanitorium with the appropriate experts.

Neither McCarthy nor The One had been able to predict the outcome regarding Elena's health. Analyzing timelines involving other Tens was difficult to begin with, since their ability to see and change the future often resulted in their prime timeline dissolving quickly. Additionally, Elena's mental instability was also affecting her line, making it even more difficult to follow.

Rhea took keen interest in the talents Elena had developed during her eighteen-year incarceration, explaining that the mind, when isolated and relieved of the burden of managing day-to-day life, often developed under-lying talents more quickly. It was a method the Primus Talentum, in charge of talent development within the Nexus House, sometimes employed, placing the subject in voluntary solitary confinement.

One talent Rhea was particularly interested in was Elena's ability to block timelines from view, a talent developed thus far only by Corvads. Rhea pondered the implications, while Ronan, predictably, disapproved of any talent that was considered exclusively Corvad, such as Lara's Touch. Upon discussing how Elena had incapacitated the combat Korilians, Rhea explained that Elena's ability was probably effective only against Korilians, who were telepathic and likely more susceptible to whatever Elena had done, since nearby humans hadn't been affected. Further analysis, however, would be required if Elena recovered.

However, Rhea offered a disapproving frown after learning Elena had used her healing talent in reverse. When Lara inquired, Rhea had replied tersely, explaining that *draining* was a forbidden talent, with a *how-dare-she* attitude in her voice. Lara almost erupted in fury at Rhea's reaction. After everything Elena had endured, to condemn her for developing the *wrong* talent seemed inhumane. Lara still hadn't become accustomed to the heart-less way most upper-level Nexi assessed things. Even McCarthy was emotionless most of the time, although he wasn't judgmental like Rhea and Ronan when interacting with those less emotionally restrained.

"Where do we stand on the attack on Darian 3?" McCarthy asked.

Rhea replied, "We haven't made much progress. The captured praetorians killed themselves, and their records have been erased from the registry. Ronan scoured the Corvad compounds again, finding no trace of surviving Corvads or any material that's shed light on the matter thus far. The House Concilium meeting, however, was a bit more revealing."

Rhea went on to explain how Claude Verhofstadt, princeps of Devinctus House, had challenged major house leadership of the Concilium.

"You think Devinctus House was responsible for the attack?" McCarthy asked.

"They're the leading suspect at the moment. They certainly have the motive, being the lead minor house aligned with the Corvads, and it's clear that Verhofstadt believes the Nexus House is weak and ripe for at least a council leadership challenge, if not outright destruction."

Lara's gaze shifted to Ronan, who didn't join the conversation. But Lara sensed his frustration. For three decades, Rhea had repeatedly declined his requests to rebuild the praetorian legion.

The meeting began to wrap up, and as McCarthy prepared to leave, Rhea asked, "What's next for you," although Lara was certain The One already knew the answer.

"I'm going to visit Elena on the way back to Fleet headquarters."

"Can I come with you?" Lara asked. "I'd like to see how she's doing."

McCarthy looked to The One, since it was her decision.

"Certainly," Rhea replied.

Ronan interjected, "Should I assign Jon a guard, in case there's a praetorian attack?"

"No," Rhea replied. "He'll be safe. There'll be no attack, at least for the next few days."

56

During the journey to Belgium aboard McCarthy's shuttle, he rarely spoke, sitting with his eyes closed most of the way. Seated beside him, Lara felt the chill from his view and wondered what he was seeing, thinking, and feeling. She considered using her Touch on him but decided otherwise. McCarthy didn't seem to be in a mood to share his thoughts, so she probed his feelings instead. As usual, it was difficult to read much from him, although she caught occasional waves of frustration.

She reached over and placed her hand on his to show her support, being careful not to invoke her Touch. "Have you foreseen anything useful?"

McCarthy shook his head as the shuttle descended through the clouds. "Elena's line fades too quickly. I can't follow it far enough into the future to determine what kind of recovery she has."

"Is it possible you're having trouble following her line because she's sedated?"

"It's possible. I haven't tried to follow a sedated person's line before."

The shuttle descended onto a circular landing pad in what looked like a country estate: nearby was a sprawling five-story stone mansion with lush, manicured gardens. Waiting at the edge of the landing pad were two men wearing white uniforms. They greeted McCarthy and Lara as they stepped from the shuttle, then escorted them into the sanitorium, the front doors closing behind them with a heavy clank. Once inside, they were led to a conference room filled with a half dozen men and women—the team assigned to care for Elena Kapadia.

A man at the head of the table stood as they entered. "I'm Dr. Elijah Guptah," he said, extending his hand. "Welcome to Sint-Pieters."

Guptah introduced the members of his team, with each doctor specializing in treating different mental disorders, then provided an overview of Elena's condition.

"We can't give a prognosis at this point," he began. "Physically, Elena is in remarkably good health, considering..." Guptah looked uncomfortable as he discussed the Nexus Ten's health. "There will be ramifications to what the Korilians did to her, which I'm not at liberty to discuss with you, but whatever they've been feeding her has kept her in reasonably good health. She'll need to put on some weight, but hopefully that won't be a problem."

When Guptah mentioned *whatever they've been feeding her*, Lara recalled their entry into Elena's chamber on Hellios 4, where they discovered her eating one of the Korilian carcasses.

"What about her mind?" McCarthy asked.

"Ah, yes. Her mind. The brain is a complex and unpredictable organ, and Elena has significant issues. What's clear so far is that she's been subjected to severe physical and emotional torture. We unsedated Elena after her arrival to get a clearer picture of what condition she's in. She remained rational for only a short time before becoming aggressive. Fortunately, we were aware of what happened aboard the Second Fleet command ship, and we kept her restrained. We had to sedate her again shortly after she regained consciousness."

"Do you know what the issue is?" McCarthy asked. "Why she becomes violent?"

"We think so," Guptah replied. "She was quite verbal during the episode, and it seems that she thinks this," he spread his arms out to signify everything around him, "is a fabrication. That her rescue from Hellios 4 is a cruel Korilian mind trick. Apparently, not only are Korilians telepathic, but they can create scenarios in a human's mind. We think Elena's violence is a symptom of her frustration at not being able to return to reality."

"But this *is* reality," McCarthy replied.

"Therein lies the problem. Typically, within this set of psychological disorders, we deal with individuals who are trapped in fantasy and we help them find their way back to reality. In Elena's case, we'll have to convince her that this is, in fact, reality. Unfortunately, the Korilians have likely done this to her many times, and her defense mechanisms are ingrained."

When Guptah finished, there was silence around the conference room table as McCarthy absorbed the information. "What happens next?" he asked.

"We'll periodically unsedate Elena and subject her to various treatments. Hopefully, one will be successful in convincing her that she has been rescued from Hellios 4."

"What's your official prognosis?"

Guptah hesitated, then answered, "It's difficult to predict with certainty, but based on our experience with similar trauma, it's unlikely Elena will ever be normal again."

Although McCarthy's face didn't betray his feelings, Lara sensed his emotions: anguish and guilt. She placed her hand on his, offering silent support.

"Can I see her?" McCarthy asked.

"Of course," Guptah replied, pushing himself to his feet. "I'll escort you to her room."

Guptah led McCarthy and Lara through a maze of corridors, swiping his badge on an access panel before entering a secure area of the facility. After a short walk down the hallway, Guptah stopped beside a door with a glass window, through which McCarthy and Lara peered.

Elena was asleep in bed. She had been bathed and her hair washed and cut, and instead of the filthy woman with matted and tangled brown hair they had discovered on Hellios, Elena's skin was clean and pale, her hair now blonde and straight again. An IV bag hung from a pole nearby, a slow drip running down the clear tubing to the needle inserted into her arm. Despite the sedation, Elena's body twitched slightly under the sheet, as if fighting demons in her nightmares.

Guptah's wristlet vibrated, and he answered. The display activated, and a man's face appeared. "Dr. Guptah. Regent Lijuan Xiang has arrived."

Guptah replied, "Escort her to Elena Kapadia's room."

The display went dark as Guptah turned to McCarthy and Lara. "I forgot to mention that Regent Lijuan Xiang will be joining us today. She's asked for a status on Elena, and I told her you'd be visiting this afternoon. She decided to join us."

Lijuan, accompanied by four aides, arrived a few minutes later, greeting Guptah, then the Nexi. "Admiral McCarthy and Lara, I want to convey the Council's appreciation for rescuing Elena, and we are saddened by her current condition. We...or at least I, feel responsible for what happened to her. We were the ones who sent her to Darian 3 and then abandoned her."

McCarthy nodded his appreciation, then Lijuan asked Guptah for an update on Elena's condition. As he explained, Lara reflected on Lijuan's visit, that she'd taken the time to check on Elena in person. Regent Alperi, however, who was the director of Personnel and therefore the regent who should have visited Elena, hadn't been able to carve time from his schedule. Elena couldn't advance any of Alperi's ambitions, so she was of no use to him.

After Guptah finished updating Lijuan, she thanked him, then stared pensively through the window at Elena. After a short while, she turned back to Guptah.

"If there's anything I or the Council can do to help, please let me know. Also, inform me if there is any change in Elena's condition."

As she prepared to leave, Lijuan shook McCarthy's hand, then embraced Lara. As the regent hugged her, Lara suddenly realized that Lijuan was a rare Council member who genuinely cared about the men and women she represented, and didn't lust for prestige or power.

Lijuan smiled warmly, then bid farewell.

McCarthy peered into Elena's room again.

Guptah offered encouraging words. "There is always hope. We will do our best."

Lijuan Xiang stepped into the Council shuttle outside the sanitorium, taking a seat as her aides joined her in the transport. As the shuttle lifted off, Lijuan reflected on her visit. Timing it to coincide with McCarthy and Lara's visit had been wise, and her talents had come in handy. She had successfully charmed Lara, convincing her that she was the rare regent who cared about her constituents, but had refrained from planting a suggestion. It was still unclear how Lara could be manipulated to the Corvad House's advantage.

What was clearer was Elena's condition. Lijuan was no stranger to pain and terror—she was a Corvad Ten. When engaging in critical long-range views of the future, she would slay a man or woman, feeding on the victim's terror in the final moments of his or her life to fuel her view. In addition to her powers of charm and suggestion, Lijuan was also an empath. Standing outside Elena's room, watching the woman twitch beneath her bedsheet, she had felt waves of emotion emanating from the Nexus Ten, emotions so intense and visceral that Lijuan had almost recoiled reflexively. It was clear that Elena was battling demons in her torturous nightmares.

But beneath the emotion, Lijuan sensed something subtler, something critical. Inside Elena's dreams, she was viewing, subconsciously harnessing her level-ten ability. For what reason, she didn't know or care. What mattered was that Elena had broken the most sacred Nexus decree—she was using emotions to propel her view.

Lijuan smiled.

Elena was already half Corvad.

The End of Time: A Colonial Fleet Novel
Nexus House Book 3

The discovery of a mysterious space station unlocks a centuries-old mystery.

Admiral Jon McCarthy, a Nexus Ten with the gift of foresight, stands as humanity's last beacon of hope against the relentless Korilian Empire. With the outcome of the brutal 33-year war tilting in the Korilians' favor again, McCarthy must lead 3rd Fleet on a perilous mission behind enemy lines.

By his side is Lara Anderson, a woman whose absence of a prime timeline —rendering her past and future indiscernible—may hold the key to humanity's survival. Joining them is Elena Kapadia, another Nexus Ten, whose years of captivity and torture by her Korilian captors have molded her into a formidable, yet unpredictable ally.

Their mission takes an unexpected turn when they discover a mysterious space station deep in Korilian territory. As the team races to determine the purpose of this facility, 3rd Fleet must endure a withering assault by the Korilian armada, buying time for McCarthy, Lara, and Elena to unravel a centuries-old mystery and the key to ending the Korilian War.

Get your copy today at
severnriverbooks.com

COMPLETE CAST OF CHARACTERS

<u>NEXUS HOUSE</u>

Rhea Sidener Ten (Placidia) / Nexus One (The One)

Elias Tanner Ten (Placidia) / one of The Three (ruled Nexus House prior to Rhea)

Valeriya Sokolov Ten (Placidia) / one of The Three (ruled Nexus House prior to Rhea

Angus Klein Ten (Placidia) / one of The Three (ruled Nexus House prior to Rhea)

Jon McCarthy Ten / Colonial Navy guide

Elena Kapadia Ten / Colonial Army guide

Noah Ronan Nine (Primus) / Legion Commander / Department Head - Defense

Dmitri Birchmeir Nine / Metu Lectorum

Siella Salvos Nine / Ten trainee

Zaheer Bhyat Nine (Lost One)

Chenglei Zhang Nine (Lost One)

Amira Bakshi Nine (Lost One)

Dewan Channing Eight (Deinde)

Lara Anderson Eight / Nine trainee

Carson Lieu Eight / 2nd Fleet guide

Angeline Del Rio Eight / 3rd Fleet guide
Chen Wei Seven (Primus)

CORVAD HOUSE
Lijuan Xiang Ten (Placidia) / Princeps
Nero Conde Nine (Primus) / Legion Commander / Department Head - Defense

OTHER HOUSES
Claude Verhofstadt Nine / Princeps - Devinctus House

COLONIAL COUNCIL
David Portner Regent - Inner Realm / Council president
Morel Alperi Regent - Inner Realm / Director of Personnel
Lijuan Xiang Regent - Terran (Earth) / Director of Material

COLONIAL FLEET
Nanci Fitzgerald Fleet Admiral / Colonial Fleet Commander
Liam Carroll Admiral / Colonial Fleet Deputy Commander
Jon McCarthy Admiral / Colonial Fleet staff
Khalil Amani Admiral / 2nd Fleet Commander
Natalia Goergen Admiral / 3rd Fleet Commander
Nesrine Rajhi Rear Admiral / Hellios Cruiser Task Force Commander
Tom Bradner Captain / Troop Transport *Artemis V*
Greg Vandiver Commander / 2nd Fleet Command Ship *Controlador* Medical Officer

COLONIAL ARMY
Sergei Lavrov Field General / Army Chief of Staff
Dutch Hostler General / Eighth Army Commander
Kurt Coleman Colonel / Eighth Army Operations Officer
Deshi Zhang Captain / Nexus escort platoon leader (Darian 3)
Trevor Romano Sergeant / Communications Specialist (Darian 3)

COLONIAL MARINE CORPS
Narendra Modi Field General / Commandant of the Marine Corps
Vern Hutton Major General / 3rd Marine Expeditionary Force Commander
Demi Kavanagh Colonel / 21st Division, 1st Brigade Commander
Drew Harkins Major / Nexus escort platoon leader (Hellios 4)
Ed Jankowski Sergeant Major / Nexus escort platoon (Hellios 4)
Narra Geisinger Sergeant Major / Nexus escort platoon (Hellios 4)
Liza Kalinin Sergeant / Nexus escort platoon (Hellios 4)
Chris Travis Sergeant / Nexus escort platoon (Hellios 4)
Tony DelGreco Sergeant / Nexus escort platoon (Hellios 4)
Reid Tanaka Sergeant / Nexus escort platoon (Hellios 4)
Deanna Riley Corporal / Nexus escort platoon (Hellios 4)
Tony Rodriguez Corporal / Nexus escort platoon (Hellios 4)

KORILIANS
Mrayev Pracep (war campaign commander)
Meorbi Pracep (war campaign commander)
Krajik Pracep Mrayev's executive assistant

OTHER CHARACTERS
Winston Albright Special Intelligence Division (SID) agent
Elijah Guptah Director, Sint-Pieters Sanitorium
Trent McCarthy Jon McCarthy's father
Claire McCarthy Jon McCarthy's mother
Kristen Tobin Jon McCarthy's grandmother (Claire's mother)
Cheryl Johnson Lara Anderson's mother
Gary Anderson Lara Anderson's husband (deceased)

AUTHOR'S NOTE

I hope you enjoyed *Descent into Hellios*!

Since I finished the outline for this series, I've been looking forward to introducing Elena. As the saying goes, the team is finally all here: McCarthy, Lara, and Elena. I particularly like Elena, because I can do a lot with her character. McCarthy and Lara are fairly predictable—McCarthy is a straight arrow, and Lara, while being somewhat volatile and lacking confidence, is conflicted only in purpose. Hopefully, I've done a decent job in this book in the small time spent with Elena, conveying how broken she is after eighteen years of torture and how unpredictable she might be in the future.

In the next book, as the tide of war tilts in favor of the Korilians again, Elena joins McCarthy and Lara as they guide 3rd Fleet deep into the Korilian Empire on a mission to locate and assault the Korilian home world. But when they reach Korilia, neither the Nexi nor 3rd Fleet are prepared for what they encounter.

I hope you enjoy *The End of Time*!

ABOUT THE AUTHOR

RICK CAMPBELL, a retired Navy Commander, spent more than thirty years in the Navy, serving on four nuclear-powered submarines. On his last submarine, he was one of the two men whose permission is required to launch its nuclear warhead-tipped missiles.

Upon retirement from the Navy, Rick was contracted by Macmillan / St. Martin's Press for his novel The Trident Deception, which was hailed by Booklist as "The best submarine novel written in the last thirty years, since Tom Clancy's classic - The Hunt for Red October". His first six books became Barnes & Noble Top-10 and Amazon #1 bestsellers.

Rick lives in the Washington, D.C. area and continues to work on new books across the submarine and science-fiction genres.

Sign up for the reader list at
severnriverbooks.com

Printed in the United States
by Baker & Taylor Publisher Services